Any Witch Way

ANNASTAYSIA SAVAGE

JournalStone

San Francisco

JournalStone books may be ordered through booksellers or by contacting:

JournalStone
199 State Street
San Mateo, CA 94401
www.journalstone.com

Because of the dynamic nature of the Internet, any Web addresses or links contained in this book may have been changed since publication and may no longer be valid. The views expressed in this work are solely those of the author and do not necessarily reflect the views of the publisher, and the publisher hereby disclaims any responsibility for them.

ISBN: 978-1-936564-03-3   (sc)
ISBN: 978-1-936564-04-0   (dj)
ISBN: 978-1-936564-05-7   (ebook)

Printed in the United States of America

JournalStone rev. date: April 8, 2011

Cover Design by Denise Daniel

Artist-Illustrator: John "Hippie" Marks

Edited by Whitney L.J. Howell

Dedication

This book is dedicated to my husband, Mitch Savage, without whom it never would have been possible.

Acknowledgements:

Nancy McKinley, Stephanie Riese, Rachel Strayer, Renee and "Hippie", Christopher C. Payne with JournalStone Publications and all the things that go bump in the night.

Thank you for the encouragement, inspiration, help, advice, picking up off the floor and dusting off, love, laughs, the belief in me and my story and for the friendship.

Contents

Happy Birthday,

Sadie

The bright red lockers lining the school's hallway became a blur as Sadie started to run. She could smell the all-too-heavily applied perfume of her tormentors, and it made her stomach churn. That smell alone, not to mention to whom it was attached, gave her all the get up and go she needed. Picking up speed, she ran as fast as she could to avoid the impending after school confrontation. *Only one turn and I'm safe in the library.*

Sadie didn't mind running away from her bullies; at least then they wouldn't see her cry should the tears come again. Tears, like her moods lately, were always so unpredictable. Anything could trigger them. She ran, trying to act like she had somewhere very important to go, but knowing it was so obvious she was just trying to get away. She wished she could just keep on running, going as far away as her legs would carry her, and then go even further.

"Saaa – die's craaa – zy! Saaa – die's craaa – zy! Look at Crazy Sadie run! Where ya runnin' to, Sadie, to find your dead Moooom – ie?"

Sadie tried to block out the older girls' taunts, but the sing-song way they tormented her rang in her ears and reverberated through to her very soul. Actually, it broke her heart each and every time she heard them say those things to her or about her. She often wondered how much a heart could take before it just quit and broke for good.

She ran into the school library, letting the door slam shut loudly, and leaned against it to catch her breath. *They don't dare come into the library, there are too many books in here, and they might actually learn something, the stupid, catty girls.* Though Sadie didn't know what catty meant, she thought it applied to anyone who picked on her since she overheard some teachers use the word on that very same clique.

Three boys looked up from their computer stations and snickered when they saw who had come through the doors. Sadie readied herself for the next onslaught of jeers. As if right on cue, it began.

"She really thinks her mom is still alive...."

"I swear, she said so to Kate Anderson--she's *crazy*...."

"They should lock her up...."

"She's weird anyway--just look at her clothes, she only wears black now...."

Sadie put her head down and sighed as she made her way to her preferred hiding place in the back corner of the vast room. The smell of all those books, all those worlds to get lost in, brought a small wash of relief. But it always took a little while for her heart to stop pounding. She thought she would be used to the teasing by now; in reality, it was like a fresh scab repeatedly picked off an old wound every single time she heard their nasty heckling.

Stupid boys, at least they didn't start singing the crazy song at me, too, I hate it; I hate everyone.

She threw her backpack onto the floor in anger. As soon as it hit, three books flew down the aisle and landed at her feet.

What? Now they're throwing books at me?

She looked around and saw no one. Sadie stooped to pick up the volumes and carried them with her to the end of the aisle. Still, she saw no one. She looked down at the books she held in her arms.

I thought all the books in this aisle were Natural History Encyclopedias. These two are about the history of Halloween, and this one's about Mythological Beasts.

Shrugging it off to lackadaisical shelf restocking by the library aides, Sadie went back to the chair, her chair, in her self-appointed sanctuary. She plopped down in the well-worn piece of furniture, tossed the books to the side, and sighed once again. Picking at the loose threads on the arm of the rickety old chair, she kicked her feet on the wooden legs and heaved a sigh so heavy it blew the strands of fallen hair from her face. The lights flickered above her head, and one of the three bulbs in the overhead lamp popped and went out.

I guess that's just more of my bad luck, she said to herself and then laughed. *All of my conversations seem to be with myself anymore. No wonder they think I'm nuts.*

She pulled the book on Irish Fairies she had recently begun reading out of her backpack and snuggled into the chair. She had at least an hour and a half before all the other kids left school, and she could leave also without anyone around to taunt her.

Unfortunately, she couldn't focus on the words in front of her, and she stared off into the deep, book-filled room to dwell some more on what her life had become. A poster on the wall adjacent to her caught her eye. It wasn't so much the poster as what was in the bottom corner that grabbed her attention.

A small ladybug had been drawn, crawling along a branch on the poster tree. Sadie's eyes instantly welled up.

My mom always called me Ladybug.

She shut her eyes tightly to stop the tears and mostly, to try and regain control of her emotions. They seemed to have a life of their own, bursting out before Sadie knew what she had said or done. Though she couldn't control the actions of others, she at least wanted to be in control of herself. As she slowly reopened her eyes through the wet blur of unused tears, she could have sworn she saw the ladybug take flight.

Maybe I'm as crazy as they say.

She shut her eyes again, trying for once not to think about anything.

She didn't know how long she had been asleep when Mr. Cuttle woke her, telling her he was locking up the library and that she should have gone home hours ago. As he waddled towards her, she thought his name appropriate and sized him up accordingly. His arms were always waving about, seemingly for balance. His mouth snapped open and closed like a sharp beak and his bulbous eyes, made larger by his eyeglass lenses, protruded from his head. All of these things gave him the appearance of a cuttlefish.

She rubbed her own eyes and apologized to the portly man, but he just kept on muttering. She wasn't quite sure if he were even still talking to her, for he was yet another person Sadie tried to tune out when he spoke. She had always thought of the library as her refuge and Mr. Cuttle a neutral party; but when even he had begun suggesting she talk to someone about her problems, Sadie decided right then and there that he wasn't worth listening to anymore.

As she stretched she heard him say, "...and I just changed those bulbs yesterday."

Who cares about your stupid light bulbs? I've got bigger problems.

Still a little fuzzy from her nap, Sadie quickly gathered her things and left the school library, only stopping to see if the coast was clear once she reached the main school doors.

She looked down the left hallway--the one lined with the bright red lockers--and saw nothing but leftover Fall Festival posters littering the floor. She turned to her right and noticed that even the principal's office was empty, a sure sign no one was around. Kicking a broken pencil that had been abandoned like last year's school books, Sadie wondered when the janitor got there to clean up everyone's mess. Satisfied she was alone and there was no chance of running into anyone who could give her grief, she relaxed a little and let her shoulders sink.

Checking to make sure no one was around to torment her had become almost second nature, like breathing or brushing her teeth. It was something she just did. She didn't want it to be that way, but it was. And it hadn't always been that way either. When her mother was still around, Sadie fit in with a small group of friends very easily. They weren't close like spending-the-night-at-each-other's-house close; but they were close enough that she had someone to hang out with at school, people to eat lunch with, and a partner or two for science class.

Books were her true friends, along with her mother. But all of that changed after the car crash and her mother's death--or her supposed death. Sadie didn't truly believe her mom was dead. No body was found, and she just had this feeling, a strong feeling, her mother was still alive.

With no father, or any other family for that matter, social services had quickly swooped in like a portentous vulture. Though they said they had her well-being in mind, Sadie didn't trust them. She hated them actually. They reminded her constantly that she had no father or other family to take her, so she somewhat blamed them for her current state of mind.

To be fair though, her life had really changed for the worse when she went to live at the Anderson's foster home. She made the very bad mistake of telling Kate Anderson, who was close to her age, that she knew her mother was still alive. Instead of being a confidant and ally, Kate had told her mother, Mrs. Anderson, and Sadie ended up in therapy sessions and being transferred to another home.   "For the safety of the other children," Mrs. Anderson had said. "Who knows what else is going on in that girl's mind."

I hate thinking about these things. Why can't I turn my brain off?

Sadie heard the strong winds outside whip up against the front windows of the schoolhouse, rattling them with great force. She shook her head while looking down and pulled on the straps of her backpack. She bent downward and tied her shoelace that had come undone while she tried hard to swallow the lump in her throat.

The sadness could be overwhelming. She didn't notice the potted tree to her right seemed to wilt in her presence as she subdued her sobs for what seemed like the millionth time that day. Still lost in her thoughts, Sadie opened the big metal front doors of Cranberry Grove Middle School. She stepped outside onto Main Street and into the early evening weather, which seemed just as miserable as she was.

The biting October wind whipped her hair around her face, framing it to look like a crazed lion's mane. Its icy fingers stung her eyes, making them water, and her own fingers began to ache from not having on gloves. Sadie fought the blustery weather, leaning into the wicked wind, as she made her way down the sidewalk towards the center of town.

Leaves didn't have time to crackle and crunch under foot as they were torn from the tree limbs with great ferocity and flung about town like so many ragdolls. Sleet began to fall in sideways torrents, causing the sensation of a thousand little wasps stinging her cheeks all at once. Pulling her coat tighter to combat the chill, Sadie thought about her upcoming birthday, wondering if her foster family would make a big deal out of it.

Since she had only been there a few months, even though it was a few months more than usual, she didn't think so. The Argyles were kinder to her than the Andersons had been. Mrs. Argyle always had fresh cookies, treats, and hugs waiting for Sadie at the end of the day--which kind of annoyed her. It made her feel like Mrs. Argyle was putting on an elaborate show to win her over. But she was pleasant, caring and motherly nonetheless. And Mr. Argyle, though he worked an awful lot, always had a smile on his face.

They were definitely nicer than the Moatses, whom she had been transferred to after the Anderson fiasco. Mrs. Moats criticized everything and everyone, always on the verge of screaming her head off. You could monitor her anger by the vein on her forehead; it was like a mood meter. If it was pulsing and pounding, get out of the way. Mr. Moats, though, was even worse. You had to be nearly perfect to please that man. Sadie assumed it was his military background.

But, as per her track record, she had made a grave mistake there as well, saying she could have sworn she saw her mother's face in the clouds one day. And she did see it; Sadie was positive about that. Sure enough though, Mr. Moats had told her counselor at school and her state appointed social worker. He said he thought she wasn't adjusting well and that, for the sake of the other "normal" children, it would be best if she were placed somewhere else. Plus, he told them she didn't like to follow rules. Who could even keep up with, let alone follow, his never-ending list of rules? Her mother's only rule had been for Sadie to let her know where she was, always.

So off to the Argyle's house she went. Mrs. Argyle was a hospice worker, and Mr. Argyle was a bereavement counselor. So Sadie's social worker thought this would be the best place for her. And she didn't mind adding that this was probably the end of the line before Sadie would have to go live in a state operated orphanage if she didn't "straighten up and fly right" at the Argyle's home.

As soon as Sadie had heard mention of an orphanage, she tried to change right there on the spot, if only for show. From that point on she kept all her innermost thoughts and feelings to herself. No one would ever know what she was really thinking--ever again. On the outside, she would agree with people when they would speak of her mother in the past tense. She even began to believe it herself, somewhat.

Yet, another summer conceded (three to be exact) and another fall had begun before she really and truly began to accept the fact that her mom wasn't coming back. Not now, not ever. Three whole long years had passed, and it still hurt every day to think about it. Sadie wondered if the pain would ever go away. She remembered the day the policemen, with counselors in tow, had come to school to tell her.

They led her from the classroom to the principal's office without speaking. All the while Sadie had a strange feeling in her stomach. Still without talking to her, they sat her in a chair while they surrounded her in a semi-circle, as if she had done something wrong. And indeed, Sadie began to recount that morning's actions in her mind to try and remember if she had broken any rules. Now that act seemed so silly to her.

Dr. Miller, her elementary school principal, had been the one to break the news. No sugar-coating, no sympathy, just matter-of-fact, "Your mother has died, Sadie."

Now, every day, Sadie wakes up with that in the forefront of her memories and hears his voice in her head. "Your mother has died." She could never forget her mother was dead; her life had changed so much as a result. "Your mother has died." It was like a CD with a scratch on it that she couldn't find the button to turn off.

Sometimes though, she still let herself believe her mom was alive. As a matter of fact, she *knew* her mother was still alive, somewhere, out there. Sadie just didn't tell anyone these things anymore. Sadie knew she had to be alive; there were too many unanswered questions about the car crash for her not to think this way. She didn't care what the counselors, her foster parents or anyone said.

Plus, there was that feeling she got. Not just a feeling, but a *feeling*--a whisper she thought she heard, a presence she thought she felt, and her mind instantly filled with her mother's face. Sadie even smelled her on the wind, a sweet lavender scent that deposited a warm, homey feeling deep in the pit of her stomach then left, as fickle as it came.

She also thought about how much she missed having someone to confide in, especially since she was on the verge of becoming a teenager and things seemed to be changing so fast for her. Like why all of a sudden did she feel the need to start wearing black? She wasn't Goth or like those punk rockers and heavy metal kids at school. She didn't feel like she fit in with any of the kids at school for that matter.

She wasn't depressed, well, not *that* depressed. And she also didn't understand her sudden interest in fairy tales and all things mythical, mystical or magikal.

Boy, I could really use a good mother-daughter talk right now.

A frosty gust blew sleet down the nape of her neck and brought Sadie back from her thoughts with a shiver. She sighed, pulled her coat tighter, and continued her journey towards her new, but unwanted, home.

Ahead of her in Winslow's Hardware storefront alcove, Sadie noticed Crazy Mary conversing with herself, yet again. Crazy Mary was, well, for lack of a better phrase, the town crazy. Averting her eyes, Sadie tried to hurry past the old woman who seemed engrossed in a conversation with the parking meter right in front of the store.

Sadie was a little afraid of Crazy Mary. Not that the old woman had ever harmed anyone; nevertheless, Sadie acted like she didn't see her. It was kind of hard to take a muttering old woman who talks to walls, parking meters and trees seriously, in addition to looking like someone out of medieval times. Just when she thought she was clear of the eccentric old woman, Sadie felt a hand grip her arm. She froze, as if the weather had finally taken her.

"They're coming for you, sweetness. I don't know when or how, but mark my words, little Lammia, they are coming. Be vigilant, girl!" Then she brought her aged face close enough that Sadie could smell her sour breath. "Evil and madness grouped together as they are…this Syndicate of Lunacy…they wouldn't dare let the likes of you get away. I can see your shine a mile away," Crazy Mary said through cracked lips and ancient, pained eyes. She began muttering under her breath, "Run…hide-away…hidey-hide…won't be long now…."

Then the old woman burst into raucous laughter.

Sadie wrestled her arm away from the old woman as panic set in, and she ran towards the bookstore across the street, not even checking for oncoming traffic. She could hear Crazy Mary still cackling behind her. As she reached the curb, she tripped in her hurried carelessness; and if Sadie didn't know better, she could have sworn the parking meter directly in front of the shop reached out and righted her on the sidewalk. She shook her head as if the action could clear things away just like it does with an Etch-a-Sketch.

Just like me not to watch where I'm going.

As her hand touched the handle of the mostly glass door, the wind grabbed it, flinging it open furiously. This commotion caused those inside to look wide-eyed at the tussled young girl entering. Though it didn't shatter, it did cause enough of a scene to make Sadie feel uncomfortable. Wrestling it closed, shutting out the horrid weather, Sadie tried not to notice how many people were staring at her.

"Rough weather, huh, Sadie," the grandmotherly Mrs. Felis said more than questioned, as she looked up from the counter. "Come have a cup of tea with me to warm your bones. I wasn't expecting to see you tonight." The woman had a concerned look on her face.

Catching her breath, Sadie smoothed her hair and replied, "I hadn't planned on…I was just going home and…I thought I'd stop in, like usual, to see if there were any more of those donated second hand books I could take home. One day I'll have enough money to really buy something. I promise, Mrs. Felis."

As if her shaky voice weren't a giveaway, her staggered words definitely did so as she choked on getting them out. She hated being so transparent.

"Sadie, kitten, what's got into you tonight? You look five shades of pale and a bit shaken," the old woman said as she came around the counter.

Her cat Grimm silently leapt from his perch on the plant stand and came to weave himself in and out of Sadie's legs. The comfort Sadie felt from Grimm calmed her almost instantly, and helped her regain her composure.

"I'm okay, really. I'm just cold; and for the first time ever, Crazy Mary spoke to me. She actually touched my arm, called me some strange name, and said something about someone or something...something evil coming for me. Can you believe it? That woman is nuts."

Sadie took a deep breath and decided to change the subject. She had an uncomfortable, unexplainable feeling that she shouldn't speak ill of Crazy Mary. "Not to mention, this weather is outta control. Where did it come from?" Sadie said, forcing a smile and unbuttoning her coat.

For a fleeting moment Mrs. Felis hesitated before she took Sadie's coat from her and hung it on the aged black wrought-iron coat stand by the door. The old woman hugged Sadie closer than usual and beamed at her through sparkling green eyes full of love. The pair walked to the corner of the bookstore reserved for Mrs. Felis and Grimm.

Two big overstuffed chairs with footstools and a table holding a tea kettle and cookies filled the space and made it a cozy place, one where you could stay lost for hours with a good book. Books had always been Sadie's friends, her only friends now as she was also considered crazy in her own way since she admitted to thinking her mom was still alive.

As Sadie plopped into the huge chair, Mrs. Felis poured her a cup of tea and added a spoonful of honey, just the way she liked it. Handing the cup and saucer to Sadie, she poured her own and sat opposite the girl in her personally familiar chair. Grimm appeared at her feet and began his winding dance between their legs. For once, he didn't go straight to the extremely large bowl of catnip Mrs. Felis kept on the table in between the cookies and tea. He liked catnip so much that Sadie often thought they may have to have an intervention on him.   Distracted by Grimm, Sadie looked up in time to see Mrs. Felis sprinkling some of the catnip into her own cup of tea.

What on earth? Catnip in her tea? I mean, I do know that Felis means cat in Latin. She told me as much, but to eat catnip is taking it a bit too far. She must be losing it in her old age.

Seeing that her action didn't go unnoticed, Mrs. Felis briskly wiped her hands together in an almost clapping fashion and chuckled, red-faced. She shook her head and tsked-tsked herself as if embarrassed at being seen making such a silly mistake.

"Oh, what a silly thing I am--thought it was the sugar bowl. I did." Clearing her throat she continued, changing the subject quickly. "So, little one, your birthday is coming in one day. To be precise, it's tomorrow. You'll be thirteen. That's a special age for you people, isn't it? Do you have any plans? Is your new family doing anything in particular?"

As soon as the words left Mrs. Felis's mouth, it looked as though she regretted them, knowing the pain it would cause little Sadie. It was an unfortunate reminder that this was yet another birthday without her mother.

You people? Mrs. Felis had always been a little *off*, and Sadie, once again, chalked it up to old age. But *you people*, what exactly did that mean?

"No, no plans. I hate that Mom isn't...I hate that my birthday is on Halloween. My birthday gets mushed into that stupid holiday, and it's not really about my birthday anymore. Or...all my presents have to do with ghosts and pumpkins and witches. Mom always made sure my birthday was very un-Halloween."

After a moment's silence, she continued, trying to sound more cheerful, "At least I don't have a Christmas birthday. I'd be swamped with snowmen and reindeer and Santa stuff."

As Sadie said her last word, she exhaled a sigh full of heavy sadness and bowed her head. As she did so, the leaves on the very tall spotted angel wing begonia began to drop in a flurry, as if sighing themselves. Sadie turned her head slowly and eyed the shedding plant. With a curious expression she turned back to face Mrs. Felis.

"Well, that was weird, about as weird as everything else that's been happening to me this week," Sadie said as she sipped her tea and hungrily eyed the cookies on the plate next to her.

With a chuckle, Mrs. Felis set down her untouched tea, passed Sadie the cookies, and looked at her with a warm, loving expression.

"You should feel proud to be born at such an exciting time of year. Halloween is actually my favorite holiday. Since it's combined with my favorite person's birthday, it makes it all the more extraordinary. You and I will do something special, just for you, something that distinctly separates those two wonderful holidays. Come by here some time tomorrow when we open, and I'll have a unique surprise for you."

Just then, the sleigh bells on the door jingled and in slinked a customer wrapped from head to toe in heavy black wool clothing, for protection from the nasty fall weather, one could only assume. Before Mrs. Felis looked away, she gave Sadie a wink, licked her fingers on both hands and began smoothing her hair back into her silvery-gray bun.

The woman and child sat in comfortable silence for the next few moments. Mrs. Felis had been like a grandmother to Sadie from the moment they first met, which Sadie thought was a wonderful thing since she had never met her own grandparents.

Sadie recounted their first meeting and smiled as a warm, soothing feeling spread through her body. The bookstore had just appeared, practically overnight, almost six months ago. While walking home from school one day, Sadie had noticed the empty building because it gave her a peculiar feeling in her stomach. And the very next morning on her way to school again, it wasn't empty anymore. How delighted she was in discovering it had become a bookstore. The old woman had taken to Sadie as soon as she had walked through the door, like she'd been waiting for her. And Sadie had taken to her as well. How could she not? With her little round glasses that slid down her nose, her grey hair pulled loosely into a bun at all times, her long grey matronly dresses spiced up with very grand Victorian boots all coupled with the warm way she smiled. She reminded Sadie of a storybook aunt or someone's kind old granny.

Being a voracious reader and always looking for a place to hide away, Sadie didn't waste any time in becoming a regular. Mrs. Felis even gave her some books to take home, since Sadie had no money of her own. Sadie assumed this was where newfound interest in all things magikal had come from. The fact being that all the donated books Mrs. Felis gave her were, ironically, about magik, witchcraft, and mythological beasts.

What she couldn't figure out was why Crazy Mary had taken to hanging around outside the bookstore. Sadie had never seen her with a book in her gnarled old hands, let alone, reading. She figured it must be because of the kindness Mrs. Felis shows everyone. The warm feeling of safety rushed through her body again at the thought of Mrs. Felis. Eventually, Sadie began to feel like her old self again and even put Crazy Mary's intrusion out of her mind. Though she still thought it odd that the woman would even talk to her and even odder still the words she uttered. She knew enough about crazy people to know not to listen to them.

With a sigh, Sadie set down her tea and spoke. "I guess I should be going home now. I left the school library much later than I thought."

What she didn't say was that she was hiding out in the library to avoid the teasing and taunting from the mean kids at school. It could be so tiring to have a daily battle of wits with those that thought you beneath them.

"Thank you, Mrs. Felis, for always being there for me. I wish you could be my aunt or grandma or something. Then I could live with you and ..." she stopped before continuing the fantasy. "Anyway, I just wish you and I were real family."

And she genuinely meant it.

A look Sadie couldn't discern flashed across the old woman's face, and Sadie chalked it up to a stack of books the still very much bundled up customer had just knocked over. Sadie was just happy to have the old woman in her life, especially now, and hugged her fiercely. As Sadie released her from the hug, Mrs. Felis held tight a few seconds longer before she, too, let go.

"Before you go, dear, I have a book for you," she said with those emerald eyes of hers sparkling once again.

Sadie followed her to the counter where she was handed a beautiful green leather-bound book. The front was ornately decorated with intricate spirals that curled into complex and even more beautiful flowers. The raised detail begged for her to run her hands across it, to feel its beauty; as she did so, a surge of happiness washed through her like a warm summer day. There was no title, no name given to this book, which Sadie thought odd. So she opened it to see what the first page held. It was blank. She turned a page; it was blank, too. As was the next and the next. With questioning eyes, she looked at Mrs. Felis.

"Call it an early birthday present. It's sort of like a book of your own to write in and make personal--all about you and what you know," said the sweet, old woman.

"But what do I write?" asked Sadie as she wiggled into her coat and grabbed her bag.

"Oh, you'll know. You'll know when the words come to you," she replied as she took the book from Sadie, turned her around and put it in her backpack. "Mr. and Mrs. Argyle will be worrying about you; it's getting darker by the minute. Best hurry home, Sadie, my love."

She kissed the top of Sadie's head and then brushed her cheek against Sadie's, an action Sadie had at first thought odd, but then had become accustomed to it since she did it every time Sadie left the bookstore. Mrs. Felis sent her out the door, into the cold fall night, and back to a home that didn't quite feel like home.

Sadie turned to face her coveted family. She smiled at both Mrs. Felis and Grimm standing in the doorway, and she braced herself for the cold walk. She always felt good when she left the bookstore and Mrs. Felis. Smiling, she fought the wind and assault of sleet and leaves and began trudging the three blocks off Main to her foster parent's home. Then she had to stop and turn around. As she did she silently laughed at the error. She was staying with the Argyle family now, not the Moatses; she lived on Main now, just three blocks up from the bookstore, not three blocks off Main.

All these foster homes were getting confusing. It had been three years, and in that amount of time, she racked up the same number of families. At least she was still in the same town. She always felt so sorry for those kids that had to learn new towns and cities all the time. Cranberry Grove, Pennsylvania, was her hometown, and it felt safe to her; plus, Mrs. Felis and the bookstore were there.   Sadie was never good at making new friends, any friends for that matter, only having those acquaintances she *used to* have at school. She always assumed the friends she did have were because they were outcasts just like her. And the families, none of them really wanted her, and they all had something to say about it. Funny thing was that it was all about the same.

"There's something wrong with this girl...she hardly speaks to us, to anyone; when she does speak, it's to say her mother's still alive." That was what Mrs. Anderson used to say. "She's too quiet, too shy, too withdrawn, too unusual and definitely strange. If she does speak and it's not about her mother, it's to ask too many questions. The girl just rambles on and on."

That was Mrs. Moats' complaint about her. Mr. Moats was more direct: "She still thinks her mother is alive. We can't afford all the therapy bills this one will need."

And Sadie's personal favorite, which she'd never forget, was from Mr. Anderson. "When she's sad, it's like a dark cloud settles over the house."

I just wish I were a normal kid. I don't know what's wrong with me.

Sadie wrestled with this in her head. The same dilemma she'd been fighting her whole life. It had become a tired old lament she tortured herself with on a daily basis. At least this family, the Argyle family, wasn't making her see a shrink anymore for thinking her mother was still alive.

Sadie quickly remembered the first time she told Mrs. Argyle she knew her mother was still alive. How she was probably wandering, lost, confused, with some sort of amnesia, trying to work things out. Mrs. Argyle smiled at Sadie and asked her to sit with her in the parlor to tell her all about it. Sadie, at first thinking it was a trick, only said a few, small things. But then, after realizing the woman really was genuinely interested *and* wasn't going to send her away, Sadie let loose and told her all her theories, starting with the body.

If Sadie knew these things, she really didn't understand why the police didn't. It made so much sense. To have a car crash without finding a body? Granted, the car careened into the river, but eventually, wouldn't a body wash up somewhere? And the police theories about animals dragging it away, well, there haven't been coyote sightings in Cranberry Grove or the surrounding towns for over three decades. There weren't any other large animals so Sadie just didn't buy that theory. And wild dogs, well, she hadn't seen any of them either. Even the fishes couldn't dispose of a body that quickly.

If her mother were dead, her body would have been found sooner or later. Sadie just knew it. She told all of this to Mrs. Argyle freely and without constraint. It felt good to actually let it all out. Mr. and Mrs. Argyle were probably analyzing her themselves, and that was okay with Sadie if it meant not going to the therapists twice a week. All they wanted to do was put her on medications that made her head feel like a balloon. And the one set of pills made it so she felt nothing. Sadie didn't like crying all the time, but at least she felt something. While on the medications she walked around in a balloon-headed stupor, numb to anything and everything. Though the pain of it all still burned deep, she would much rather deal with it as opposed to feeling nothing. She just wanted to feel like herself, even if that meant she were sad all the time. At least there might be a chance at feeling happiness again without all those medications to cloud her mind.

As she made her way home, Sadie stopped torturing herself with thoughts of her mother. Sadie didn't think about Crazy Mary and what she said. She didn't notice the pelting sleet and cold evening autumn air. She didn't think about not having her mom anymore. She didn't think about her upcoming birthday being combined with Halloween. And she didn't notice the large man in a long black wool trench coat with his hat pulled down over his eyes standing in the alleyway between Johnson's Title and Tag Service and Dipsy's Doughnuts watching her every move.

* * *

As Sadie lay sleeping in her bed, an ominous dark cloud, not unlike the metaphorical one her prior foster families always said hung over her, settled over the house. It only hovered over this house, her house, and it seemed to breathe as it enveloped the rooftop. It was a strange, dark cloud, unusual in its appearance. Its appearance was as curious as those times when it rained in the front yard, but not the back yard.

Sadie stirred under the covers and began to blink her eyes. A noise awoke her. It was a noise that much was obvious. It wasn't music or singing or a sound. It wasn't anything like that. It wasn't anything that denotes something good sounding. It was noise, but it was an attractive noise. It drew her in like a moth to the flame. The noise grew louder yet was not an assault on her ears. It was a cacophony of sounds all blended together to make "that noise." Humming, fragments of sentences and the clink, clatter, and clash of daily objects all blended together to make that attractive noise the background music for something that made her feel good. It made her feel good because it was home, and it had been a long time since Sadie had a "home."

It's all been just a horrible nightmare.

She smiled like she hadn't ever before and opened her eyes completely. Silence. Grey light filled the room, and Sadie's smile faded as she realized she was home and not "home." Home was where her mother was. Home was where Sadie felt like she was okay. Home wasn't the Argyle's big old empty house. It was her and her mother's cozy little apartment. Home wasn't the nightmare of foster care at all.

Yeah, it's a nightmare all right, a waking one, she thought as she rolled over and tried not to let the sadness creep in yet again. *I miss my Mom.*

Three hours later Sadie woke and dressed quickly, for she was in a hurry to get back to the bookstore. She tried to avoid her foster family as much as possible. They were nice, nicer than most had been, but they still weren't "hers." And Sadie had the sneaking suspicion she was just filling a void since they couldn't have children of their own.

Mrs. Argyle was at the head of the table with her needlepoint accoutrements in the two remaining chairs as Mr. Argyle had already left for work. The new, un-matching one had been placed carefully amongst the other two just for Sadie, but she felt as awkward as it looked when she sat there. It wasn't a part of the set and neither was Sadie. She said her "good mornings" and "goodbyes" as she grabbed a piece of toast from the clutter of threads and hoops on the kitchen table.

"Sadie, where are you rushing off to? It's your birthday, and I thought we'd do something especially Halloween-y since it's both Halloween and your thirteenth birthday. And I wanted to ask you why you're always wearing black now? Are you trying that whole Goth thing? I do understand children expressing themselves through their clothing. Where are…" said Mrs. Argyle to no avail. Her voice was fading in Sadie's ears as the woman shouted out, "Happy Birthday, Sadie! Make it home in time for the trick-or-treaters!"

But Sadie was already out the door.

She felt bad for ignoring Mrs. Argyle; she tried really hard to make Sadie feel at home, but talking about her Halloween birthday was something she just didn't want to do. Kicking at the sticks and leaves that last night's wind had left in piles around Main Street, she didn't look up in time to see the moving van and boxes piled high on the sidewalk. Just then, she smacked into a very large, very solid wall made of dark clothing. It wasn't really a wall, but it felt like one. What Sadie had really run into was a very large man.

"You should watch where you're going. A little girl like you could run into all sorts of dangers," said the man through a wide, beaming grin.

"I'm s-sorry. I wasn't paying attention," she said as she tried to sidestep him and the mess of clutter in front of her.

"Hey, what's the rush?" he boomed as the statement began to make Sadie uncomfortable. "I've got a son about your age; you should meet him. Since we're new to town, maybe you could show him around? He's not helping out here that's for sure," he said as he motioned for someone in the house.

Why does he seem, I don't know, familiar?

"I...I don't know..." Sadie stammered, feeling very uncomfortable, "I'm supposed to be somewhere. It's my bir...I just can't...."

But he cut her off. "Nonsense!" he said a little too forcefully for Sadie's liking. "He can go with you, can't he?"

The man looked at Sadie with condescending eyes and a disgusted smirk, yet his voice had become softer. "Well, at least you two can meet so he has a friend come Monday morning. I understand you can't just go off willy-nilly with a stranger. I'm just anxious for him to meet people since we're new in town."

Why do all adults think that children don't have important things to say or do? How rude, Sadie thought to herself. *And isn't he being a bit forward?*

She softened a little remembering how hard it always was, and still is, for her to make new friends. She smiled up at the tall man.

Stranger-Dangers she heard her mother's voice say in her mind, yet clear as crystal.

As she stood on the sidewalk feeling confused, awkward and on the spot, Sadie watched as a dirty-blonde haired boy, about her age, appeared at the door. With his hands shoved deep in his pockets, he begrudgingly came towards her and the man who was his father.

"David, come meet..." he slowly turned to face Sadie again. "I'm sorry, what do they call you, girl?"

"S-Sadie," she said shyly, "I'm Sadie."

And I HATE being put on the spot.

"Come meet Sadie, David."

David sulkily walked up to Sadie and without looking up, said hello. At least, she thought it was a hello. It was a low mumbling of a hello, and it reminded Sadie of how painful it was for her to meet new people--let alone a boy. His dirty- blonde hair hung down in his eyes, not like he was going for a look, but like he was in desperate need of a haircut. His clothes were black, which she didn't know why but she liked, and he was shoving a stick into his pocket as he drew near.

Just like a boy! I bet he's got a frog or snake or something in those pockets, too.

He didn't look too happy about having to meet her, or it could have been the fact that he had to unpack all this stuff; but he looked disturbed enough that Sadie warmed to him a little. She felt genuine pity for this kid, especially with a dad like that. But...at least he had a dad.

I never had a dad, and now I don't even have a mom.

"Hello, David," Sadie replied with a hint of pity.

After a few moments of awkward silence consisting of Sadie looking at David--*I have nowhere else to look*--David looking at the ground--*poor kid*--and David's father glaring down at both of them--*I can feel his eyes boring into my flesh.* Sadie finally broke up the standoff by clearing her throat.

"I have to go now," she said, sounding sure, but feeling unsure.

Mumbled goodbyes began and just as it looked like David's father was going to touch Sadie, to pat her on the back or something, he pulled his hand away as if he thought better of it.

Like he would get cooties or something, she thought. *Even strangers think I'm a weirdo.*

The last two blocks to the bookstore went quickly, and as Sadie opened the door, once again the wind took it and flung it wide. But...this time Sadie noticed there was no wind.

"Sorry, Mrs. Felis, I guess I don't know my own strength," said Sadie as she wiped her feet on the mat.

"It's okay, Piseag. The hinges are just too loose," Mrs. Felis replied, bearing a huge grin not unlike that of the Cheshire Cat.

Sadie hung her coat by the door and made her way to her usual overstuffed chair with Grimm tagging along behind her. Following the two of them was a very eager, very glowing Mrs. Felis carrying a large box wrapped in Happy Birthday wrapping paper which had NO markings what-so-ever stating that today was also Halloween. Sadie grinned to herself and acted surprised when she turned to sit down and saw it. Though she had seen the gift out of the corner of her eye, she still wasn't convinced it was all birthday and no Halloween. Looking at the present, she smiled wider when she realized that pink and yellow wrapping paper in no way would make someone think of Halloween.

Just like Mom used to do, she thought before taking the gift from Mrs. Felis.

"Happy thirteenth Birthday, Sadie. May you have many more!" Mrs. Felis said with a slight tear in her eye.

Grimm had jumped on top of the package and rubbed his face along Sadie's cheek. Little bits of catnip fell from his fur to Sadie's lap, and he quickly scooped them up with his paws and put them on his tongue, all the while still rubbing on Sadie.

"Leave her alone, you cheeky cat," Mrs. Felis said as she picked him up. "Let Sadie open her gift and then you can monopolize her time."

"Oh, he doesn't bother me. I kinda like his touching me. For some reason, it makes me feel good," said Sadie as she played with the ribbon on her present.

Mrs. Felis cleared her throat, set Grimm down, and began pouring the tea. Grimm did figure eights at Sadie's ankles as she smiled inside, wondering what on earth her gift could be. It was only nine o'clock in the morning, and, so far, it was turning out to be a wonderful birthday day.

I only hope something doesn't mess things up like usual. I've got that weird feeling in my chest like I always get right before something comes along and WHAM! My world is upside down again.

Handing Sadie her cup, Mrs. Felis began to speak after she took a quick sip of tea. "Sadie, my pet, I want you to make a wish before you open that gift. It's not every day a girl turns thirteen."

Mrs. Felis looked as though she bit her tongue. Sadie suspected it was because she was about to say it was also Halloween.

Sadie took a lengthy, unhurried sip. She let the honeyed, warm liquid wash down her throat slowly. She then took two more to give herself time to think about her wish. One more sip and she set the cup and saucer on the side table so that she could be very serious about this birthday wish. She always wanted to make Mrs. Felis happy. Plus, for some reason, she really felt that whatever wish she made could come true.

As she looked up at Mrs. Felis, about to speak, Mrs. Felis's face began to contort and blur. Sadie saw Mrs. Felis grab the arm of her chair and slowly, awkwardly begin to sit down. Sadie tried to move, but felt as though she weighed a thousand pounds. Her head was thick and her tongue matched. In her distorted vision Sadie saw Mrs. Felis's lips move, but just barely heard her words.

"Sadie, the tea, I think something's wrong. This smells like my sleeping tea, not chamomile." Then, everything went black.

Somewhere

Between Dreams and

Reality

A cold wash of air blew over Sadie, causing her to shiver. *Where am I? Last thing I remember, I was in the bookstore.* She looked around, not recognizing her surroundings, and became alarmed. It was getting dark here, wherever she was, and fear began to prickle up her spine. *I think I'm going crazy. I have no idea where I am or how I got here.* She spun around, trying to take it all in and ground herself in the situation.

"I'm coming for you, Sadie," cried a vibrating voice in the menacing darkness.

She inhaled quickly, but the cold air bit into her lungs with its icy fangs and took her breath away just as fast. Resisting the urge to cough, Sadie struggled to capture just a moment of controlled breathing. As she focused on equal inhaling and exhaling, she tried to take notice of her surroundings. That horrible sleet was back again, coming at her from all directions and assaulting her brutally. She pulled her coat closer to shield herself from the new burst of weather as she searched for a way out. At least the moon was full and bright, giving her some sort of light in the darkness.

In front of her lay a vast, murky peat bog, sure to filch her to her death. If the quicksand waters didn't get her, then Tod Lowery would.

Children steer clear of the Tod Lowery's bog; they'll drown your soul and turn you into a frog. Oh, my God, how do I know these things?

To her left, the immense forest began. It was undulating and moving like fabric in the wind. The wicked storm tore the vestiges of fall's leaves from their branches and didn't give them time to alight on the ground. It swept them away forever. Not bending to wind's will, limbs began to snap and crash to the earth violently.

Too many dangers in the forest, both living and dead.

To her right the immense lake pounded the shoreline with angry intentions of utter destruction. Cold fingers of surf seemingly reached out for her, to snatch her away to a chilly and painful dark blue death.

As she stared out at the angry loch, the mast of a large sailboat broke and crashed into the furious waters, taking the handful of sailors on board with it. All disappeared rapidly below the ever-changing surface in the blink of an eye.

The Undines will have fun tonight. Wait! Who is putting these thoughts into my head?

Sadie turned widdershins, trying desperately to spot a safe place amongst so many threats. As she did so, she noticed three ethereal wraiths appear from nowhere known. She crouched behind a cluster of abandoned fishing gear and remembered once again to breathe, as the hideous ghosts glided in the opposite direction from her position on the beachhead. Further up the beach, five algae-draped, calcium-encrusted corpses trudged slowly out of the waters, oblivious to the surf. Slick black eels slithered from their homes within eye sockets and crayfish dropped from the flesh they had been feeding on. These rotting and stinking pieces of water-logged tissue moved precariously towards shore to begin their part in the hunt for Sadie.

How is it I know they're after me?

From the wood emerged the Hell Hounds, shaking off moist clumps of black earth, their fiery red eyes glowed bright in the fury of the gale. Their rancid, hot breath could be seen in puffs steaming forth from their nostrils and lather had formed around their mouths. With enlarged new claws clicking and clacking against the sound of gnashing teeth, the beasts assembled to carry out their orders. Before the Hell Hounds ran off towards the swamp, Sadie thought they had caught her scent as they furiously sniffed the air sweeping from her direction.

Where are all the good magikal creatures when you need them?

A gust blew up and scattered her cover, exposing her to whatever entity should come for her next.

RUN.

Staying on the middle ground between forest and lake, she ran as fast as her legs would carry her.

She ran, not feeling the pain in her chest. Somehow fear gave her back her ability to breathe. She ran, not caring what she ran towards. She knew she had to run away. She ran, like a sneak thief coveting her prize. She barreled towards what she hoped was safety.

When hope ends, grasp for anything to stay alive, but use your heart before your head.

As if Mother Nature were against her as well, the sleet came harder, faster, causing her to shut her eyes from its attack. A voice in the darkness began calling her name.

"Sadie...Saaaaaaaadieeeeeeee...."

When she opened her eyes again, the sheer impact of her surroundings struck her like an angry open hand. Everything was silent. Gob-smacked, she realized she was staring into her mother's smiling face.

"Sadie, you were having a dream, a very bad dream. I'm here love; it'll be okay," said her mother in a soft and gentle voice.

Relief flooded Sadie as the warmth of her bed, her mother's presence, and her new-found safety encompassed her entire being. She stared at her mother's soft expression and relaxed a bit.

"Oh, Mom! It was awful. I couldn't get away. They kept coming. I couldn't breathe, and I was scared and...."

Wrapping her in the time immemorial safety that her mother's hugs always brought her, Sadie slowly began to calm down and relinquish her urge to flee.

"Sssssshhhhhh, sweetie. I'm here now. It was all just a dream."

Sadie smelled the sweet lavender, her mother's scent, and inhaled deeply. She felt the warmth of her hug and, in an instant, felt safe and secure. The strength in her mother's arms somewhat surprised her, she had never known her to be so strong, but Sadie chalked it up to a mother trying to calm a distraught child.

When her trembling had stopped, Sadie pulled back a little to look at her mother's face, wanting to ground herself in reality after such a nasty, frightening nightmare. She was smiling down at her and moved her hand to caress Sadie's tear-streaked cheek.

When did Mom's hands get so rough? They're usually so soft and un-calloused? She must have been working in our little garden plot out back of the apartment without gloves.

"It's all better now," she whispered to the child.

Sadie buried her head and hugged her mother back as if she hadn't seen her in years.

Something's not right.

Her senses came alive again, tingling with reception.

My mom's dead.

Her own heart skipped a beat as she tried to reconcile what was now happening.

My mom's car went into the river. My mom died in that car crash.

Slowly, she released herself from her so-called mother's hug and with new fear, lifted her gaze to face her latest obstacle.

Her mother's beautiful red hair turned black and grey while her smooth skin aged centuries in seconds before Sadie's eyes. Her nose began to hook and crook and her eyes turned to narrow red slits. Yellow, broken teeth bared themselves from between thin, cracked lips that dribbled greasy spittle onto its now caved in chest. The smell of rotting flesh emanated from this creature, causing Sadie's stomach to turn. She put her hand over her mouth to quell the urge to vomit.

A slimy grey tongue flicked in and out of the repulsive mouth like a snake scenting the air for prey. Black shadow creatures flitted about the space surrounding this new witchy creature, weaving an invisible web to ensnare their victims. As Sadie stared, horrified at the thing before her, festering boils appeared on any exposed flesh and oozed pus that sizzled like bacon grease. She opened her mouth, maybe in protest, but she couldn't speak as she stared into its ominous eyes.

"I told them I'd get you, Sadie, any which way, we are going to get you," the witchy-thing before her rasped as Sadie's world turned to black yet again.

"SADIE!"

From some vast distance a voice called to her across the black abyss. She struggled, as something had a hold on her consciousness, to open her eyes once more.

"Oh, Sadie, thank ye gods, you were having such bad dreams, and I couldn't wake you," said Mrs. Felis as she hugged her tight.

Sadie remained motionless in the old woman's arms, afraid, yet ready, should this be another trick of the mind or some crafty concoction from those "otherworldly" creatures that had been after her. As she slowly regained her composure, her head pounding, Sadie tried to focus on something, anything, not to remember the wretched breath or horrid eyes of the witch-thing that had only moments ago been breathing in her face.

"W…what's going on? What happened? My head really hurts." Sadie said as she rubbed her eyes to try and get the blurriness out.

How can dreams seem so real?

"Oh, Sadie, I must have mixed up a batch of Sleeping Aid tea, and a bit too much I might add--you fell sound asleep." Mrs. Felis released her hug and picked up her cup of tea, obviously freshly brewed. "You've been out for many hours. I would have been as well, had I taken a bigger sip of that tea and been as small as you. Luckily I wasn't and could take care of…."

"WHAT? What do you mean? How? How on earth did you mix up the teas? THEY ARE CLEARLY MARKED! I've SEEN the jars!" Sadie yelled, cutting Mrs. Felis off mid-sentence. "I don't understand," she said in a lower voice, realizing she had been screaming.

"Sadie, my little kitten, to be completely honest with you, someone must have switched them…and I have a feeling I know why," replied Mrs. Felis, a bit frayed at the edges.

She took a sip from her teacup as though nothing suspicious had just happened with the drinks.

Sadie, still trying to digest what she had just been told, sat quietly thinking to herself.

Who goes around switching old ladies' tea jars?

The idea seemed preposterous to her.

She is getting old. She must have done it herself; maybe she needs to get those glasses checked.

Grimm jumped up onto Sadie's lap from the gift box that lay at her feet. *Some birthday,* thought Sadie.

"I've only been awake for about two hours now, and already my bad luck has ruined it," she said trying not to sound too depressed.

"Sadie, it's almost midnight, Halloween night, eleven thirty to be exact, you've been out for the entire day and evening," Mrs. Felis said softly.

As new panic set in and Sadie's fingers dug into the upholstery of the chair's arm, Mrs. Felis noticed her alarm and tried to calm the now-again-distraught Sadie.

"I'm afraid, dear, there's some things I need to tell you--some information that you might not find too easy to digest," said Mrs. Felis.

"Could I have a drink of…no, wait, never mind, not after what just happened," said Sadie through a dry throat as she thought better of drinking anything else she didn't open or pour herself.

"We don't have time, anyway. What I need to tell you should have, would have, taken me all day today; now we've got but a mere half hour," Mrs. Felis stated much to the shock of Sadie. "No use having that stunned look on your face now, little one; wait 'til you hear what I've got to say," she finished, with a big cat-who-ate-the-canary grin.

Sadie took a deep breath and braced herself for the worst. The worst was what she was used to, at least since her mom died three years ago.

Here it comes; she's probably gonna say I'm being given to another foster family. Oh, NO! The Argyles! They've probably called the police by now, thinking I've run away.

"The Argyles, I have to call them or…."

"The Argyles are fine, Sadie," replied Mrs. Felis.

She twitched her nose a little, which reminded Sadie of Grimm, and then put catnip into her tea right in front of Sadie. Sadie's eyes opened wide, as did her mouth, and then she pulled her jaw shut quickly.

There's no reason in letting her know that I think she's gone absolutely mental.

Sadie straightened up in her chair and tried to look as though she were intensely listening to the old woman. In reality, she was rationalizing the situation and circumstances in her mind.

Poor Mrs. Felis, she's finally lost it in her old age. See, she probably switched those tea jars. I wonder what crazy thing she's gonna say or do next. Is she going to tell me that my mom was an assassin or something, and she killed someone so important that now they're after me?

Mrs. Felis set her tea cup down very matter-of-factly. She smoothed her dress with her hands and then folded them on her lap. Crossing her legs at her ankles, she wiggled back further into her chair. She then cleared her throat and looked Sadie right in the eyes.

"Not an assassin, Sadie, but a witch; yes, people are after you to capture you. And I'm not sure, but I think to kill you. That's why I'm pretty sure they had to be the ones who switched the teas in the jars, so that they could get to you without incident. You see, I'm NOT crazy or losing it in my old age. I couldn't have, would NEVER have made such a mistake on such an important day. Oh, and you're a witch, too, at least at midnight you will be."

What on earth is Mrs. Felis talking about? Sadie quickly, internally, tried to understand and digest those three sentences. *I think the poor old thing has really lost her mind. I am so confused.*

Once again, she felt like someone had rung her bell. Head spinning, hurting, and body numb from shock, she began to consider Mrs. Felis' words. Her emotions ran the gamut from sadness and fear to joy and laughter back to panic and uncertainty. Rationale went out the door as she noticed that outside the bookstore windows, it was indeed nighttime.

Okay, so I was *asleep for a long time that much is true. But this witch stuff-- that's just crazy.*

Taking deep, measured breaths, Sadie continued to process this new and crazy information.

Be calm, Sadie told herself; *let's just try to figure this out. Mrs. Felis must be completely insane. As crazy as...well, as crazy as Crazy Mary.*

Her eyebrows scrunched as her brain tried to assemble and sort this new information.

Witches aren't real, but maybe that explains my dream. No, maybe it's me; that's gotta be it; I'm crazy! Yeah, that must be it; I'm nuts or...still dreaming.

She stared at Mrs. Felis who had deposited herself in her usual chair and the old woman and young girl were locked in the heavy, paralyzing silence of the bookstore until a revelation smacked Sadie out of her internal thoughts.

"Wait, I didn't say that out loud, the part about my mom being an assassin, or did I?"

Sadie hated that she was second guessing herself, but after everything that had happened, it was to be expected she thought. "You read my mind. So...I guess there must be something to all of this, or it's that I'm crazy or I'm still dreaming or...."

"No, Sadie, you're not crazy, not yet. You might be though after you hear the rest, or should I say, *see*," said Grimm as he jumped up onto Sadie's lap and began grooming himself ever so casually and with a bit of cat-smugness.

Before Sadie's mind could register a talking cat, little sparks of colored light began to pop and crackle throughout the bookstore. Each pop and crackle appeared like colorful fireflies and just as quickly, blinked out as if they never happened. From these little bursts of multi-colored light, creatures and beasts of every sort began to appear--the types of creatures and beasts you only read about in mythology books or see in the movies.

There was a centaur vigorously pulling his tail which had been caught in the front doors as they shut. His long black hair and mane ran down his human back to his horse body from the Mohawk on his head.

I didn't even hear the bells on the door jingle.

A green-skinned elf jumped down off the top shelf of books closest to Mrs. Felis without a sound, his pointy ears twitching back and forth. Five twinkling faeries fluttered and then alighted on the shoulders of Mrs. Felis, who had taken her usual place in the chair next to Sadie. Two lumpy gnomes put down books they had been reading on urban mining techniques and began to waddle towards her. Grimm looked up at Sadie while she sat in utter amazement; if cats smiled, he did so.

Everyone was right about me. I am crazy! There is no way this is really happening!

A group of ghosts, seven old women carrying knitting bundles to be exact, came in chattering amongst themselves. Sadie heard one of the two gnomes tell the ghosts to stay out of them, as they passed in and, well, out, of the little guys while they formed their semi-circle before the sitting nook. From out of the aquarium splashed two blue water sprites, leaning over the side with big wide grins and twisting their deep azure hair around their webbed fingers. Three old women, dressed in long black flowing clothing and covered in what looked to be fireplace ash, popped into existence next to Mrs. Felis. Each one carried a very large bag with her. The one stroked Mrs. Felis's frazzled hair and smiled at her as the others began to brush ash from their clothing and mutter to each other about "the trip."

Sadie took it all in as Grimm began to purr on her lap. A smile spread across her face and then she laughed out loud, a laugh so strident it silenced the now chatter filled bookstore.

All eyes were on Sadie. Heat rushed to her cheeks, and she felt the familiar knot of uncomfortable tension twisting in her stomach. She tried to clear her throat, but it came out a loud, choking squeak.

"Well, does this human speak or does she only make animal noises 'cause I can get that at home from him?" asked one of the gnomes as he hooked a gnarled little thumb at the other one.

"Hey," the other one said thumping the first one on the head. "Watch it or I'll feed yer lumpy carcass to the Hell Hounds."

(Though as he spoke, his speech came out sounding like a tea kettle boiling over.)

"All right, all right, Elgarbam and Whistle, stop the bickering or I'll turn you both into a plate of Forgur cookies and everyone else--be diligent, time is of the essence," said the tallest of the three old women.

"May I?" queried Mrs. Felis to the woman who was just speaking.

"Yes, Abigail, you may. I know this has been, well, difficult for you to maintain," she replied with a smirk.

As Sadie sat staring in amazement, Mrs. Felis's entire body began to shrink. Her clothes began to become too big. Arms went up into her shirt sleeves. Legs disappeared under her skirt and her head and neck were lost within her blouse. Within a matter of minutes, all that was left of Mrs. Felis was a pile of clothing. Sadie stared in amazement. What had happened to her only friend? Just then, the pile of clothing began to move a bit. The movement was not dissimilar to that of a mole tunneling underground. Two seconds later out of the neck of the blouse popped a very plump, very grey, very unusual cat. The only thing that let Sadie know this was, in fact, Mrs. Felis, was that she still wore her glasses.

"Well now, that's better," said the cat while adjusting her glasses with her paws.

Sadie was speechless, not that she would have spoken or even taken a breath at this point. Too much had happened, too many fantastical things, too many unbelievable creatures stood before her very eyes, and Sadie thought she might faint.

"I'll take a drink now...and I don't care what's in it," Sadie rapidly spit out.

All of the creatures laughed and one of the old women clapped her hands. When she did so a table full of every drink known to man (and some not) appeared before Sadie's eyes.

"This is just too much; I'm going to go now," said Sadie as she tried to get out of the chair and leave. As she went to stand her legs gave out on her, her sight became a little blurry, and she plopped back down again.

"All of this can seem a bit...much, can't it, my dear? Take a moment to catch your breath. Let it all sink in, and we'll get started," the taller old woman said very matter-of-factly.

She then turned to Grimm and Mrs. Felis and asked, "How much does she *really* know? And be quick about it, we've got fifteen minutes 'til the midnight hour."

Sadie checked her pulse by her wrist, much to the amusement of the fairies who giggled in unison. She also noticed that the bookstore smelled less like musty old volumes and more like a pine forest. Since Mrs. Felis had turned into a cat, the fairies had taken to flitting around the gnomes' heads. Their giggles sounded like a high pitched twinkling of bells as they fluttered about the bookstore alighting here and there to poke about. The two gnomes, who she now knew to be Elgarbam and Whistle (Whistle, for obvious steam-propelled reasons) went back to their reading and arguing, thumping each other along the way. The centaur was busy in conversation with the ghosts, and the water sprites kept splashing water onto him, much to his dismay.

Sadie sat in utter amazement as the three old women spoke with Grimm and Mrs. Felis the cat, all of them talking about her like she wasn't even there.

As Sadie sat and watched and listened, she began to get very irritated and annoyed. She was mad that all of these…people…were paying her no mind, still speaking about her like she was invisible and all after abruptly revealing themselves to her without warning.

She started chewing her bottom lip, wringing her hands. When that didn't work to calm her fury or get attention, she began tapping her foot on the floor in a very loud, very hurried fashion. When no one still paid her any mind, she began to feel the pangs of resentment much like those she felt towards the mean kids at school who teased her and caused her so much pain.

The anger took over, making her tremble; when it filled her up like an overstuffed omelet, she stomped her feet, stood up, and yelled, "ENOUGH!"

As she did so several books flew from their places on the shelves and crashed into the wall opposite.

Once again, the bookstore became silent and all eyes were on Sadie when they weren't on the books that had flown off the shelves by themselves. The centaur started clapping.

"Bravo, little human child. Such power, such a display of it and when it's still ten minutes to go before you're a witchling…and three years 'til you're a full witch I might add," he said with his deep and gravelly voice as his applause died down. "You must be carrying some power within you the likes of which we haven't seen in millennia."

"I'M NOT A WITCH!" Sadie screamed. Lowering her voice she continued, "Nor do I want to be a witch. This is not…normal; I just want to be normal, like everyone else, like every other kid, with a real family, with friends other than my books. Normal, where you don't see knobby little dwarfs and sparkly fairies or GHOSTS! What's that all about? I just want to be normal. NORMAL!" her voice rising as she spoke. "NORMAL not...not...THIS!"

"Look at that, the human is hysterical, someone slap her," said Whistle.

"Oh, oh, oh, I will!" shouted Elgarbam and raising his stubby little arm.

"And I'm not a dwarf, I'm a gnome. Dwarves are so...tall," said Whistle, trying to cross his arms in defiance.

"Yeah, and what's wrong with ghosts," asked one of the disgruntled knitting circle.

"Once again, everyone calm down. No slaps, Elgarbam. Or pinching either," she said to a very small imp Sadie failed to see earlier. "She's okay, a bit in shock maybe, but she's seen and learned lots so far tonight. All of this can be a bit much on a human child first coming upon the change. Imagine if it were you seeing and hearing things you had always been told only existed in fairy tale books," said the tallest old woman as she approached Sadie.

It was all said to no avail though, for Sadie had fainted dead away in her chair.

Out of the

Frying Pan

and Into the Fire

The shock of the cold water brought Sadie back with a start. She heard thunder boom and lightning strike somewhere close by as she blindly wiped water from her face. She slowly blinked her eyes open, gradually taking in her surroundings and remembering. She remembered something about teas being switched. She remembered Mrs. Felis saying something crazy about her being a witch. And then she remembered all the magikal creatures she had seen, and her heart began to race. She was not happy--again. When she decided to genuinely focus on what was before her, she was looking into the face of the centaur and the tallest of the three old women.

"Sadie, listen to me. You MUST get out of here. Just trust Zeno to get you where you need to be. SADIE, FOCUS! Your very life depends on it!" said the old woman while she shook Sadie by the shoulders.

In a quick scan of her surroundings, Sadie saw that the only two "beings" left in the bookstore were the Centaur and the tall, old woman.

And me, thought Sadie, *'cause I'm a witch.*

Lightning struck again, illuminating the outside as though a light switch had been flicked on. Sadie thought she saw odd shapes in the darkness just outside the bookstore doors.

"Why do I have to go somewhere? Where am I going? What's ...," but she was cut off by a very loud, very angry, and very persistent banging at both the front and back doors of the store.

"Quick, get on my back," said the centaur named Zeno as he grabbed her by the arm and deftly swept her onto his muscular body. "Hold on tight; this may not be easy."

"I'll meet up with you after you get her to Tara's safely," said the old woman sternly. Raising her left hand to the sky, she snapped her fingers and was gone.

"Who is Tara? Why do I have to go there? What's happening?" questioned Sadie but to no avail. Zeno just looked at her with a firm jaw and bared teeth.

He then pulled a quiver full of golden, glowing arrows and an ornately decorated golden bow from somewhere behind some books on a shelf. Sadie thought he must have hidden them so those two impetuous gnomes wouldn't steal them. She didn't like anyone who wanted to smack her so she didn't feel bad for thinking them thieves. He possibly hid them so he didn't have to wear them. They looked heavy.

No, that's silly, how could they be heavy to a very muscular centaur named Zeno? And he's probably magikal, too, isn't he? I mean, he is a Centaur. Aren't they magikal?

Zeno began to move towards the large bay window in the front of the store. Out in the darkness Sadie could see eerie red eyes, flashing green ones, and some angry yellow slits peering in at them. She almost thought she saw gnashing and snapping teeth, very large dagger-like teeth, but she couldn't be sure. As Zeno pulled an arrow and placed it, ready to shoot, he looked back over his shoulder at Sadie with his eyes flashing intensity.

"Lie low on my back, little one. Hold onto my mane, and use what little power you have to help get us out of here alive," he said to her, voice low and deep.

"But I don't have any power, and I don't want it anyway. This is crazy; I'm not a wit...."

"YES, YOU ARE!" he shouted and then lowered his voice. "Yes, you are not a full one yet, but in the beginning stages. We don't have time to argue this point, child of the moon, just do as I say if you want to live to see tomorrow," and with that he turned around and aimed.

The glowing arrow smashed through the window without a sound, save for the whooshing through the air. Miraculously, the glass had all fallen away and outside could be heard an agonizing moan. The magikal arrow must have reached its mark. Roars and screams and cackles rose up out of the night, and Sadie felt Zeno's muscles ripple under his skin. He took off at remarkable speed towards the now-open window, his bow and arrows flying at supernatural speed. Sadie held on tight to the thick, black mane that ran down his back as she tried to see what was happening. They flew through the window in one colossal leap, out into the night to put faces to their foes.

Immediately Sadie felt someone or something grab her ankle. She looked down to see some sort of half snake-half man thing trying to pull her off of Zeno's back. She screamed at the sight of it and kicked furiously as she tightened her grip to the point of making her knuckles white. Its scaly, razor-sharp fingers raked her leg, leaving rips in her pants as Zeno turned and shot the beast between its cold, steely eyes. It imploded upon itself in a mess of green ooze and then disappeared completely into the ground.

"Do what I told you, Sadie! Use your magik! Remember the books flying off the shelves!"

He tried to shout above the mayhem as he spun this way and that, rapidly shooting arrows at the creatures that were trying to get them.

Sadie was scared. Really, beyond doubt, frightened to her utter core. Though she didn't truly believe she was a witch, she did know their lives were in danger and she should listen to Zeno.

It's worth a try.

She closed her eyes and tried to concentrate amongst the chaos.

What do I concentrate on? In the book store I was angry, though I still don't believe I did that to the books. I guess anger is the key here.

Sadie thought hard and went deep into herself to find what angered her most. A thousand memories flashed through her mind, and she settled on the anger she felt at Death. She was angry with Death for taking her mother from her so soon and without goodbyes. She felt the anger she had towards Death for not even giving her as much as a body to say goodbye to or have a proper funeral for.   She was angry at the lonely little plaque at the graveyard, placed without a service, and the absence of family to rally around her. She remembered the very moment she'd realized what it meant for her mother to be gone and to have no one else in the world she could rely on. It was the first time Sadie had felt utterly alone.   Her anger began to change form. The anger had turned to sadness and a lump caught in Sadie's throat. She tried to fight it, but it was no use; she was overcome with sadness. The tears welled up in her eyes, and her stomach turned sour. Her heart ached, and she couldn't help but cry. As she held on tight to Zeno, she relived the pain her mother's death had caused, and she felt as though she could die herself.

As she was consumed with this wretched feeling she had lived with for the last three years of her life, she felt something pulling on her shoulders with a bony, claw-like grip. She turned to face this next opponent, and saw, hovering above her, a creature mankind could not imagine. It had the body of a bird, a vulture quite possibly, with scaly vulture legs. Its enormously long and sharp talons were trying to maintain a grip on Sadie's shoulders. The head was that of a man, contorted in anger and fierce warlike determination. Its wings were vast and leathery, bat-like, and flapping up quite a wind.

If these things had been female, Sadie would have thought them to be Harpies since she had read about such beasts recently. Through tear-filled eyes, full of sadness and despair at the memory she was wrapped in, she almost gave in and let the man-vulture take her.

Why not? I can be with Mom again, and I won't have to deal with all of this.

She started to loosen her grip on Zeno's mane and her body began to lift off his back.

NO! Sadie--LIVE!

She heard her mother's voice saying very clearly in her mind. Warmth flooded her body from head to toe. It was the warmth that love can fill you up with, and it gave Sadie a surge of energy and newfound strength. She faced the man-vulture and grabbed one of its wings when they flapped downward. It was tough and leathery and horrid to the touch, but she didn't care.

I WILL NOT GIVE UP, MOM, she screamed in her mind.

Pulling as hard as she could, trying to knock it out of the air and get it to release her from its talons, Sadie's outlook began to change. Because of her newborn determination and strength, it became off-balanced, and it was hard for the creature to remain hovering above her. It began to drop a little in altitude. Sadie wrestled with the thing frantically, and they soon were at a stalemate. It was just too strong. Sadie grew weary and became frustrated.

"I WISH YOU WERE GONE!" she shouted. And in a burst of white light, the man-vulture was flung across Main Street and hit Winslow's Hardware store, knocking out one of its windows.

"Good shot, Sadie," said Zeno while he shot a troll who had a club the size of an oak tree. "Hold on, we're going to make a mad dash for our very lives, and it may get messy," he yelled over the explosion of the troll.

Grey goo rained down on everything, including them, as they made their getaway. Sadie was surprised at how much grey goo a troll was made of; as Zeno ran, she tried her best to get it off of her. It smelled like liverwurst, and she wanted no part of troll slime.

They ran down Main Street until they reached the end where farm country began. The troll explosion provided good cover for their escape, and no one seemed to be following them. The storm that had been raging began to subside as they continued on, never slowing their pace, just going deeper and deeper into vast open country.

"Why didn't anyone in town hear what was going on?!" yelled Sadie towards Zeno's ear.

"Because when we are in your world, we wear a glamour. You'll soon learn what that is, how to use a glamour, and how to see through them. Just hold on and try to rest a bit 'til we reach Tara's neck of the woods," shouted Zeno back at her. Sadie could hear fatigue in his voice.

At last, after what seemed like ages, they arrived at their destination. At least, Sadie assumed it was their destination because they began to slow. They were at the edge of a very large, dark forest, and in a great clearing stood a tiny stone cottage with a thatched roof. It seemed much too big a clearing for such a small house. It looked like the country cottages Sadie had seen in postcards of England that one of her foster families had stuck on their refrigerator. It was small enough that Sadie knew it could only be one room, and she wondered how she, Zeno, and this Tara person along with whomever else was there would all fit inside together.

Smoke was coming from the chimney in circular puffs and light shone through little square windows that bordered the front door, making it look strangely inviting. The closer they got, the more Sadie relaxed.

"Are we here?" she asked Zeno.

"Yes, but still, be on alert," he responded.

Sadie's eyes darted all around, taking in her immediate surrounding and looking for any signs of danger--not that she even knew what to look for. Apparently what she thought she knew of the world didn't apply anymore. Either that or the rules had changed.

They walked on, not on a path or anything, for nothing led to this cottage. Sadie realized that the forest had become quiet, not that she knew anything about the woods or what was in it. She was a town girl. To her left, the imposing trees seemed to be pushing themselves in a defensive line around that side of the house. To her right, where the cottage was, she saw the same thing. There was also a huge pile of firewood that rose up and above the roofline of the house. As they came within twenty yards of the dwelling, she heard a noise in the darkness of the trees. Zeno appeared unaffected by it and kept walking. She wondered if he were too tired to notice.

"Don't you hear that?" she asked in a hushed whisper as she gripped his mane tighter.

Zeno didn't answer and kept walking. Sadie was growing annoyed; this was the second time he hadn't answer her questions tonight.

The storm was gone completely, and the air smelled crisp and clean, like fall air does. Sadie inhaled a long, sweet breath of fresh air just as they reached the door. As Zeno raised his hand to knock, from around the corner came a hulking, great figure much larger than the house itself. Sadie froze on Zeno's back, prepared for him to either shoot the beast or run. Her stomach went upside down as she realized it was a troll. She was frozen and sick with fear, still remembering the liverwurst smell.

"Hello, Zeno, it been long time no see you, what say? Who small human?" queried the dark, mountainous shape before them in a voice so deep Sadie thought that only elephants in India could have heard it.

"Greetings and peace be your friend, Alroy. We're here to see Tara. I'm pretty sure she knows we're coming," replied Zeno as the creature stepped out of the shadows and into the light cast from the tiny windows.

The troll began to lower itself down, kneeling on the ground next to them, grunting and groaning all the way. Sadie could hear bones cracking and skin squishing as it settled on the ground. Its huge head bent forward on its muscular neck; with eyes as large as Sadie's head, it looked at her with the gentlest expression, all things considered.

"Human smell funny, not all human, not all witch, what give here?" asked the creature with a worried look on its face.

It began to scratch its bald, lumpy head and study Sadie with its gigantic puppy dog eyes. Sadie realized trolls were completely different when they're alive and not reduced to grey slime and goo. She even thought she may like this one, though it still smelled like liverwurst and its breath was what she thought a camel's butt might smell like. (Not that she wanted the opportunity to find out.)

"This is Sadie, and I'm sure she does smell funny. She's in the middle of the change. And if what I've seen and my instincts are correct, she's going to have quite some power in her. It's been a long night, Alroy; if it's all right with you, I'll find you later and fill you in on the battle. I know how you love a good battle. Right now, I've got to get this child in to see Tara," said Zeno as he knocked on the door.

Before he had finished his second rap, the door swung open and in they stepped, his hooves clacking on the stones of the floor as he ducked to fit through the frame. What Sadie saw inside was enough to shake her senses once more. She questioned her eyes and rubbed them as a gesture of sight correction.

The small cottage she saw from the outside opened up into one large room, a sort of kitchen/living room combination. It was much larger than the outside made you believe. The ceiling went on forever, it being an enormous cathedral-type, supported by great wooden beams. A large, black cauldron was bubbling as it hung over the fire in the fireplace, giving off a delicious scent she couldn't quite place. A table was in the center of the room, large enough that ten big comfy chairs encircled its thick, wooden, circular presence.

There were two closed wooden doors on each stone wall. The walls were lined with shelves holding books, candles, plants and other objects along with bottles, jars, and containers of all sizes. They also held everyday objects like plates, bowls, and glasses. As Sadie looked around the room, Zeno began to speak.

"Um, witch child, you can leave my back now. You're not as light as you think," he said with humor in his sleepy voice.

"Oh, sorry," said Sadie as she slipped from his back like she had been riding centaurs her whole life.

While she stood in awe of what she was viewing in this small but not small cottage, one of the doors opened and there stood one of the most beautiful women Sadie had ever seen. She was wearing a long deep green velvet dress and an even deeper green shawl was wrapped around her bare white shoulders. Her hair was a brilliant, bright red and hung in long spiraling curls well past her waist. There were vines and flowers woven in a sort of tiara on her head, and three butterflies fluttered around her as she stood while a wren sat on her shoulder. She had milky white skin that looked smooth as sea glass, and her smile was as wide and bright as the sun. As she lifted her dress to walk, Sadie could see she was barefoot.

She spread her arms wide and began to speak. "Zeno, how wonderful to see you, me old friend," she said as she approached the centaur and circled her arms around him in the warmest of hugs.

Unwrapping herself from the centaur, she turned to face Sadie. As she looked at her, studied her, an expression crossed her face that Sadie could not recognize.

"And you must be Sadie. I've been waiting to meet you, lass. 'Tis an honor to meet the daughter of my best friend," she said as she then wrapped her arms around Sadie in the same warm manner as she did Zeno.

She smelled of cinnamon and vanilla and hugged Sadie with the strength of ten men. When she finally released her after what seemed like a yearlong embrace, Sadie noticed there were tears in her forest green eyes.

"You were my mother's best friend?" asked Sadie. "How come I never met you or even heard of you?"

Sadie felt a pang of regret as soon as she asked this question for this woman looked as though Sadie had stabbed her through the heart. In the same second, she was a little angry that if this woman had indeed been her mom's best friend, where had she been for the first ten years of Sadie's life and the last three after her mother's supposed death?

Besides, her head hurt something awful, and in her chest there was a pain, a pain that felt like her heart was going to explode. As a matter of fact, she felt downright horrible, like she had the flu. Sadie didn't care if she hurt the woman's feelings; she herself was feeling way too bad to be concerned with manners.

Looking at Zeno, who had retreated to stand near the fire, the woman named Tara spoke to him.

"Does she know nothing? Is the lass completely unaware of what's happening? Ach! We must be gettin' her prepared and in a circle right away, centaur! This is of the greatest urgency it is or my name isn't Tara of the Isle."

When she spoke the last part of the sentence, her voice had risen and immediacy was felt in the words. The earth seemed to respond to those words and a rumble was felt, not so much like an earthquake, but more like an earth shiver. The creatures that seemed to live in her aura flitted about nervously before settling back down on her shoulders and hair. Tara herself seemed to become illuminated from the inside out, and her radiance shown brilliantly in the fire lit room, her brilliant red hair giving off the most intensity. The centaur smirked a little and cleared his throat.

"It's true, Your Greatness. We had to leave before she was told of anything, and midnight came and went in a small battle with the turncoats. I didn't think it my place to tell the girl because...well, I couldn't very well run, fight and carry her on my back, at least not very well, and all the while telling her very vital details about her life. It just didn't seem plausible. I have delivered her to you safely, and if I am no longer needed, I shall take my leave," Zeno said with the utmost respect towards Tara.

He looked tired, and Sadie felt a pang of sympathy for him.

"Aye, of course ya cen. I'm sorry, my friend; it's been a long night here, as well. I've 'ad six dozen or so winter elves to heal who suffered terrible wounds from their battle with the Syndicate and I...." She took a deep breath. "That's not your worry; take your leave warrior, and I'll see you again soon, my dear comrade," spoke Tara as she hugged the centaur once again.

She went to the door with him, put three fingers up to her face, touching her forehead and then her heart and then touched them to his chest. She hugged him once more and sent him into the night. As Tara was shutting the door, Sadie ran to it, wanting to tell Zeno thank you and goodbye, but he'd already disappeared into the cool dark night.

"Let him go, Sadie; he's got work of his own to do. Fighting the Syndicate takes all of our manpower. And he has his own personal demons to conquer when it comes to them, pardon the pun. I'm sure you'll see him again, you can thank him then," said Tara with a warm smile.

"How did you know I wanted to thank him?" queried Sadie.

With a chuckle, Tara responded, "I'm Tara from the Isle. The Isle being Ireland in case you've no learnin' 'bout that as well. No worries though, I'm 'ere to take good care of ya now."

Sadie felt her stomach growl long before the sound resonated up and all through the room. Her face flushed red and she looked down at the floor.

"Aw, you're hungry, little lamb. Don't need me powers to figure that one out. 'Ere, come sit and I'll fix ya something. You can eat and then sleep. You're probably feeling a bit wonky at this point."

"I do have the worst headache I've ever had, and my chest feels strange," said Sadie as Tara led her to the table and pulled out a chair for her.

"That be the change, love, you're okay. 'Tis best to sleep through it, I always say," Tara said as she spooned something wonderful smelling from the cauldron.

She then swept her right hand over the table in front of Sadie; as she did so, a steaming pot of tea appeared as well as desserts of every kind.

"Eat now, then you'll sleep, and I'll fill you in on everything tomorrow. My shamrock! 'Tis almost three in the mornin'. Oh, and don't worry, you be safer 'ere than anywhere else on this planet, our world or your former one. Remember, I'm Tara fr...."

"From the Isle, I know, I know," Sadie said in unison with her.

The two smiled at each other, and Sadie dug into the bowl before her with all the ferocity of a crazed badger. It was filled with the most delicious chicken and dumplings she had ever been witness to and privy to taste. Before Sadie could make it to her fourth spoonful, her head was lying on the table, and she was fast asleep.

Happy Birthday,
Sadie, Again

Waking up to the smell of cinnamon buns just coming out of the oven is one of earth's greatest pleasures, and Sadie's mouth was watering even before her eyes had fully opened. She felt something on her chest, a vibrating of some sort, and slowly opened one eye to peek. The last twenty four hours had taught her to be careful, if anything, and to expect the unexpected--always.

"GRIMM!" cried Sadie as she maneuvered her hands from under the covers to stroke the purring feline.

"Good morning, or should I say good evening to you, Sadie, pet?"

Through half-opened sleepy eyes only inches away from Sadie's face, Grimm stretched and yawned.

Sadie was startled for a moment at his speech; she had forgotten he could talk. She stroked his head and scratched behind his ears as she looked around. Someone, most likely Tara, had put her in bed, a very large, very comfy bed covered in thick, down blankets. The window-lined room let the outside in as Sadie saw the forest illuminated in twilight's pink light. Everything was quiet, peaceful and Sadie felt safe. She remembered she was at Tara's bigger-than-it-looked-from-the-outside house and smiled at the thought. Her stomach growled, boldly and loudly, causing Grimm to open his eyes again.

"Grimm, get off of me; I am STARVING! Those cinnamon buns smell delicious," said Sadie as she began to scoot the cat and the covers away.

She slipped out of the warm, snug bed; as she began to head towards the door, she stepped in something that felt grainy on her bare feet. Looking down, she saw she had stepped in salt and that it encircled the entire bed. She looked back towards the sleepy Grimm, who was grooming himself at the foot of the bed, and gave him a questioning gaze.

"For extra protection. Not that you're not safe here already. No one would dare mess with Tara, but still, you can't be too safe these days what with the Syndicate having their fingers in lots of pies," said Grimm right before coughing up a hairball.

"Ew. That's gross, Grimm," responded Sadie.

She wrinkled up her nose in disgust and put her hand to her mouth.

"Sorry, these things happen when you're a cat. Not that I complained about the sounds that came from you as you were sleeping. And the smells that followed, my gosh, you'd think you were part troll," Grimm stated as he waved his one paw in front of his face while the other went around his throat in a choking gesture.

It was all in mocking, of course, but Sadie felt her usual self-conscious flush rush through her body.

Embarrassed, Sadie turned red almost immediately and changed the subject just as quickly. "Where's Tara?"

"Oh, about the house somewhere. I'm going back to sleep. You'll find her, I'm sure," said Grimm as he quickly resumed cat nap status, but not before covering the hairball with the bottom of the comforter.

Sadie turned and smiled to herself as she headed towards the only door in the room.

I wonder how many other thirteen-year-old girls have ever talked to a cat.

As she turned the crystal knob of the door, she thought to ask about Mrs. Felis and changed her mind at the sight of Grimm all spread out with his legs in the air sound asleep. Most cats slept curled in a ball. This one was as different as they came. Sadie smiled to herself.

Stepping out into the grand room of the house, Sadie saw it much as she remembered from the night before. Without a moment's hesitation, Tara stepped through the door that led outside, as though she were expecting Sadie at that very instant. Sadie gasped at the sight of her; she was even more beautiful than she remembered.

"Good evening, witchling, how are you feeling?" asked Tara in her sweeter-than-honey voice.

Her beautiful red curls were pulled back from her face with a silver barrette, and she was wearing another green dress. This one buttoned down the front all the way to the floor and had a black cinched waist line. She was still barefoot, and this time three birds circled her as ivy made a crown around her head. Butterflies alighted on her shoulders, and a little white mouse clung to her sleeve. Inside, Sadie hoped to be as beautiful as Tara one day. Tara smiled at the girl and asked her again how she felt.

"I feel okay. My head doesn't hurt anymore and neither does my chest," replied Sadie.

"Good, good. 'Tis complete then and without incident. Oh, how are your fingers?"

Sadie looked at her hands. All seemed well, and she shook her head. "Okay, I guess, but why?" she asked.

"Oh, no reason in particular, love, 'cept that sometimes witchlings gain an extra finger during the change," Tara responded matter-of-factly as she lay a basket of gourds on the table.

Sadie looked at her hands again, this time in a hurry and with much worry. She checked thoroughly for any sign of an extra digit. The last thing she needed was an extra finger. That would make her even further from normal than she ever wanted or thought she'd be.

There's no hiding, or hiding from, an extra finger.

"So, when can I go home?" asked Sadie. "Or should I say back to the Argyles. They must be worried sick about me, or at least concerned enough to call the police. And...with all the commotion last night from the bookstore, they've got to be at least a little worried. I really don't want to be kicked out of another foster home."

Tara laughed a full-throated and gorgeously amused chuckle. She brushed her spiraling red locks towards her back and studied Sadie with a curious expression.

"So, you really don't know a thing do you, lass?" asked Tara.

"I know lots!" cried Sadie, hating feeling stupid and in the dark.

Tara laughed again.

"I meant 'bout what's goin on with ya, lass," she said as she headed towards the cauldron.

"I know that some crazy things happened last night--things that now seem like a dream, and I wouldn't believe them save for the fact that I'm talking to you right now. I know people keep telling me I'm a witch and...."

"Witchling," corrected Tara.

"Witchling, right, whatever," responded Sadie with hands on her hips, "and I know I have to get home so I don't get kicked out of that foster home like all the rest!"

"You don't ever have to go to another foster home as long as you live, Sadie," replied Tara with a serious stare on her face that made her look like the powerful witch that she really was. She had turned to face Sadie and was holding a book in her hands that wasn't there a moment ago.

"I thought we'd start with your family history and then go from there. What do you think?" Tara stated more than asked.

Sincerely confused and a bit hungry, Sadie took a seat at the table.

What's a girl to do? She thought to herself. *I'm curious to know what's going on. I am interested in knowing how it is that I don't have to live in foster care anymore. I can at least have some of those cinnamon rolls I've smelled before I tell her I just want to be a normal girl.*

"You will never be just a *normal* girl, never again, Sadie. As a matter of fact, you're more than just a girl now," responded Tara ever so seriously. "And the cinnamon rolls are to your left."

Sadie turned her head; the rolls were there, steaming and oozing frosting down their sides.

"Stop reading my mind!" Sadie halfway shouted. "It's rude, don't you think? Plus, you may hear something you don't want to hear."

She then grabbed a bun and shoved half of it in her mouth.

"You really are the clever little daughter of Adrienne MacDougall, and a bit feisty like her as well," Tara said with a smile as she waved her arms and supplied the table with all sorts of breakfast foods and drink. "I promise I'll try my best NOT to read your mind anymore, although it's my inborn gift, and I have a hard time turning it off. Some people do find it hard to be around me because of it. I understand it bothers you. So I'll do my best, lass."

Tara laughed, her voice tinkling like bells. "At least I don't have the problems of the Lorelei."

Sadie thought for a minute and decided that Tara really wasn't all that bad. It was the fact that she was being feisty, as Tara said, or persnickety, as her mother would have said, that made her so quick to argue. She didn't want to be a bother, especially since this woman had been so nice to her from the start. Sadie did, however, want to know more about Tara and her mother's friendship. She took a long drink of milk and then looked at Tara.

"Will you tell me about you and my mother?"

"Of course I will child, in due time. We've much to go over, much for you to learn, and I feel we're at the disadvantage as I wasn't able to guide you through your change," said Tara, a bit dismayed.

"What's this change? And why do you people keep calling me 'witchling?' I'm not sure I believe or even want all of this. And I'm really concerned about Mrs. Felis. She was really good to me, cat or old lady or whatever she is. And another thing, I will let you in on a secret about me, Tara, I just want to be a normal kid," Sadie said with defiance as she stuck out her chin.

"You sound just like your dear mother, lass. She always complained 'bout wanting to be normal. Always wanted something other than what she had. And when you were born and she took you away to live in the human world, well, that was just unheard of. Upset quite a few in the Guild, I can tell ya that, lass," Tara stated with a grin before continuing on. "That be one of the reason I loved her so much. She was always one to tip the scales of balance. I do understand why she took you away though, musta been hard for her...."

Tara's voice trailed off.

Sadie had never thought of her mom this way. Her mother seemed so--uptight. Always watching over her, always right there and quite literally always one to follow the rules. Sadie guessed if she were the witch Tara said she was, she probably didn't want to draw attention to herself in "the human world," as Tara called it.

Then it hit her: *Mom was a witch!*

Her own curiosity grew exponentially, and she could hardly contain herself. What did this mean? She didn't really die in the car crash? Did she blink or snap her fingers and disappear somewhere?

She really is still alive! I KNEW IT! Could she be...?

"No, Sadie, she's not still alive," said Tara softly, gently, as she moved to stroke Sadie's hair.

Sadie herself softened a little and lost her appetite at the thought of her mother. She pondered what it meant that her mother was a witch.

What good is being a witch if you can't save yourself?

She contemplated what it would mean if she accepted the fact that she was a witch, as everyone kept saying, and what she could do. She thought about waving her arms and making things happen, and it didn't seem all that bad. Then, a thought struck her that had so much weight to it that she came alive with excitement.

"If I'm a witch, can't I bring her back? If I'm not powerful enough, can't you bring her back? What's the use of having power if you can't do something to save someone's life? Why didn't she try to save her own life? What if she did and you just can't find her 'cause she magikked her way out of the car crash to somewhere else, and she's still trying to find her way home? Or what if she did all that and hit her head and lost her memory in the process? If she were really dead, she'd be a ghost like the ones I saw in the bookstore. She would come to me; I'm her daughter. We can find her, Tara! It's possible, I mean, until yesterday I never thought any of this was possible," said Sadie with excitement and the tiniest hint of sarcasm as she opened her arms to encompass the entire room.

"I'm sorry, Sadie, that's just not the way things work," said Tara with a tear in her eye. "If she were alive, I'd know it. Believe me, I tried to find her. Reading minds extends to those minds out of your immediate viewing area."

Sadie bowed her head and tried not to let Tara see her sadness. She felt somewhat ashamed that she still let her mother's death rule her world after three years of dealing with it.

Why can't I get past this? Why can't I move on with my life? I've been to so many counselors you'd think I'd have at least resolved some of the issues with her dying.

"All the counselors in the world couldn't take away your sadness, Sadie," said Tara with a soft voice.

"I thought you weren't going to read my mind anymore?" asked Sadie with a small smirk on her face, trying to lighten the mood she'd created.

"Sorry. Habit," responded Tara, smirking back.

Just then Sadie passed gas louder than anyone she had ever heard. Tara burst into laughter as Sadie's face turned five shades of red.

"Well, now, I thought that'd be finished by now," Tara said through giggles.

"I'm sorry," said Sadie, "I don't know what got into me. That just sort of sneaked out."

"It's okay, lass. It's the sleeping potion I gave you yesterday. For some reason it makes people a wee bit full of gas. Sometimes magik, like life, doesn't go as we plan no matter how good at it we think we are. I've been working on it for some time now and can't seem to fix that one unnecessary aspect of the wonderful brew. Other than that, it does work wonders, doesn't it? I mean, you've been out for quite some time and you feel totally refreshed, do you not?" Tara looked at Sadie with raised eyebrows as she waved her hand in front of her face. "But maybe you should spend some time outdoors until it's completely over. That'll give me time to get things ready for your first lesson. And, at the same time, I can air out the room."

The two laughed and Sadie felt relief instead of embarrassment. For once in her life, it felt okay to just be herself. Tara was a perfectly sweet and wonderful woman that was impossibly beautiful. Sadie felt she could spend the rest of her life with her.

"Now, here's a scarf, coat, and mittens. It's a bit brisk out there this evening," Tara said handing her items that weren't in her hands a few seconds ago, "I'll call you when I'm ready for ya."

And with that, she ushered Sadie out into the crisp fall evening.

The warm sunlight setting behind the trees temporarily blinded her, and she felt the brisk air fill her lungs. She felt renewed by the fresh air in combination with the long sleep she had. Sadie felt good, better than she had in months, or even years, and she smiled wholeheartedly. Her vision adjusted to the light of the setting sun. She decided to follow a path she hadn't seen the night before that led off towards a field of huge orange pumpkins and gourds of every color. As soon as she took her first step, a booming voice called her name.

"Sadie," said Alroy as his hulking figure came from around the side of the house.

He's gotta stop doing that.

Being unsure how to greet a troll, she didn't want to offend so she smiled and did a curtsy.

"Haven't seen curtsy since King Arthur was around," said Alroy. "Your kind still do such things?"

Embarrassed for the third time this morning, Sadie felt sure it wasn't the last. "No, I...um, I didn't know how to greet you," she stammered.

"How 'bout hello?" Alroy said matter-of-factly. "Seems to work for everyone else these days."

Sadie chuckled. "Hello, Alroy, how are you today…I mean, this evening?" she asked with a smile.

"Hungry. Want to go walk?" he asked the girl.

Sadie felt so small next to this goliath of a, well, troll. Though he was a troll and her first encounter with a troll had been less than nice, she felt safe with Alroy. Stifling a nervous giggle, Sadie took in the reality of her situation. She was about to have a conversation with a troll before beginning her magikal lessons and, probably the craziest thing of all, she was a witch. She tried to think about what all of this could mean. She also began to wonder about Cranberry Grove, her foster family, and exactly what was going on back there. She had a quick, fleeing notion about the possibility of getting even with all of those kids at school who tormented her, but tucked that muse away for later. As all these things raced through her mind at breakneck speed, she looked back up at Alroy who was still waiting patiently for her answer.

"Okay," Sadie replied as he picked her up and put her on his shoulder.

"Travel faster you up here," said the troll.

"Understood," said Sadie and the two set off in the direction of the pumpkin and gourd patch which, incidentally, only took a few steps for the massive giant of a beast.

Alroy set Sadie down on a pumpkin the size of a park bench and picked up a slightly smaller one and popped it between his jaws. He began to throw pumpkins, hand over hand, into his large cavern of a mouth with all the ferocity of a determined machine. It reminded Sadie of how fast she could throw miniature marshmallows into her own gob. Bits of orange pumpkin juice dribbled down the sides of his chin and then splashed to the ground. Before long there was the start of a puddle about the size of a bathtub. When Sadie thought he had slowed down enough to talk without choking, she began to speak.

"Alroy, may I ask you a question?" she queried.

Between chomps he garbled, "Yes."

"Why am I here? I mean, who decides who becomes a witch…and why? I just want to know these things. And what about my mother, she was a witch, too? How? How did all this come about? Can I fly? Will I make magik potions? Do all cats talk? Are there other creatures out there besides the ones I saw? Where do they all live? I mean, I'm so confused, I have a thousand questions, and I just want…." Sadie looked at Alroy who sat motionless.

She realized that though the creature had some limited speech, he was clearly confused by her fast paced ramblings.

"Sorry, Alroy, I've just got so many questions. How 'bout I start with one easy one?"

Alroy nodded, wiping his hands on his juice-stained shirt. He sat down clumsily in the dirt next to Sadie, squashing many, many pumpkins in the process. He crossed his legs and laid his hands on his knees. When he looked to Sadie as if to say I'm ready, he let out such a belch her hair blew back from the gale force winds it produced.

Green with nausea from the stench (troll burps were nastier than rotten eggs), Sadie formed the words, "Why are people trying to kill me, Alroy?"

The troll seemed to think hard for a moment. His brow furrowed into trenches deep enough that if they were on the sides of the road, the state would fill them in. He put a big calloused hand to his chin and closed his eyes. His other hand rubbed his head. This went on for several moments, and Sadie thought for sure she would get all the answers she needed from the determined and stoic look on Alroy's face. When at last he put his hands back down on his knees and a few moments later opened his eyes, his giant lips quivered as though he couldn't wait to speak.

Then they opened, slowly, and in his deep troll voice Alroy said, "Don't know. But Alroy sure it be Syndicate that after you."

Sadie exhaled a sigh to rival the troll's own loud breathing.

I'm not going to get anywhere with this big lump.

As she looked up from her despair, Alroy had begun munching on more pumpkins. Sadie thanked him kindly for his time and decided she should ask Tara if she was going to get any real answers. The troll nodded acknowledgement as he continued shoving the great pumpkins into his even greater mouth. Sighing again, she wiped the garden dirt off of her pants and began the walk back up the path to the cottage.

I guess things aren't easy in any life, whether it be a witch's or normal human's.

Realizing she was absolutely famished, her walk turned to a trot; she reached the door to the cottage in no time. As she turned the handle, she had that familiar feeling she always gets in her stomach when something's about to happen.

What could happen here?

And then the door flung wide open as what sounded like a hundred voices shouted, "SURPRISE!"

The main room in the cottage had expanded three-fold to accommodate   what looked to be at least 200 creatures and people. All were smiling and staring at Sadie as if she would say something utterly amazing. When she found her voice, all she could choke out was, "Wow!"

Tara took her by the arm and led her to the familiar table by the hearth. A dozen or so fairies flitted around her head and five brown-skinned elves hopped onto the chairs surrounding her. A gnome, one Sadie thought to be either Whistle or Elgarbam, sat in the seat next to her after pushing one of the elves out of the way. Floating in a bubble of water, three sprites drifted over and began to hover above the table in their water filled sphere. All three were looking down at Sadie with love.

The knitting circle of ghosts Sadie had met yesterday was chattering to her all at once while several satyrs played the Happy Birthday song on their flutes. Presents began piling up on the table in front of her as creatures of all sorts said "Happy Birthday, Sadie," in every type of voice. Sadie was beleaguered and looked up for some support from Tara, who was setting a pink and yellow wrapped gift in front of her.

"I couldn't let you *not* open mine first," said Mrs. Felis as she jumped onto the table beside the gift. "I'm sorry our birthday party yesterday didn't go according to plan."

The old cat finished as she licked her paw and ran it over her head, only stopping to straighten her glasses.

"Mrs. Felis?" asked Sadie.

"Abigail Felis at your service," the cat replied, "as I once was in your mother's service. I used to be her cat you know. Since her dea…since the accident, I just work for the Guild now. And, Sadie, please don't be mad with me for not telling you my true nature. I simply couldn't do it before you went through the change."

Mrs. Felis looked at her and even though she was seeing her as a cat now, Sadie could see all the love in her eyes that the old woman always had for her.

"You see, I was sent to keep an eye on you and to help bring you through the change since your dear, sweet mother is no longer with us. I was sent because I belonged to your mother long ago when she still lived in our realm; like I said before, it was before the accident. I was attached to you even before you were born. It's always been that way and always shall be.

"I guess in a way, I'm kinda your cat now. Well, once you've become a full witch. Please try to understand though I know you're probably still reeling from all that's happened. Oh, your mother was a stubborn one. I should have known, with what the Syndicate did, that she probably was holding out on telling you what you really were. But we'll get to all that in time; right now, we celebrate your party, and tonight should be all good times."

"Sadie, my love, I was hoping you weren't on to me. I wanted you-- we ALL wanted you to have a wonderful birthday party despite all that's happened. It was actually Mrs. Felis's idea," said Tara as she nodded to the cat. "We're all here to celebrate your thirteenth birthday AND the fact that you've gone through the change without incident. We'll party tonight, and then tomorrow start your training. So, without further adieu, let the gift unwrapping commence!" shouted Tara whilst clapping her hands.

As she did so, confetti and balloons rained down on Sadie and the guests as the music started up again. Then Tara leaned in to speak more directly to Sadie.

"Oh…and, Sadie lass, we only have a cake *without* candles this time. You see, making a wish and blowing out the candles is a form of magik, if only those humans knew…." Her melodic laughter added to the flutes played by satyrs. "Since you're a witchling now and know nothing of your powers, it could be quite disastrous, me little friend, if you were to go about making wishes on flames. Candle magik is very powerful, and I'm sure you won't be wantin' to hurt any of your friends here tonight. Accident or no."

Sadie looked around at everyone there to celebrate with her. Creatures and people she didn't know that actually wanted to be around her, patted her on the back, or kissed her cheek.

Is this what it's like to have friends?

She felt happy and filled with so much joy and delight she thought she might cry. Sadie couldn't really believe there were that many people in the world that wanted to celebrate her birthday.

I guess I do have friends.

And the presents. The table was quickly filling up with gifts of all sizes. Trying to catch her breath, Sadie couldn't believe this was all about her. No one had ever made such a fuss about her before. Well, her mom did, but not on this scale.

And NONE of it has to do with Halloween.

Sadie wondered if this was really happening or if she were dreaming, yet again.

"Yes, Sadie, this is all for you," said Mrs. Felis as she nudged her present closer to Sadie with her nose.

An Unlikely

Friend

When the last wood nymph was leaving the party, somewhat drunk on pumpkin wine, Sadie sat at the table staring at her gifts. Tara helped the inebriated creature from flying into anymore walls and ushered him out the door, trying not to laugh at his silly behavior.

The gift table held a huge varied array of items from seven league boots and magikal monocles, to a hair brush that was enchanted to brush hair all by itself. There was also a sweater that made you look thin no matter what you weighed. Mrs. Teak, the shorter and definitely rounder one of the original three ash-covered women from the bookstore, had told her in the attached card: all girls should have one "because you never know."

Sadie continued un-wrapping the remaining presents. Ripping through the paper and tearing off the lid to the box, she was somewhat surprised. This one looked nothing like all the magikal gifts she had received. Someone had given her a rather opulent, ornately decorated silver box. Taking the gem out of its packing, she lifted the lid to peer inside. A rather loud "OH MY" escaped her lips when tiny musicians floated up and out, playing a delicate tune on their miniature instruments.

Little ballerinas danced to the music, in circles, around her head. Their pale pastel outfits sparkled when the firelight hit them, and the twinkling melody caused Sadie to begin to sway in her chair. With a smile on her face, she closed the lid; and when she did, all of them disappeared. She opened it once again, and they were back. Closing it quickly, they vanished once more.

This is the best music box ever!

Looking for a card, she found none and made a mental note to ask Tara to find out just who gave it to her. She just had to thank them for this.

Grabbing the last gift on the table, she saw that on the plain brown wrapping paper someone had handwritten something.

Dear Sadie, I hope your second birthday party is all you ever dreamed of. I also hope you never need my gift. Love, Zeno.

Her heart skipped a beat.

What kind of present would someone not want you to use?

As she untied the string, her mind raced at the possibilities.

It's too small to be a sword. Oh, maybe it's a dagger or knife; if it is, I also hope I never have to use it.

Removing the paper from the parcel, she found a cardboard box, much like the wrapping paper--plain and handwritten on.

Relic only can be used once. So use wisely.

Now her curiosity had reached its peak, and she ripped off the lid to reveal the present inside. What she saw in no way belied all the messages and warnings she had read through to get to it. Snuggled amongst wads of brown tissue paper was just an ordinary ring. But it was a pretty ring. It was silver and gold with a large onyx stone as the centerpiece. The stone was fixed on one side with large silver clasps which looked similar to hinges. On the other was a single prong.   *Odd way to adhere a stone, but I guess jewelry is made differently in the magikal world. I'll have to ask about it and thank Zeno for this.*

She slipped the ring on her finger and slid the discarded wrappings to the pile on the floor.

Sadie admired all that she had received and was thinking how she never had so much attention, good attention at that. She wanted to write each and every creature and person there a personal thank you note. Her heart was filled with happiness--a happiness she hadn't felt in about three years now.

If only Mom could see me now. I'm not such an outcast anymore.

Sadie sighed long and deep. When she did, leaves fell from the potted plant by the door and three candle flames fizzled out.

"What's wrong? Tired, lass?" asked Tara.

She was surveying the damage done to three of her chairs by some woodland dwarf children. Apparently when a dwarf child teethes, they *really* teethe, and they do it on anything available. Three of Tara's big comfy chairs had been literally eaten down to the springs. With only the half-devoured wood frames left, it looked as if giant termites had stopped by for a snack.

"I guess I am. I'm mostly shocked at everyone who came to the party. And I'm really shocked at all the gifts I got. I have to thank everyone, as soon as possible, especially Zeno. I need to ask him what his gift is all about," replied Sadie through a yawn as she brushed her long, brown hair from her face.

"Oh, there'll be plenty of time for that later. Right now, why don't you go to sleep so we can start lessons fresh in the morning. Remember, you're going to be learning quite a lot and you'll need a clear head," Tara said with a wink as she spun widdershins three times with her hands in the air.

As she did so the mess from the party began to spin with her as bursts of multi-colored light popped in the air like miniature fireworks. Within minutes, the entire cottage was clean and fresh, as though there had never been a party. The three dwarf-eaten chairs were right as rain, the cauldron was bubbling over the fire, and the house smelled of cinnamon and honey. Amazed, Sadie smiled at Tara and spoke.

"Boy, I coulda used that magik all the times I was told to clean my room," she said. "I absolutely HATE to clean--anything. Do you think I could learn that?"

With a smile that was more a giggle on her face, Tara replied to Sadie and tried not to let the girl's burgeoning sense of humor take over her.

"Sadie, you don't ever have to worry about foster families again, I told you. It will be your choice if you *ever* want to return," Tara replied. "You'll have so many decisions to make soon enough without that to worry about. Plus, we've taken care of the Argyles--the whole town actually, just in case."

Sadie felt a pang of fear surge through her body at the thought of the Argyles and the whole town "being taken care of." They had been nice enough to her, and she definitely didn't want any harm to befall them, any of them. And she actually liked her small town of Cranberry Grove--from the ridiculous way they celebrated fall with a squash festival, parade, and Squash Queen competition to the summer time swimming at Miller's Pond-- what they considered their community swimming pool.

She felt a lump in her throat at the thought of what some magikal creatures might be able to accomplish given full leave of their abilities. The look on Tara's face told Sadie that she had read her mind once more, even though she promised to try not to, and Tara choked back yet another laugh.

"Sadie, I didn't mean it the way you're thinking. I simply meant we put a memory spell on them, on the whole town really. They won't remember you were even there until we change the spell to fit our liking. And let me tell ya, lass, it took lots of energy to do so. The apprentices assigned to carry out the task slept for the whole day. Calm down, nothing bad has happened to anyone, lass. If I didn't know better, I'd say your special gift was compassion," Tara said to Sadie.

That's right. I get a special gift. Being a witch might not be so bad after all. I have friends, even if they are "different." I mean, I've always been different. And I get special powers, heck, I get powers!

Sadie pondered these ideas as she started to pick up her gifts.

"Let me," said Tara, "I'll take care of this." With a quick snap of the fingers all of Sadie's gifts disappeared.

"Hey, wait a minute..." responded Sadie.

"Don't worry, Love; they're in your bedroom."

"But which is my bedroom?"

"Whichever one you choose. The gifts will always be in your bedroom. No matter which door you pick, you'll always end up in your bedroom," Tara said with a wink.

Sadie, amazed at the whole idea of it, immediately tried the door opposite her.

Yep, presents are there.

She then turned and ran across the room to the door opposite the one she had just tried.

Yes, there, too!

She tried one more door, the one farthest from her, and to her chagrin the gifts were there as well.

"But how?" asked Sadie, genuinely wanting to know.

"Magik, my sweet little witchling. You'll soon learn that magik is only the power of belief. You'll also be made well aware that magik will do wonders for anyone if she practices and does the right thing with it," Tara said.

She spoke as if someone other than herself and Sadie were in the room.

As Sadie turned and started to head to her bedroom (she chose the door opposite the front door), Tara suddenly shouted, "BE STILL!"

Sadie froze immediately.

What have I done now? The last thing I ever wanted to do was make Tara mad; she's been so good to me. Leave it to me to screw up.

Instantly, very sad and a little frightened, Sadie ever so slowly began to turn and face Tara. What she saw made her cringe a little inside. Facing Tara was a grey skinned, wart covered, bony creature about three feet tall. It had tufts of greasy dark grey, wiry hair sprouting from inside its ears, and its spine jutted out and ended in a long, twitching bony tail to compliment its emaciated physical features. It was barefoot and had long yellow nails on each toe, except for the left foot pinky toe--it was missing. All it wore was a sash made from what looked like human hair, all different. There was a scar that ran from the corner of its cracked and bloody mouth all the way across its cheek ending right by its left ear. Its teeth looked as though it ate concrete blocks for snacks.

As Tara stood facing it, pointing three fingers at the creature with her left hand and her right hand in the sign of a W over her heart, its yellow eyes glared at her full of hatred and revulsion.

"I see that the turncoats sent their most disposable goblin," Tara said, still frozen.

"They sent their best, sent their best, hag," said the goblin. When the goblin said the word hag, it enunciated it with the utmost disgust.

Neither witch nor goblin moved, just stared at each other as the long slimy stretch of drool on its lips that Sadie had been watching finally touched the floor though still connected to its mouth. Even though she found this utterly repulsive, she didn't dare say so, much less move.

"I'm not sure how ya made it through my magik walls, ya filthy beast, but you're here nonetheless. Now, I'll be havin' to deal with ya, you nasty fiend. Do you prefer death or eternity in the dungeon?" quipped Tara, no fear at all in her voice and looking fierce as ever.

Sadie wondered where on earth a dungeon would be in this house. Then just as quickly she shrugged it off, remembering all the bedrooms. She also noticed how unafraid Tara seemed and hoped that one day she could-- would be as brave. From the looks of this goblin, Sadie doubted she could ever face one with no fear whatsoever. Then, as if it knew she were thinking about it, the goblin slowly turned its warty, bony, pus-covered head to look directly at Sadie.

"I see you have the human child we're after," said the creature. "The human child."

"She's not human; she's a witch," said Tara.

Sniffing the air and apparently sucking up much snot, the creature began to cough a little before speaking again. "I can smell the human in her. She must be witchling. Still, not hard to kill, not hard to kill. Your lies won't work on me, Tara of the Isle. I have more power now than you. It was a gift from...let's just say, a friend, a friend. It's a good thing I got here when I did, when I did," the repugnant creature said as it pointed a crooked finger at Sadie. "She's beginning to stink like witch. But still has some human stench within her, so killing her will be easier than I thought, easier than I thought. Working for the Syndicate, I tend to lose track of days, I get so involved in my carnage. She must have turned...what...a day ago...the sooner I murder her the better, the better," it said matter-of-factly while flicking a piece of meat from between its snarled, broken, and decaying teeth.

Sadie tensed.

I don't want to die!

Her body seized up with fear.

YOU WON'T DIE IF YOU LISTEN TO TARA!

There was her mother's voice once again, clear as crystal, yelling instructions at her.

In the deepest, most sinister voice Sadie had ever heard, the goblin spoke directly to her. "I'm going to wear your skin, girl, wear your skin. The best part--you'll still be alive to see what a beautiful fit it is."

"Sadie, run into your room and don't come out 'til I say, lass," said Tara as though she was exerting great energy.

"No, I want to help!" shouted Sadie.

"Do as I say witchling, I can handle him," Tara responded through her set jaw.

Sadie began to back into the closest door, never taking her eyes off the nasty goblin. She backed right into her room and didn't stop until she had backed onto her bed. When this happened, the door to her room flew shut; she heard a great commotion on the other side of it.

The sound of wood splintering combined with glass breaking and grunts and groans and moans from who knows was all Sadie heard for the next twenty minutes. Her muscles began to ache as she realized she was tense and holding her breath. As she exhaled and relaxed a bit, the fight noises reached a crescendo. Then, with one thunderous boom, all went silent.

Releasing her grip on the bed, Sadie inched towards the door. Everything remained quiet except the sound of her heavy breathing. She inched closer, straining her ears to hear.

Nothing, not a sound.

She inched closer and closer. The sound of a glass shattering broke the silence and caused her to squeal and jump a little. She quickly put her hands over her mouth and waited for something to happen. Nothing. As Sadie reached the door, she somewhat shakily put her hand on the knob. Slowly and a bit reluctantly, she began to turn it.

Tara said wait for her to come out.

Sadie kept turning the knob.

Where is this courage coming from?

Sadie asked herself. She stooped to pick up the umbrella she had received as a birthday gift from one of the ghost knitting circles. It was the only weapon she thought she had, not that an umbrella was all that much of a weapon. She didn't even know how to use it other than as an umbrella.

Out loud she said, "I'm either becoming very brave or even more stupid," and she flung the door wide open.

Nothing. The cottage was in a shambles, but it was empty of any life. Both Tara and the goblin were gone. Sadie scanned the entire room. A bit of fear seeped into her belly and made her feel nauseous.

What am I to do? Where have they gone? I must find Tara.

As she moved towards the front door, she noticed there were none of the birds or butterflies that usually accompanied Tara; the room seemed so void of warmth and happiness. So void of Tara's essence. This made her sad. Just then Sadie thought she heard something outside. She ran out the front door in a flash.

"Tara!" Sadie shouted, but to no avail.

Tara was nowhere to be seen. What Sadie did see, however, was more than a little disturbing. Down the hill leading to the pumpkin patch were about twenty torches all in a huge circle. Holding those torches were creatures similar to the goblin that had done battle with Tara. As the light of the torches danced in the darkness with their creepy holders jerkily and unnaturally moving about, Sadie could make out the figure of Alroy pinned or tied down in the center. He looked dead; at least, he wasn't moving. She gasped, putting her hand over her mouth again.

When she did so, one of them began to yell, "There she is!" And the mob began running her way.

Sadie turned and ran back inside the house, bolting the door behind her. As she leaned up against it, she tried to figure out her next move. She looked up and sighed, then gasped at what she saw. Above her, floating up in the beams of the ceiling was a giant shiny bubble. Within this bubble were Tara and the goblin. Both were looking down at her--Tara with an urgent expression and the goblin seemingly full of smug satisfaction.

Tara began pounding on the walls of the bubble which sent ripples all over it, just like when you poke your finger in the still waters of a pond. Each time her fist hit the walls, it sent ripples fanning out until the entire bubble was vibrating from the effect.

Tara then urgently started pointing at one of the doors along the cottage walls. Not knowing what else to do and thinking that inside that door was a way to help Tara, Sadie ran as fast as she could towards it. At the same moment the wood splintered on the front door. Looking over her shoulder as she ran, Sadie saw the scaly, knobby head of a goblin poking through a hole in the slats. Using its broken teeth, it was slowly eating its way through the wood and into the house.

Slamming the door behind her, Sadie turned to see she was in yet another one of 'her' bedrooms. On the bed were her backpack and a tiny twinkling blue butterfly.

"Come closer," she heard the butterfly say.

As Sadie did what she was told, not wanting to upset one of Tara's butterflies and not being able to think of anything else to do at such an urgent moment, she drew in close. When she did, she realized it was not a butterfly at all, but the tiniest of the tiniest fairies.

"Take your backpack and go out that window. Once outside run as fast as you can, never stopping, never looking back, just run. Do not lose your backpack, for we've filled it full of your most useful gifts," said the minuscule, glowing blue fairy.

A loud noise could be heard outside the door.

The goblins must be inside.

"Don't worry about Tara. She'll be just fine; you might not be. So RUN!" shouted the fairy and Sadie listened.

She was up and out the window as the pounding started on the bedroom door. She ran blindly into the night, into the forest, and for once she was not afraid of where she was going, but what she was leaving. The light of the moon gave her some ability to see so that she didn't run smack dab into a tree, but she still had trouble with briars and ferns that were as tall as she. She fought her way through the flora and eventually, after what seemed like hours, she came out on the other side of the tall dark woods.

As she emerged, she could see the pink of sunrise over the trees in the distance; she took a few steps forward. A squishing, wet sound came from underfoot, and she stopped to gain some sort of idea as to where she had ended up. Sadie stood along the edge of a vast swamp. She knew it to be a swamp from the foul gases bubbling and burping up at her feet; in the coming daylight, she could make out the outlines of swamp grass and reeds.

This all seems so familiar, she thought as she began to walk the perimeter between forest and swamp.

A few yards ahead of her Sadie spotted a pile of downed logs and decided she would take a much needed rest there. Upon closer examination she found them to be trees that looked beaver-cut at their base. She walked around the formation, studying all its nuances. They formed a small hidey-hole for her on the inside while looking like a pile of logs on the outside.

This will make a great place to hide for a minute, to rest, to give my legs a break.

As she crawled inside, there was a bed of thick green spongy moss with the pungent aroma of pine needles floating in the air.

What kind of place is this? Who built this and why? This could be a trick, but I didn't get any strange feelings so....

There was moss tucked in between the logs and branches and ivy hung down in places. Crunchy dead leaves seemed to be sprinkled here and there, reminding Sadie of the season; she shivered, not from fear but from cold.   *They must be nice or good people, I mean, creature, because I can't imagine anything slimy wanting to live so, well, nice.*

Sadie crawled around inside and sat up against the back wall. She unhooked her backpack from her body and unzipped the main compartment. It was packed full of things she recognized to be some of her birthday gifts--lots of the things she had no idea what they were, much less how to work them.

Oh, I wish Tara were here. But if Tara were here, I guess I really wouldn't be here.

"How are these things going to help me if I don't even know what they are," Sadie said aloud to no one in particular.

"I can help you," said a small, calm female voice right next to her, causing her to jump sideways and almost squeal.

"Who...who are you?" questioned a shaky-voiced Sadie while desperately scanning her surroundings for who or whatever had said that.

"Don't be afraid; I'm an elemental. A woodland elemental if you want to get technical. We are usually earth, air, fire or water. I'm earth and of these woods. A spirit of the forest if you will," the voice said. "I will not harm you, Sadie, daughter of the MacDougall clan; you are safe with me to watch over you. So long as you are in my forest, no harm will come to you."

Sadie relaxed her stance a little and remembered to breathe again. She had yet to meet, hear about, or come across an elemental in her journeys, but this one seemed nice enough, and Sadie was so tired. What that really meant was she didn't get that bad feeling in her heart or stomach--that wretched feeling in her chest and belly. The one, that always made an appearance when things were about to go bad, was nowhere to be found. This elemental must genuinely be on her side.

"Did you build this...hut?" Sadie questioned.

The elemental seemed to laugh, if indeed she could. It was a bit unnerving that Sadie couldn't see whom she was talking to, but she began to relax nonetheless because of her melodic and soothing voice.

"No, I just asked a favor of some beavers, which I already have a deal with, and some swamp fairies along with some wood elves. They put it together. I knew you were coming even before you did, Sadie. I wanted you to have a safe place to rest. Though I'm neither human nor witch, I do understand it's not easy being a witchling without guidance."

"What are you exactly?"

"I'm what I said, a spirit of the woods. I am the spirit of the Green Man, yet the female personification. As he cannot be everywhere at once, I'm his representative in this forest. There are many of us all over the world. It's kind of like how certain men will "play" Santa Claus because he cannot be everywhere all the time. We also transcend the barriers between the human world and the magikal realm. We always have been and always will be--should humans not destroy all the trees or this wondrous planet they live on as parasites."

For a moment, Sadie was a bit offended as being referred to as a parasite, but in the time it took to think about it, she realized humans kind of were a parasite of the planet. Not all of them, but lots of them fell into this category. Also, not wanting a confrontation with the elemental, Sadie decided to change the subject, as this new "person" obviously knew things.

"You said you can help me. How?"

"I will tell you about your objects, and I will point you in the right direction when you leave here," replied the elemental. "I will give you cover now and when you leave, should you need it, and call the winds to hold back any foes."

Sadie smiled. Elementals must be powerful.

"I do not take sides. Normally. I stay out of the goings-on between humans and non-humans, but Tara beseeched me protect you, and I respect her as she respects me. Let's just say we, Tara and I, work together sometimes and because of that, I'm now an unlikely friend to you as well," replied the invisible elemental. "Not that I don't suspect you are worthy, it's just that as I told you before, I stay out of all the drama humans and magikal beings seem to thrive on. I have trouble trusting your kind. For me, trust must be earned."

"Can you show yourself?"

As soon as the last word left Sadie's lips a slight wind began to rustle. Fall's colorful leaves began to spin in front of her, a kaleidoscope view of every shade, while moss and ivy joined in, adding green to the mix. The swirling mass began to shape and form into a face.

When all was done, a female countenance made from bright red, yellow, and orange leaves appeared in the air before her. Brown leaves formed what looked like hair draping down to the ground. Ivy and other vines made a crown while moss formed a neck line to what would be clothing. It all left Sadie somewhat speechless. It was nature, or more specifically, the forest incarnate.

"Is this better?" the now-visible, and in a different way, very beautiful face asked.

"Y...yes," said Sadie, "it's easier to speak with someone when you have an image or idea of what they look like."

"Well, if it works for you, so be it. Now, let's get to work on the items in your backpack."

"Wait, what can I call you?" asked Sadie.

"I do not have a name, per say, but you may call me the Green Woman."

An Unlikely

Enemy

"It's a shame you don't have some seven-league boots in there," said the elemental as Sadie dumped the contents of her backpack on the cushy floor.

"If you mean ugly dark green rubber boots, I got some for my birthday. I guess they didn't fit in the backpack when the fairy packed it," Sadie responded while picking up a beautiful glass orb and tossing it from hand to hand. "What's this, some sort of crystal ball?"

"Careful! Careful with that, little witchling. That's a Sinking Sphere. I'm surprised you received one of those; they are quite rare from what I understand and remember," said the Green Woman as she looked fondly at the ball. "What that object does is to sink whom or whatever it hits and shatters on."

Sadie wondered how that would ever come in handy and why on earth would it be rare, but she was not one to complain. She looked at the pile and grabbed another item. They looked like very small, very unusual binoculars. "And what are these?" she asked.

"Ah, yes. I've seen a few of those in my days. Those are called Magikal Monocles. If you look through them, they will show you the immediate future of whomever you're looking at."

"Now that's cool," Sadie quipped.

"Okay, looks like you've got your standard sleeping potion in that bottle, a handful of frog pebbles, three battering bats, a freeze wand, two Giganticus Snailicus pills, some Forget Me Dust, ohhh…wait…there's Remember Me Dust, too. How unusual! And you've got some Forgur Cookies, Green Vomiting Swamp Eel Snot, and some…."

"Wait, slow down, you have to tell me what all these things do," Sadie said somewhat desperately. "I'll never know what to do with them or how to use them if you don't tell me."

With her leaves rustling, the Green Woman smiled at Sadie. It was a warm, almost motherly smile, and it made Sadie relax a bit. She regained her train of thought and slowed down her urgency. It may have been the Green Woman's intense gaze or maybe it was the warm sunlight beginning to stream through the branches and wood of the lean-to.

"What are frog pebbles? Are they dehydrated frogs?" Sadie asked, wondering what the importance of dried frogs could be.

The Green Woman seemed to laugh a moment and then spoke. "Frog Pebbles will turn anyone into a frog so long as you place a pebble on their person. They can only be turned back into what they were or are by placing a Reverse Frog Pebble on their frog person. That can be dangerous though as Reverse Frog Pebbles are three times the size of regular Frog Pebbles, and frogs can be quite small. I personally see no problems with being a frog, seems a simple enough life to me."

"Do I have any reverse Frog Pebbles? I might need them."

"I don't think they thought them necessary, as I don't see any. If they had, I'm sure they would have included them when they packed your bag."

A rustling was heard outside in the leaves. It was too loud and crunchy to be a mouse and too small and crackly to be a human. Every muscle in Sadie went tense.

"Relax, little witchling; it's just your guides," the Green Woman whispered through her leafy lips.

Sadie wondered.

Guides to where? And what kind of creature could or would guide me?

The rustling grew a bit louder and amidst the crunch of the leaves, chatter could be heard. At first it seemed to be light conversation between two…what-or-whomevers…that were coming her way, but as they got closer, Sadie could make out an argument.

"…and I'll smack you on the head with ten Troll Boulders!" (A loud whistling was heard at the end of this sentence.)

"If you think you can, you morally corrupt little lump. Troll poop is much too big for you to pick up. And why would you want to touch it in the first place, you sick, dirty little gnome. You're a disgrace to gnome-kind. Why don't you just go over to the dark side? You seem to have such an affinity for violence and nasty things."

"Only towards you, you…you…" (yet another whistle).

Sadie recognized that high pitched whistle of a voice. "Elgarbam, Whistle!" she shouted as she poked her head out of the hut.

Sure enough, right before her and eye to eye with her, as she was on hands and knees, were the pair of gnomes.

"Hello, Sadie, you look tired and out of sorts," said Elgarbam. "You looked prettier at your birthday party."

"Hello, Sadie, what a mess your hair is--too many knots and sticks in it for a human or, uh, er, a witchling," said Whistle.

Sadie, remembering that these two gnomes weren't exactly the most congenial, smiled as she felt her hair and began to pull sticks and leaves from its rumpled state.

"Well, what do you expect? I've been running through the woods all night," Sadie remarked, defending her apparently offensive appearance.

Elgarbam whacked Whistle on his little head, knocking off his cap, and exposing his bald scalp. With a flustered rush of stumpy little fingers, Whistle picked the cap up and replaced it almost immediately. Sadie smirked as the pair continued to do battle with each other. She looked at her pile of magikal objects on the moss-covered floor and picked up what looked like a fairly large icicle.

"And what can I do with this," she asked as she waved it about.

"WHOA!" screamed Elgarbam.

"Look out!" exclaimed Whistle as he ducked.

"Sadie, just put that down carefully and slide it back into your bag. That's a freezing wand," said the elemental.

"What's a freezing wand?" a curious Sadie questioned. She wondered what kind of icicle could get that much of a reaction from the three of them. She also felt a little bit tougher knowing it was in her possession.

"Whatever you point that wand at will turn to ice and not thaw for at least a week. They usually have about twenty freezes in them. If my powers of observation serve me correctly, yours has a full twenty charges on it. Whenever you run out, you can recharge them at any one of the Society for Magikal Beings Supply Outlets," responded the Green Woman.

"Oh, I want to go to the supply outlet now. I LOVE to shop," Sadie said.

"Well, you have to be in the Guild for Magikal Beings territory first before you can go to any of their shops," said a disgruntled Elgarbam.

"You mean we're not there right now?" Sadie asked. She was genuinely confused. How could Tara's home, all of this, everything she'd seen exist in the human world?

As the two tiniest beings laughed in unison at Sadie's question, the Green Woman was perfectly still. Sadie felt her cheeks turn a little red, and she began to feel somewhat like she should stand up for her question, but inside she knew she wouldn't dare. When the laughing had died down and Sadie was thoroughly embarrassed, the elemental spoke.

"No, Sadie, we're still in the human world. Whatever gave you the idea that you, us, all of us, were in the magikal dominion?"

"I just thought, I just...well...since I've been around all these creatures and whatnot," she stammered as she waved her arms towards the two gnomes, "that we were already here. I mean, I didn't see these types of things back in my world."

"Oh, we're all around in your world. You just don't see us as our true selves. We remain hidden from human eyes though we're here, living and working right beside you all the time. We wear a glamour when in your world so no one spots us and can expose..." Whistle started, but was cut off by Elgarbam.
"...our true forms. There are some out there who can see us magikal beings, but they're mostly considered crazy and either left alone, ignored, or locked up if they speak about us."

Sadie took all this in; as she did, her mind drifted almost immediately to Crazy Mary.

If that's the case, that would explain what she said to me. But how did she know? Could she see through the glamours? Does she have some sort of magikal powers? If so, she probably saw our town filling up with all sorts of nasty beasts. I guess she's not so crazy after all.

Sadie thought and answered her own questions in her head. The implications of what this new information could possibly mean made her eyes open wide.

So anyone could be a magikal being?

Her mind raced with this information as well.

Anyone I've ever spoken to could have been...otherworldly, and I didn't know it. That could explain that strange little man who runs the movie theatre and the lady who...OH, MY GOSH--I've got to find out about the parking meters. I just knew I saw them move....

"And I'm afraid that the Society of Magikal Beings or the Magik World is much, much different from what you're used to in your world. That's why no witchling is allowed to go there until she's a full witch at age sixteen. That's when you more fully understand what it all means, and you are in control of your powers, which, I might add, don't come into full effect until you're sixteen," stated the Green Woman.

Sadie pondered this new information for a moment, digesting what it all meant to her. She began pocketing bits of pertinent information into the files and folders of her mind. She also took a few moments to mull certain ideas and kept coming back to the fact that the gnomes had laughed at her, very loudly.

"And this is for laughing at me for asking a question," she said as she punched both Elgarbam and Whistle in their arms. "I won't punch you, Green Woman, since you've helped me so much. Not to mention, I think if I made you mad enough, nothing in my backpack of tricks could help me."

The two gnomes sat rubbing their arms in stunned silence as the Green Woman chuckled a little, causing some leaves to shed. "You're wise not to upset me, Sadie."

"What about us? You think you can just punch us with your giant pink fist, girl child? Witchling or no I ought ta...."

"There are NO stupid questions in this world or in the magik world, and you laughed at hers. I'd say the two of you deserved those punches. It's just a good thing she's still unsure how to use most of these items from her bag. Although, she does know all about the Frog Pebbles she has. I might add, little gnomes, there are no Reverse Frog Pebbles."

The two gnomes held each other and backed away a bit from Sadie, eyes wide, like they might've been turned to frogs before.

"I'm sorry, Sadie, it's all Whistle's fault. He's so rude. I blame his upbringin'. He was raised in a mixed marriage, Gnome and Sprite, very nasty business if you ask me, and I would...."

"She didn't ask you and since when are you against mixed marriage? You yourself have been after me sister Whisper for the last so many years, and she's half gnome and half sprite." Elgarbam punched Whistle; then Whistle punched him back. "You're just scared of the witchling now."

"ENOUGH!" the Green Woman exclaimed, "I don't know how anyone can be around you two with all the arguing. Now stop it!"

Some more leaves fell from her face. "The time has come for you to guide Sadie to one of the Society of Magikal Beings offices. Tara sent me word saying you are to go to the office in her hometown, Cranberry Grove, isn't it? Put your glamour on to look like adults so no questions are asked as to why this young lady is in your company."

"Done," said the bickering pair in unison.

"I can still see you," Sadie said.

"You will always see magikal creatures now, Sadie; you're a witchling. Glamours for the human world no longer work on you unless you let them," responded the Green Woman. "If only you were a full witch and you could glamour yourself, dear child, for the Syndicate will be looking for you full force. It's a shame these two can't perform magik on you; gnomes just don't have it in them to glamour someone else."

Elgarbam and Whistle looked down at the ground, pretending they didn't hear what The Green Woman said. It was obvious they were embarrassed by their weak magikal skills.

"What is the Syndicate I keep hearing about?" Sadie asked. "Zeno did mention something about the glamours, but I've really heard nothing about the Syndicate, 'cept for their name, 'til now."

"Elgarbam and Whistle can fill you in on the journey. I have other matters that need my attention immediately. I'm sorry I couldn't help you more, or explain more of your objects to you, Sadie MacDougall. Good luck!"

As she spoke, her moss began turning brown, the ivy began to curl, and leaves began to drop just like from the trees in the fall. "Be safe and vigilant, and if you really need help, remember everything in the world is whispered on the wind."

As she spoke her last word, the elemental known as the Green Woman completely disappeared in a little gust of wind that scattered her vegetation about the hut as if she had never been there.

Silence filled the tiny shelter as Sadie gathered her objects back into her bag. She felt a little sad The Green Woman was gone. She had really liked her.

Was she even really here?

That thought was immediately interrupted by a very loud burp.

"No couth!" said Elgarbam as he, yet again, smacked Whistle on the head with a loud crack.

"I'm surprised one of you doesn't have brain damage with all the smacking and hitting about the head the two of you do," said Sadie as she hooked her arms in her backpack straps. "Shall we be off?"

The two gnomes began inspecting each other's heads for brain damage as Sadie left the lean-to. The sun was shining bright, yet brought little warmth on this most beautiful of all fall days. Just about all the leaves had left the trees, and Sadie wondered why she hadn't noticed before.

Laughing a bit, she thought *'cause I've been a little busy.*

She looked around and the vast, murky swamp lay to her right and the forest she had run through last night lay to her left. In front of and in back of her was a sort of dirt road that ran the length of the two. Not knowing which way to go, she yelled for the gnomes. The two creatures waddled out and put up their hands to shield their eyes from the sunlight.

"Smells like snow," shrilled Whistle.

"Which way do we go?" questioned Sadie.

"This way," said Elgarbam, pointing along the track of road between swamp and forest that seemed to Sadie to lead north. She had worked this out from the time on her watch and the position of the sun. For once, she was glad she had paid attention at Outdoor Girls Camp when her mother had sent her.

As the threesome walked together, Sadie asked once again about the Syndicate. After several attempts and much arguing about who would talk, Sadie set the rules, and they all came to an agreement about the conversation at hand. They walked on and the two gnomes (who looked very much like they could be Sadie's mother and father to our regular old human eyes) told her all that they knew of the Syndicate.

Elgarbam began to explain how years before in the human world's history, around the year 1487, a book had been written called the Malleus Maleficarum.

His story went on something like this: A loose Latin translation of Malleus Malificarum is The Hammer of the Witch or Witch's Hammer. It is said that in 1486 it was written by two men--two human men--named Heinrich Kramer and Jacob Sprenger. Who really wrote the book and what this book's intended use was is still up for discussion to this day. The one thing that is known for sure is that following its publication, the hounding of any witch became crueler and much more widespread. This was because, at the time, witchcraft was accepted in human society as a very real fact.

Human society also thought witches were very dangerous and, thusly, should be killed. Eventually, humans realized how ridiculous this was (the dangerous part) and that they were burning and torturing lots of innocent people. They weren't even killing magikal beings most of the time. Mostly poor innocent women, midwives, and people who just didn't quite fit into society's norms were the ones accused and tortured. The book-and-witch-hunting were stopped. At least, on the surface, they stopped.

Out of all of this hoopla formed a secret society determined to keep witch hunting and destroying alive. This group believed all witches to be an abomination, and that they should be disposed of accordingly. They called themselves the Exterminator of Witches Syndicate. As time passed and they somehow found out about other magikal beings and creatures, their name changed to the Witches and Magikal Beings, Hunters, Trappers and Exterminators Syndicate. It was commonly known as just the Syndicate because the latter is such a mouthful. Though the humans who directed and lead the Syndicate hated all magikal beings, they would use them to suit their purposes.

The gnomes went on to explain that they, the Syndicate, are a very real and very dangerous threat to Sadie's life. Their mission is to seek out and destroy all witches, as well as witchlings. They try to find all humans who are about to turn and kill them before they even become magikal. It's still not sure to the Society of Magikal Beings how they, the Syndicate, find these witchlings. The gnomes reminded Sadie of her thirteenth birthday at the bookstore and how that turned out.

"But those were magikal beings that came after me at the bookstore," said Sadie.

Elgarbam went on to explain that just as there are bad and evil humans there are bad and evil creatures in the world of magik as well. And some have taken to working for the Syndicate, (as he had mentioned) even though ultimately, they will be their own destroyers. The Society, which is short for The Society of Magikal Beings, is made up of good and bad magikal creatures.

The good or light creatures belong to the Chaste Commonwealth and the bad or dark creatures make up the Dark Domain. With the enticement of power and riches from the Syndicate, there were some that could turn their cold hearts even colder and kill their own kind. They were the creatures who were the darkest of the dark and could not be trusted anymore. A deal was struck between them stating that the Turncoats, as they came to be known, would be given great rewards and eventually would rule the Society once all the good witches and creatures were destroyed. As long as they stayed in the magikal world and did not return to the human world, the Syndicate would not harm them--and vice versa.

Whistle continued, "As far as we know there is only one human in the entire human world that can see the creatures of the magikal world though he has not been fairy struck. He is the leader of the Syndicate. We have no idea how he got this power or how he uses it, except to hunt out about-to-be witchlings. He is one devious and shady human, that's for sure."

"That's how they spotted you and sent some of the Turncoats to kill you, Sadie. I'm sure you've figured out by now, even without any training, that you're a witchling," said Elgarbam.

"And that on your thirteenth birthday you turn," said Whistle.

"And that usually some important member of the Society will whisk new witchlings away before the Syndicate can, let's just say, dispose of you," said Elgarbam.

"But you were found out quite quickly and almost couldn't be saved in time," said Whistle.

"So it must have made them mad, and that's why they're still after you, unless, there's some other reason we don't yet know about," said Elgarbam eyeing Sadie.

"But how did they know I was going to turn? Do I have some sort of Neon sign on my forehead that says hey, I'm gonna turn into a witch? Oh, this is all too much," said Sadie putting her hand up to her head.

"It's something like that. When a young person, such as yourself, is about to turn, they get a bright purple glow all about them, sort of like an aura. The leader of the Syndicate sends out his people to spot these soon-to-be witchlings so that they can destroy them before they even get a chance to turn," said Elgarbam. "The scary thing is it's like he knows before we even know. For quite some time we've been trying to discover how he's able to do this, but we've got nothing. He's all human. I mean, it makes no sense. And these poor witchlings? What becomes of them?"

"And before you ask, no, you don't have a choice since you're so worried about being normal all the time--whatever that, 'normal,' means," said Whistle, a bit frustrated. "You were one of the ones born a witch."

Sadie smiled. She hadn't thought about fitting in or being normal or even having a family since the surprise birthday party at Tara's. As a matter of fact, that was the first time in her life she actually felt like she fit in and was normal. The only thing abnormal was that she was the only one without full powers.

But that's okay; apparently there are lots like me out there. I belong in the magikal world more than in the human world. When all this is said and done, I'm never going back to the human world. I'm staying where I'm not made fun of for being different.

"I have so many more questions: like what if an adult wants to become a witch or what if some kid who wasn't born a witch wants to become one. Or wait, how 'bout this. Do you guys, I mean, you magikal beings, ever recruit people to join? Or what if someone wants to decline who was born a witch, not that I want to decline, I'm just wondering...oh, sorry, I'm babbling. I can't help it; there's just so much to learn and...."

Before she could finish, a shape in the distance distracted Sadie from her line of questioning. A bit nervous at the thought of running into someone or something else, she surveyed her surroundings. The threesome was approaching a road. Sadie recognized it as one of the four roads that led to town, and on this road stood a figure about the same size as Sadie. Sadie's strange feeling in her stomach and chest returned.

"Hey, guys, you see that person up there? I'm getting a weird feeling about this," Sadie said to her two traveling companions.

"Whoever it is, they are about the same size as you. What harm can a human of your size do?" questioned Whistle. "I mean unless, of course, they have magikal powers," he continued when Sadie shot him a warning look.

They resumed their approach despite Sadie's uncomfortable feeling. The person had his back to them and was looking through a pair of binoculars at a great and vast lake on the other side of the road.

All of this seems so familiar, thought Sadie, *like I've been here before. I know this place. Wait! IT'S MY DREAM!*

"Guys, when I was knocked out from that sleeping tea, back at the bookstore, I had a dream and this place looks…."

Before the words had completely left her mouth, two giant vulture-men swooped down from out of the trees and grabbed a hold of Whistle and Elgarbam. The person standing in the road turned to face Sadie.

"David?" she questioned.

It can't be.

David, the boy she had met on Main Street, held a black velvet bag in one hand and with his other, threw some sort of dust at Sadie. He turned around just as quickly as he threw the powder and buried his head in his free arm. Through blurry vision she watched David's strange actions, and she watched the gnomes being carried off into the distance. This dust caused her to sneeze and then fall over--not asleep, but paralyzed--watching everything that was happening to her.

Things That

Hurt

As she lay helpless, seeing David walking towards her, Sadie felt confused and angry. Only a few days ago she had met this boy, who seemed shy and reluctant, and now he was somehow involved in what's going on in her life.

What does all this mean? What could he possibly want with me? And...he's obviously magikal...and why can't I move?

Sadie's anger began to build; as it did, the trees in the forest to the left began to sway and shift about. Whatever leaves that were left on them came loose and began to swirl around Sadie and David on the isolated dirt road. Ripples first, then white caps appeared on the lake. From the swamp, the reeds rustled and bent in unison with the rest of nature. If she had been able to speak, she would have demanded to know what was going on. The anger in her eyes flashed that knowledge.

David raised one of his arms, snapped his fingers, and with a crackle and sparks of light, there appeared two large vulture-men. With a whoosh of leathery bat-like wings, they settled on the dirt road where Sadie lay and David stood. Sadie's anger faded as fear replaced it, and the weather seemed to worsen. The first bits of winter snow began to fall and a northerly wind began to blow.

"Let's take her to the Syndicate," said David, puffing out his chest. "I'm going to be a hero."

A strong wind almost knocked him over, and one of the man-vultures shielded him with its wings.

"We have to go now. The weather's getting worse, and I'll bet this little abomination has something to do with it."

His eyes had narrowed to slits, and he practically spat as he directed the word "abomination" at her.

How can he be calling me an abomination when he's using magik himself?

As the man-vulture's scaly talons grabbed Sadie, its almost featherless body brushed against her, making her cringe. The smell coming off the creature was enough to upset anyone's stomach, and the oily long hair that was attached to its scalp in clumps had bits of bloody, raw flesh stuck in it.

Sadie thought she heard the sound of bells twinkling on the wind as the creature over her raised its wings. There were little holes in places and its wings looked quite tattered. Sadie wondered how it could fly let alone carry her as well. She heard the twinkling again.

In a massive rush not unlike that of a swarm of killer bees, David and the two man-vultures were besieged by the largest multitude of fairies Sadie had seen to date. She had no idea they could amass like that and was quite amazed at the large numbers. They appeared as one heaving, unified object. Sadie had only seen maybe ten fairies together at once. Orange, yellow, brown, and red flashed before her eyes as the fairies began to torment the three foes.

These must be fall woodland fairies. Maybe the Green Woman sent them.

David began swatting the air, and the man-vulture next to him flapped its wings in vain. The creature above her tightened its grip and fought to take off. The fairy swarm was relentless, but in the end they were no match for whatever was in David's bag.

Sadie watched helplessly as David snapped his fingers and gas masks of some sort appeared over his and the man-vultures' faces. He began sprinkling his powder through the fairy swarm. Their fast flying swirled the powder amongst them quickly. Little by little the fairies began to drop, the same way bees do when sprayed with poison. As the man-vultures carried Sadie and David away, she looked down at the amassing pile of fairies on the ground; they looked like someone had raked the fall leaves into a pile. Sadie stared at the horrid mound; it was getting larger even though she was being carried higher and higher into the sky.

Just before everything became ant-like from her sky-high position, Sadie saw Zeno running full speed down the road towards the spot where they had just been. He looked angry, fierce, and had his bow drawn.

If he shoots, I'll fall from the sky and probably break every bone in my body.

As if Centaurs could also read minds, Zeno lowered his bow. Sadie felt a pang of pity for him; he looked utterly in despair discovering he was too late to assist her. He stomped the ground with his hooves, pranced in a tight circle, and shook his fists and bow at the sky. The last thing Sadie could make out was Zeno's shouting something at her. Then he reared up and took off at break-neck speed.

* * *

When they began to alight, Sadie noticed they were back in her hometown of Cranberry Grove, above the old abandoned whiskey storage warehouse at the edge of town. It looked the same except there were many vultures covering the roof and clinging to the sides here and there. She wondered why no one on the street saw these horrid things and then remembered the glamour.

It was no use to try and get anyone's attention; they couldn't see her or they saw her as something else. She also wondered how the glamour worked, how it covered them, and what they looked like to the people below. Otherwise, some people may just get excited at the sight of man-vultures carrying two human beings through the sky.

And why don't the magikal beings down there see us? I can see them. That's another question I'll ask whenever we get where we're going, and I don't care who laughs at me.

Sadie had amassed quite a collection of questions during her flight. She also felt what she had begun to call the paralyzing potion was wearing off. She didn't dare let on, though. Who knew what David would do to her? She was still having a hard time believing this shy boy she had met a few days ago was a malicious magikal creature.

Decreasing in altitude, Sadie noticed uniformed guards posted every nine or ten feet along Main Street.

What on earth?

The closer they got, the more Sadie realized something strange was happening. These guards, or soldiers, were dressed in dark purple uniforms with silver ornamentation. Every time a human pulled up in a car, they gave the soldier something before walking away. Every time a magikal being approached them, they seemed to have a simple conversation. Some even looked as though they were giving directions. Then it hit her.

The Parking Meters! They stand like silent sentinels all along Main Street! But why? What exactly is their purpose?

This was yet another question for Sadie to add to her list of many.

They flew into the warehouse through a very large window. Sadie prayed the jagged, broken glass would not slice her as they went through. Finally, she was dropped on the dirty, grimy floor and lay there perfectly still as the man-vulture perched on some discarded crates nearby.

"I've brought you the witchling that has caused everyone so much trouble," David said to someone Sadie couldn't see, for her head was facing the opposite direction. "She's still alive so that should count for something. I want my reward, and I want what you promised me. Oh, and here's the rest of that nasty paralyzing potion. By the way, don't you think it's a bit hypocritical to use magik when you're trying to kill all magik and magikal beings? I've been meaning to ask you that for some time now."

If Sadie had not been more careful, the snort and humph she suppressed at David's own hypocrisy would have given her away. She did, however, let a little bit of her anger get the better of her, and a small pop of magik burst above her head.

Whatever or whomever David was talking to moved closer until they were standing just behind Sadie. She felt a knot form in her stomach and her chest began to tighten; simultaneously, she felt calm. A feeling she wasn't quite sure of rippled through her body, causing her to tremble. It was too much to hope they hadn't seen the little burst of magik. But she really didn't want them to see her body trembling, for surely then they would know the potion was wearing off.   The being began to walk around Sadie until it stood in front of her face. She recognized it to be a man from his feet, but she didn't dare look up at him.

It's probably David's father.

Inside, she sighed with relief; it wasn't another creature. Outside, she just lay there.

"Do not question my methods, boy. I will fight fire with fire if need be. I have my reasons for doing what I'm doing and *how* I'm doing it. You didn't seem to have a problem using magik yourself to contain this monstrosity. And…better safe than sorry. Look at the trouble she's caused so far." Sadie heard the man say. "By the way, how did that new magik I gave you work? I'm assuming well since none of the beings in town saw you fly in."

"Yes, sir, it worked very well. Thank you. It feels good to be superior."

She felt something being sprinkled on her person.

"Let's take her and chain her up until I figure out how to get what I need from her. We don't know what this one can do yet either."

He poked his toe into Sadie's ribs.

Sadie sneezed and then felt herself completely unable to move again. Even her eyes were fixed in front of her, and she felt her eyelids slowly closing. The tight feeling in her chest began to subside, and her stomach wasn't quite as nauseous. She felt arms or what she thought were arms lifting her, carrying her for several moments until they dropped her quite hard onto the floor, but it didn't hurt. Maniacal laughter could be heard as more dust was blown into her face. Within moments, Sadie was not only paralyzed, but also fast asleep.

* * *

Blinking her eyes to clear the bleariness, Sadie woke slowly, very groggy and slightly befuddled.

Where am I and why do I always seem to be dazed, sleepy or actually falling asleep?

When her eyes had adjusted to the darkness, she took note of her environment. It was gloomy and smelled of damp neglect. There was a chill in the air, and the sound of dripping water echoed in the dark. Then in a rush of mental pictures, the memories of what happened came charging back like a movie being fast forwarded.

David is a bad guy. I'll bet his dad runs the Syndicate; I got one of my feelings when I met them. I knew it! I need to find out what's going on. I need to tell someone. Oh, my head hurts, must be from all that powder of whatever they gave me. I have to be smart and careful about what I do now. I'm at their mercy.

She moved slowly and ever so slightly to rub her head and found chains on her wrists in the process. Following the links back to their origin, she found that she was chained to a stone wall. It seemed to be a thick stone wall that went up forever and was damp and cold to the touch. A trickle of water ran down it on her right to pool in the center of the room.

She heard the scurrying and scampering of creatures unknown in the shadows around her and trembled a bit. For the first time since her life had been thrown into this turmoil, Sadie fought back tears of defeat. She tried to sit up and realized that whoever had chained her forgot to take off her backpack.

I can use some of the magikal objects to get away.

She shrugged her shoulders and let the backpack fall a little off her back. The chains were making it difficult though she was trying so hard to be quiet. She didn't know who or what was out there guarding her, and she didn't want to draw attention to herself and find out. Hard as she tried though, being chained was not conducive to taking off her backpack, much less getting into it.

I will not give up. They say I'm a witch so what would a witch do?

Into her mind popped Zeno and what he said the night of her birthday. *Use your magik! Remember the books flying off the shelves!*

She remembered what had happened in the bookstore. She remembered fighting the first man-vulture from on top of Zeno's back; when she had become frustrated, it seemed as if her feelings materialized into action. Sadie began to concentrate all her emotions and feelings into the pit of her stomach. She controlled her breathing and focused all her energy on how angry she was at being kidnapped by David, at the gnomes being taken, and at those disgusting man-vultures.

She tried to focus the emotions and energy on the chains that were binding her. If there were one thing she had figured out without any help either, it was that all magik came from energy. Sparkles of white light began to crackle and pop in the air around her, but they fizzed out very quickly and nothing happened. *No change.* She tried again, harder this time, so hard that her head began to hurt again and her stomach went into knots. The same thing happened--little pops and crackles of white light, but no change.

"I guess it's 'cause I'm just a witchling and not a full witch," she said aloud though no one was there to listen. Or so she thought.

"It's because those chains are made of iron, and iron disrupts any form of magik and can bind magikal creatures for eternity," came a voice from the darkness. "Even a full witch, or a massive troll for that matter, couldn't break those chains. But I must say, that was quite a display for being bound with so much iron. You must be one powerful little witch in the making."

Sadie thought for a moment before she spoke. Much had happened to her in the last few days, and she wanted no more trouble than she thought she could handle.

See, if only I were a normal kid, none of this would be occurring.

"Where are Elgarbam and Whistle?" she asked the disembodied voice.

Laughter could be heard echoing in the dank musty room. It was such maniacal laughter that it chilled Sadie to her very bones. When it eventually stopped, all that was left was the sound of the trickle of water running down the walls of her dungeon, along with her breathing.

"You're chained up in a dungeon quite possibly about to die, and all you can think about are two worthless little gnomes? You are a strange child, Sadie MacDougall; no wonder you've had such a hard time in the human world. "

A smug humph could be heard in the blackness.

A huge flash of white and gold light cracked in the air above Sadie's head, illuminating the darkness around her. In the split second it hovered before burning out, Sadie saw the figure of a man with his arms crossed over his chest further away in the room.

"What? Did that make you mad? Oh...I get it now. You don't want to be strange or different do you, Sadie? It hurts you that so many foster homes have traded you in for normal kids. It hurts you how much you've been teased and taunted by the children at school."

More bursts and crackles of light appeared above her head for a second before fizzing away just like the last two times.

"You've been weird your whole life, and now you find out you're a witch. So you're even weirder. An abomination. Oh, you'll never be normal now, Sadie; all your chances for that went out the door that night at the bookstore." The man laughed again, a full, deep evil laugh that came from thinking he was superior. How well she knew that laugh from the cruel kids at school who used to make fun of her!

Sadie tried not to cry, but his words hurt. Her whole life she had tried to fit in. She had been tormented, teased, bullied, and ignored, and now, even though she was a witchling, it was no different.

What good is this new life then?

"I don't care what you say. I don't care what you think of me," said a saddened Sadie, trying to sound defiant.

"Oh, yes, you do. It's been your life's problem--bullied at school, teased by the other children, foster families passing you around like a Christmas fruit cake. And all because you had that little episode where you, what do you kids call it, freaked out, in front of the whole class. You remember that, Sadie. You told everyone your mother was still alive--that you knew it. What a stupid and crazy girl! No wonder all the kids shunned you after that. Didn't your foster family make you see a shrink after that? Didn't you go around town telling everyone your mom was still alive and coming back for you? Now that I think of it, did your mom even want you?"

A tremendous explosion rang out above Sadie's head. She had conveniently forgotten about that little disaster in front of her whole science class. The snap and pop of the light burst had lingered a little longer than the others, giving Sadie some hope at magik working. But it was just as useless as before because the magik fizzled out like a spent sparkler. The man laughed once again. Then, he lowered his voice and spoke once more.

"I see I've found your weak spot. That's good; I'll just think on it and figure out how to use it to my advantage. For now, here's something for you to think about. I was the one who killed your mom; it wasn't a fiery car crash into the river like you were led to believe. And I enjoyed it as well."

In a huge burst of red light, sparkles, pops, crackles, and fizzles, Sadie sprang forward a bit--as forward as the chains would allow before yanking her back to her three foot radius she was given. The man began laughing, and his laughter faded into the distance as he disappeared further into the dark.

When his footsteps could no longer be heard, Sadie began to cry. It was a deep, belly-hurting cry that came from her very soul. With each shudder and wave of tears, sparks and crackles popped and fizzled overhead. Her entire body heaved with sob after sob and her shirt became wet with all the tears. She missed her mother, she missed being at the bookstore before all of these strange events had happened, she missed having tea with Mrs. Felis (when she was a human), and she definitely missed being normal.

Wow, I guess I'm normal compared to what I've seen and know now. I just wish I had appreciated it before all of this.

She smiled to herself.

*If only I had…*but she didn't have time to finish her thought because an imp about the size of a Jack Russell Terrier came into view. *I must not have heard him 'cause of my bawling.*

The imp walked right up to Sadie, right through the cell bars and stared directly into her eyes with its own beady black ones. Some of the wax from the candle it held dripped onto her cheek, but she dared not flinch.

They'll not see my fear, the disgusting things.

It was so close Sadie could smell its foul breath and see festering boils on its bald scalp. She also noticed that a piece of its pointy, dirty ear was missing on the right side, and on its left was a zigzag scar across its belly.

What do these things do that they get so…beaten up?

It held a Mason jar in one hand and in the other was a tube about two feet long. On one end of the tube was what looked like some sort of suction device and on the other end, an open hole. Two more imps came forward from the darkness and each carrying the same instruments. They approached Sadie as the first imp blew powder in her face.

"What did you do that for?" asked one of the imps.

"'Because she can see us, you stupid twit; she'll fight," the first one replied.

"It's so much easier on regular humans," said the third imp in.

"Yes, but hers will bring such a good price," said the first imp and the three started laughing in tiny dark chuckles.

Sadie realized the powder the first imp blew on her was that same paralyzing powder David had used. She was getting tired of this happening to her and made a promise to herself that if she got free, she would do her best to come up with an anti-paralyzing powder that prevented that one from working. Reality set in again as the imps moved forward, and she watched in horror as the first imp approached her even closer than the others.

He stuck the suction-looking end on to her index finger. He then stuck the open end into the little bottle he held. He went back to the end with the suction cup and touched a button on the top of it. Sadie didn't feel anything, but when he did this, she began to see a purple spiraling smoke fill the little jar. The other two imps had begun doing the same to her other hand and to her arm.

All three jars were filling rapidly with the purple smoke, and Sadie began to feel more and more tired as the jars filled. Eventually, she would have yawned, she thought, if she could have moved. When the jars were filled to the brim, each imp stuck a lid on them, pulled the tubes off of Sadie and walked away in silence. The scarred one stuck the candle in a chink in the wall before walking away into the darkness of the chamber.

Sadie, still mostly paralyzed, was beginning to regain control over her body, but it didn't matter at this point. She wanted to move out of the way of the cold trickle of water running down the stones of the wall behind her, but she was just too tired. All she wanted to do was sleep. With her arms chained, she scooted a tiny bit back so that she could put the backpack between herself and the wall. Then, Sadie did something she had never done before. She fell asleep sitting up.

Though just before she drifted off, Sadie could have sworn she saw a large, dark, cloaked figure carrying a sickle, floating down the hallway away from her cell. And when this figure came into view, all the air seemed to be sucked out of the room.

Gypsies, Stinking Slather Bugs, and Forgur Cookies

Sadie woke to the sound of snoring. It got louder and louder in her ears, so loud in fact that she opened her eyes even though she wanted to keep on sleeping. She sluggishly readied herself to give someone a piece of her mind.

"Will you please be quiet?" she demanded more than asked, as she rolled over to see the cause of the noise.

Four more candles were stuck in the crevice where the imp had left his, though only one was burning. The others were reduced to waxy stubs with spent wicks. In the flickering light of the single flame, Sadie saw a small figure. Elgarbam. He lay chained like she was, but a few feet away.

When Sadie realized to whom she was yelling, she softened almost immediately. She had been very worried about Elgarbam and Whistle; at least, she thought she was. She couldn't really remember exactly what happened or for that matter, what she was thinking.

"Elgarbam! Wake up, how did you get here? Where's Whistle? What time is it? We got to…." She was interrupted by the gnome.

"Quiet, please! My head hurts immensely!" shouted the disgruntled gnome as he struggled to sit up.

Sadie looked at the grumpy little guy. He was tattered and torn. Scratches down his cheeks led to the rips in his clothes, giving him a beat-up garden gnome appearance. He had bruises on his face, as well, and looked the worse for wear. She took all this in, with heaviness in her heart, and gave him a moment before the barrage of questions began again.

"How did you get here? What time is it? Where's Whistle?" Her questions were more like an assault than a query.

And even though she had tried to be gentler, their situation demanded urgency so she tried to sound serious.

"I don't think shouting is necessary. As a matter of fact, another three more days of sleep wouldn't matter much at this point, and it would probably get rid of my headache," Elgarbam said as he pulled his cap down over his eyes and tried to go back to dozing.

"NO!" shouted Sadie. "You MUST wake up and talk to me! Wait, what did you say, three more days? What does that mean?"

The very tired and more than a bit rumpled gnome slid his hat up and out of his eyes while he straightened his little spine to sit flat against the cold stone wall. He eyed Sadie while she sat, somewhat agitated and anxious, and let out a sigh. He rubbed his stubby little fingers through his long grey beard and seemed as though he were considering something. Then a loud grumbling, gurgling noise interrupted the silence.

"Sorry. I'm a bit hungry," said Sadie.

"It's okay, witchling. So am I. You've been asleep for three days; I'm sure you're much worse off than I," he replied in a subdued voice.

Sadie looked shocked. Slowly, it was all coming back to her. "When I get out of here, I'm going to put a curse on each and every one of them, especially those nasty little imps with the suction cups and bottles," she said as she held her rumbling belly.

It was Elgarbam's turn to look shocked. "What do you mean 'imps with bottles?' In here? Where?" He seemed a bit disturbed and began looking around their dark, dank dungeon of a room.

"It was before you were here; I'm sure they're long gone," Sadie tried to comfort the gnome. She went on to tell him her ordeal of the suction cup tubes and jars filling with purple smoke. When she had finished, he was rubbing his beard once more.

"So that's how they do it," was all he said as he stroked his beard. Then, he continued, "I really thought they only did it to humans, but I'll bet yours will fetch a nice sum. Not to mention, I'm sure you're much more potent than any regular human. Being as you're a witchling and all."

"Do what? My what? What are they doing?"

"Stealing energy."

It was now Sadie's turn to look perplexed. She sat back along the wall, making sure not to sit in the stream of water, for the trickle had become a heavy flow now, and she took a huge, deep breath.

"I don't have any idea what you're talking about. You're going to have to explain *this* to me as well," she said. *And I thought human life was complicated.*

"Remember when you were all human how you would sometimes feel very tired, and it was only, say, the middle of the day? Well, what most likely happened is this: the imps stole your energy. You see, they steal it, bottle it, and then sell it on the black market back in the magikal realm. They do it all the time. Human energy, to a magikal being, is quite, well, quite a high.

"But, just like other drugs, it comes with a lofty price to pay for partaking, and I'm not just talking a gold coin price. I'm sure you'll see what I mean soon enough when--if we can get out of here and you meet some of those addicted to the stuff. I've never heard of their zapping the energy of a witchling, but they've probably never had the opportunity before. I'll bet there are magikal creatures already strung out on you and just begging for more."

"Ew. That's creepy, Elgarbam. It's almost like, well, I don't know, I just know it's creepy. I guess I should be glad they're not drinking my blood or anything," said Sadie with a shiver.

Elgarbam just looked at her.

"What? They do that too?" Sadie asked.

"Not the imps," Elgarbam replied matter-of-factly. "You haven't met any of the vampires or werewolves yet, have you? Well, let's just hope your first meeting is with the ones on our side."

The little battle-worn gnome crossed his arms and tried to roll over and away, his chains interrupting the process.

Sadie rattled her own chains. "I'm not liking this, Elgarbam. You never told me where Whistle is, and I want to know why."

The gnome looked sad. This made Sadie stop talking.

Something must have happened to Whistle.

Elgarbam wiped a single tear from his cheek and sat in silence.

"When I get out of here, I'm going to curse whoever did this to us and to whoever did whatever to Whistle," she said through clenched teeth as little sparkles of light popped above her head.

Though she had only met the two little guys a few days ago, she had grown quite fond of them.

"Well, I'll tell ya what's wrong with all that," he replied. "You can't curse anyone. Only Gypsies can curse objects and people. That's why they're always on the move. In life, both human and magikal, everything you do comes back to you and usually threefold. If you do something good, then good things will come to you. If you do something bad, bad things will come to you. You see how it works? So, the Gypsies have to keep moving so the curses can't catch up with them. It usually takes about three months for a curse they brought into play to find them. So they can stick around that long, but not much longer. That's why they're always on the move."

"So why don't they just not curse anyone or anything anymore? Seems simple enough," said Sadie.

"That'd be like asking a Stinking Slather Bug not to stink or asking a mosquito not to bite. It's in their nature; it's what they do. Doesn't make them bad. It's their job in life. Oh, there are bad gypsies just as there are bad humans and bad magikal beings, but just because it's in their nature to do something, doesn't make them inherently bad. There are good gypsies, too. Kinda like snakes. Not many like them and most think of them as evil, but they have a purpose in life--everything does."

Sadie thought about this for a moment before speaking again.

I've got so much to learn.

"So where's Whistle?"

The little gnome took off his hat, exposing a full head of grey puffy hair growing in all directions, most unlike Whistle's little bald head. He lowered his face to the ground before speaking.

"I'm afraid he didn't make it; he couldn't have made it," said Elgarbam in a quiet voice. "Last I heard the poor wee man, he was screaming bloody murder as they were branding him with hot irons, trying to get information. I'm sure I'm next."

Sadie didn't know what to say. She felt that familiar knot in her stomach and throat, the same knot that tied her up when her mom had died. She twisted her hair around a finger and thought for a moment.

My captors must be the most vicious men on the planet to torture a poor little creature like Whistle. And all because he's different than they or because they want information. Maybe it's just 'cause he was good and they are bad. It happens in the human world. Why wouldn't it happen in the magikal one as well? I wonder if I can run for government in the Society so I can try to change things. No, no one would listen to me there, just like they didn't in the human world.

Sadie thought to herself a bit more until her stomach growled so loudly it seemed to echo through the darkened room.

"It looks like some things have fallen out of your bag. Do you think we could somehow use your magikal objects to get out of here?"

Sadie wiggled in her chains just enough to see exactly what had come out of her bag. The string keeping her bag closed had come untied and sure enough, one of the items had fallen out. Sadie was able to grab a small wrapped parcel that she hadn't seen before.

Written on the outside of the wrapping in bold, black lettering: **To Die for Chocolate Cake.** Her mouth began to water and her stomach growled louder. She quickly ripped the wrapping from the cake and flung it aside, hitting Elgarbam in the face in the process. Elgarbam pulled the paper away with a grunt as Sadie looked like a dog with a bone. Just as she was about to shove half of the chocolate cake in her mouth, the gnome screamed.

"STOP!"

Sadie, a bit put off by this, turned to look at Elgarbam with what she thought to be an intimidating stare.

"What? I was going to share," she said icily.

"I don't want any of that and neither should you."

"What, gnomes don't like chocolate?"

"We love chocolate when it won't kill you."

Sadie was confused and, looking at the cake, even more hungrily.

"What do you mean 'when it won't kill you?' You're just trying to get all of the cake for yourself when I throw it down. You're trying to trick me out of my cake. I can't trust anyone around here! I already told you I'll give you half." And with that she raised the cake to her mouth, opened wide, and was in the midst of taking a giant bite.

"SADIE, STOP!" she heard Elgarbam say and in unison, like it was in stereo, she heard her mother's voice, as well. She stopped and looked around.

It was like she was right next to me.

Bits of cake crumbled from her shaking hand as she peered into the darkness around her.

I swear she's here; it was like she spoke into my ear.

Turning to face Elgarbam, she looked for any signs of recognition.

"Did you hear that?" Sadie asked the gnome.

"I heard nothing but your gluttonous ramblings," said Elgarbam. "But like I was saying, you don't want to eat that. There's a reason it's called To Die for Chocolate Cake. Think about it."

Sadie sat the cake down on the cold wet floor and slowly, reluctantly, pushed it away from her.

Why would they give me something that could kill me?

She looked at Elgarbam who was trying to keep the steady stream of water away from his little leather booties. Using her foot, she pushed the cake to the edge of the darkness. No sooner than she had drawn her leg back up to her chest than two beady-eyed, fat black rats ran to devour the cake. Within seconds of their first bite, they both fell over dead.

"Wow, works quickly. I'm glad you stopped me," said Sadie.

"I don't understand why they would give you something as dangerous as that and not explain it to you," Elgarbam replied.

"I was thinking the same thing myself."

The pair of captives sat in relative silence and watched as two bigger rats dragged off their recently deceased companions. Sadie didn't want to think about what they were going to do with them; she knew rats didn't have funerals. Her stomach growled even louder, and she tried to think of something other than food. She wondered how long they would have to be there before she and Elgarbam started eating rats. In the end she figured she didn't want to know or find out.

As she sat, a strange tingling began to filter through her body. She looked over to Elgarbam who was very busy trying to look uninterested in her and their situation. The tingling traveled from her toes, up her legs, and into her belly. It then moved the rest of the way up and through her body. When it reached her head, it was accompanied by a ringing in her ears. Sadie wondered if some of that wretched chocolate cake had actually gotten into her mouth. She began to wipe the inside of her mouth with her sleeve.

Is this what it feels like to die from magik cake?

She looked over at Elgarbam once more to see if maybe, just maybe, he was feeling this strange tingling, too. The gnome had pulled his hat down over his eyes and seemed to be sleeping again.

In an instant, the tingling grew more intense, and Sadie felt as though she were being pulled apart at the seams. It felt as though ever molecule was going in a different direction and that she needed to hold on to something. She grabbed for the chains holding her captive, and her hands went straight through them.

Did I die? Am I now a ghost?

Sadie grabbed frantically at the wall behind her; once again her hands swiped air like the wall wasn't even there. That all too familiar panic set in as Sadie tried to understand what was happening to her. She looked over at Elgarbam and shouted his name, but her voice sounded hollow, almost distant.

I am a ghost!

She shouted at Elgarbam again. He rolled over with his back facing her, oblivious to her yelling. As the anxiety settled in the pit of her stomach, her vision started to blur. Then, with a whooshing noise in her ears, she felt as though she were being ripped apart at the seams and her vision was a smear of colors.

* * *

"For Gur?"

Sadie tried to focus, tried to gain control over her faculties.

What just happened to me?

"For Gur?"

She heard someone or something speak, but she still wasn't quite sure what had just happened to her. All she did know was that it wasn't Elgarbam's voice she was hearing.

Is it that horrible man who is holding us captive? If I really am dead, I guess it doesn't matter now.

She blinked her eyes and looked around.

There were tombstones to her right, old ones that were cracked and riddled with green fungus. To her left there were more tombstones, except these were newer, smooth and polished. With a gasp she realized she was sitting smack dab in the middle of Cranberry Grove cemetery. She heard the voice speaking to her again; this time it sounded a bit more urgent.

"For Gur?" it said once again and with more force.

Sadie turned ever so slightly to see who was talking to her. She looked at the tattered denim and very colossal shape in front of her; as her eyes traveled upwards to gaze upon its face, it held a hand out in front of it, right under Sadie's nose. Sadie realized she was looking at a very large troll and went on the defensive.

"For Gur?"

Sadie had no idea how to respond. She looked around; there was no one to interpret or help her. She didn't know if this troll was good or bad. There was no way to tell from looking at him. As she moved to sit up straighter, her backpack slipped from her shoulders completely, spilling one of its items on the ground. The troll became even more excited. Looking to her left, she saw what the troll must have been talking about.

"Ooooohhhhhhhh! I get it! You want these, don't you?" she asked as she grabbed the parcel labeled For Gur cookies.

"For Gur," the troll said as it pointed to itself.

"Is your name Gur?" Sadie asked.

The large troll nodded his head and smiled at Sadie, revealing only two teeth in his mouth that were the size of washing machine lids.

Well, I guess he's not going to kill me, she thought. *That's a relief.*

She handed the cookies to Gur and watched as he devoured them without even unwrapping the parcel paper they came in. With regret, she wished she had kept one for herself as her belly began its rumbling once again.

"We try not to give him too many. There's nothing harder to manage than a troll with a sugar high," said a voice behind her.

Sadie turned to see a girl, somewhere between the ages of fourteen and sixteen, smiling down at her. She was wearing long purple robes and had her blonde hair in one long braid that hung over her shoulder.

"Gur makes a great watchdog, but forgets everything when there are Forgur cookies around," the girl said as she stuck out a hand to help Sadie up. "And the energy he gets…I'll bet if we could find a human-sized gerbil wheel, he could generate enough electricity to power all of Cranberry Grove. If only the humans knew what we could do for them…."

Taking her hand, Sadie stood, leaving her backpack where it lay.

"You're gonna need that magik bag of yours," the girl said extending her hand again. "I'm Hannah."

Sadie shook the girl's hand and rubbed her temples with the other one. She was starting not to like being so confused all the time, but she guessed it beat sitting in a dank basement chained to a wall, starving, and not knowing if and when you were to die.

"Why am I in the middle of Cranberry Grove cemetery? How did I get here? Where's Elgarbam? I can't just leave him chained up to …."

"Whoa, slow down, first things first," said Hannah. "We need to get you inside to Ms. Cabot. She has some questions she needs to ask you. And I'm sorry if I'm a bit cranky; that spell took lots out of me. I'm sooooo tired."

Grabbing her backpack off the ground, Sadie ran to catch up with Hannah who took off at break-neck speed for someone who claimed to be so tired. They were headed towards the large Victorian house that everyone in Cranberry Grove knew to be the cemetery owner's home and offices.

Everyone also knew the owner to be somewhat mysterious, only being seen at night or if someone died and needed tending to. Instead of asking so many questions, as she usually did, Sadie kept quiet. They walked the path that wound out of the cemetery and up the hill toward the house. The house itself overlooked the graveyard and the town as it sat on the highest hill in the county.

Sadie could see a bird's eyes view of everything from Main Street and its eclectic collection of shops and houses to the side streets where most people lived. She could see the four roads leading out of town, like a dirt drawn compass--to the woods, lake, and swamp. She even saw Miller's Pond. Her eyes went back to the roads again, for they were full of magikal creatures, all of them coming into town. Sadie recognized one of the roads--it being the very same road that only a few days ago she and a centaur named Zeno took to Tara's house.

She smiled to herself at the thought of her friend Zeno and then frowned remembering how she left Tara's. She pictured Tara trapped in that bubble with the horrible goblin and shuddered. She really hoped she wasn't still stuck there.

"You look deep in thought. No doubt you're wondering what you're doing here. Before you hear any rumors, it was I that transported you. I'm spending my last year of training here at the Society's offices in Cranberry Grove. I'm just glad this transporting spell wasn't being graded," said Hannah as they climbed the steps to the house. "I can tell you this, though, it took every last bit of energy I had. So now, thanks to you, I won't be able to do any really good magik for about three days."

"So it was you who made me feel like I was being pulled apart in every direction," Sadie replied.

"It wasn't that bad, was it? And you're alright; still have all your parts, don't you?"

Sadie gave herself the once over, checking all her bits and pieces to make sure she didn't lose any in Hannah's botched transporting spell. As they climbed the steps, Sadie noticed that Gur had taken up a position at the giant wrought iron gates that gave entrance into the graveyard. He was nodding and greeting creatures as they entered. She briefly wondered how many people in town would travel thirty miles to the next town to be buried if they knew that a giant troll guarded the gates.

*Crazy Mary would be the only person to...*but her thought was interrupted at the sight of Crazy Mary wandering among the old tombstones on the east side of the cemetery.

As Hannah put her hand on the huge doorknob to let them inside, Sadie finally couldn't contain herself anymore and asked a question. "What is Crazy Mary doing here?"

"Who? Crazy Mary? Oooohhhh, you mean Mary Cabot, the Wonky One--Ms. Cabot's poor, unfortunate sister. She's just waiting to see her sister which may take awhile now that you're here." Hannah winked at Sadie as they went inside.

Sadie decided not to ask any more questions about Crazy Mary, not until she knew what was really going on. Plus, she had also decided, right then and there, that she wasn't sure if she liked this girl Hannah. Her attitude was bit too smug.

They entered into a large, formal parlor lined with ferns on plant stands and comfortable chairs for waiting. There was a row of hooks on one wall that held people's coats and, on the other wall, horizontal hooks for, apparently, broomsticks. Two broomsticks were being supported there along with one very old, very used pointy hat. It was hung on the same rungs as a very taped up, very beaten up broomstick. The other broomstick looked as though it had just come right out of the box, if indeed, that's how broomsticks came.

"Oh, good, you're here," said a voice.

It was coming from the tall, thin old woman Sadie recognized from the bookstore. She was one of the three ash-covered women that had been there that night. The night all hell broke loose in her life. Sadie tensed a little. But, Sadie also remembered her from her birthday party at Tara's where everyone had been so kind to her. So she relaxed again.

"Now tell me, Sadie, however did you manage to get into such a horrible situation? We equipped you with some of the best magikal objects Society money could buy--along with leaving you in the hands of the very capable Tara from the Isle."

No Tears

Left

Sadie stood with her jaw slack, twisting her hair between her fingers. As her eyes scanned the so-called funeral parlor, she realized just how much the outside belied what was inside. It showed nothing to the human world to say it was chock full of magikal beings.

This must have one heck of a glamour on it.

An image of the townspeople being greeted by a huge troll at the gate and their reaction had Sadie stifling a giggle. Sadie didn't know if it was from all she had been through in the last week, if it was from lack of good sleep, or if it was hunger, but she felt completely giddy.

"I don't know what you think is so funny, witchling. We've had four attacks in as many days and lost lots of good people in the process. Come into my office and maybe you can explain your impudence," said the tall, thin woman. Sadie noticed that all the ash and cobwebs were gone from her clothes and she looked much different than she had on Halloween night. The old woman's lips were pursed tightly. There were lines on her forehead, and there was a heavy aura hanging around her. She appeared to be a very powerful person. As a matter of fact, the old woman seemed downright scary.

"Yes, sorry, I just...."

"Shhhhh." The old woman hushed her and took her firmly by the shoulder. "We'll talk inside," she said as she led Sadie to a room at the furthest end of the entry hall.

Walking down the long corridor, Sadie thought of Tara's little-big cottage. This funeral parlor-come-magikal beings meeting place seemed bigger than it should rightly be from the outside.

The same magik must apply here.

It was heaving with what Sadie thought to be décor from the Middle Ages. If anything, it looked as though they were inside a castle. When they reached the end of the hallway, they entered a room to the left. A huge, carved wooden chair stood behind the very large matching desk the old woman was heading towards. She motioned for Sadie to take the seat opposite. As Sadie started to sit, she could have sworn the face on her carved wood chair winked at her. Slowly, she sat and faced the imposing desk and old woman.

"Well, Sadie. Sorry to have taken such an angry tone with you out in the hall, but there are so many people and creatures around; we don't know who to trust so I just...well, I have to keep up appearances," she stated with a smile.

Clearing her throat, Sadie responded with, "Yes, ma'am."

"You've obviously been through much in the last week since you've become a witchling. I can't think of another put to the test as you have been. I can see you've fared well, despite having to be rescued from who knows where. Very impressive for such a young witchling incapable of any real power. I can only imagine what you'll accomplish once you completely turn." She cleared her throat and continued. "Let's start from the beginning, and we'll see where we go from here...depending on your answers."

Sadie felt nervous. It wasn't the nervous, strange feeling she got when something was about to happen. It was more like the nervousness she felt when she was in trouble. She fidgeted in her chair.

Is it hot in here?

She wrung her hands and then wiped them on the upholstered arms of the chair before beginning to speak.

"Pardon me, lady, but would thou please stop tormenting the young witchling with thine power. She's noticeably leaking on my hand-stitched embroidery."

Sadie froze. She looked around to see where this accusing voice was coming from and realized it was the very chair in which she was sitting. Not wanting to move for fear of reprimand, she remained motionless.

"Arthur, please do not quibble with me over such a trivial and minute detail. There are more important issues to discuss at the moment. We've much to talk about, Sadie and I. I'll speak with you later regarding your latest demand on my attentions. We both know this is more about that furniture polish the brownies used and less about Sadie's sweat. For right now, please, be quiet," said the woman.

"Now, Sadie, let me properly introduce myself. I am Ms. Moriganna Cabot; you may call me Ms. Cabot. I am from a long line of witches from the northern lands--Lammia from Scandinavia, of Viking decent, though most recently the British Isles. My family has survived longer than I dare try to comprehend. I'm also the head of the Guild of Magikal Beings. Along with Mrs. Teak and Miss Bruja, we run this show both here and in our realm of being. We aim to keep all witches, witchlings, and magikal beings alive and prosperous, despite the continuing efforts of the Syndicate to eradicate all of us from existence."

"Did you say Lammia? That's what Crazy Mary called me," said Sadie.

Ms. Cabot laughed. "I see you've no doubt met and know my sister."

"I've not really met her. I've always steered clear of Crazy Mary; I...." Sadie didn't finish. She put her head down as her cheeks grew warmer. She wondered if it were an offense to call Ms. Cabot's sister "crazy" to her face.

"It's okay, dear; out there in the human world, I'm sure she does seem a bit 'crazy.' Besides, we've known since her birth that something was...different about her," Ms. Cabot said. "She is a bit 'touched' but then again, if she chooses to live as a wild creature on the streets...who am I to argue? Besides, her visions are getting a bit out of hand. Why just two weeks ago she started making insane accusations about some of our best supporters."

As she finished her sentence, the door behind Sadie slammed shut. Sadie, not wanting to move for fear of disturbing Arthur the Chair, sat deathly still, facing forward, and just about holding her breath.

"Ah, Miss Bruja, Mrs. Teak, you've made it just in time," said Ms. Cabot. She motioned for the two women to come into the room. Sadie could hear skirts rustling as they approached and smelled a strange combination of sweet, hot tea and chili peppers.

Sadie slowly turned just her face so she could see the two women as they came into view. Mrs. Teak was her short and chubby self.

Maybe she could use the sweater she gave me?

She was wringing her hands and had one of her arms in a cast of some sorts. Miss Bruja was strikingly beautiful as Sadie had remembered and stood next to the portly woman with an arm around her shoulder. The pair looked oddly disparate, yet remarkably similar--Mrs. Teak so round and motherly and Miss Bruja so supermodel perfect. Miss Bruja's tight black clothing left nothing to the imagination; she was every human man's dream. Mrs. Teak's rustling skirts and apron made her look the perfect matronly mother. They nodded at Sadie and then Ms. Cabot.

"I see your arm is healing, Mrs. Teak. Miss Bruja, you look...in good health...as usual. Well, where were we? Oh, yes, that's right. Sadie was about to tell us how she got into such a fine mess. It's a good thing we had a personal item of hers so we could whisk her back here when the fairies reported her capture to us. I think we ought to find out exactly what happened though. Sadie, what do you say?"

Sadie thought for a moment over everything that had transpired since the day of her birthday. She had never been on such a crazy misadventure, never been so out of her element. Heck, she had never been outside of Pennsylvania and had only lived in one other town besides Cranberry Grove, and that was only for a very short time. She rubbed her eyes. It seemed too unreal, too fantastical to be her life, but like it or lump it, it was hers now.

I'll never again have to worry about where I'm going to sit in the cafeteria, she thought with chagrin; *never have to worry about being so different now.*

Somehow, it didn't seem to bother her so much anymore and, without realizing it, Sadie was starting to come into her own. She sat up straight, looked directly at Ms. Cabot, and began to speak.

Sadie told the three women of all that happened at Tara's the night of the impromptu birthday party. She told them of Tara in the bubble with the goblin creature. She told them of Allroy being subdued by other goblins. She told them of running, of the elemental, and of Elgarbam and Whistle. She told them of David, the man-vultures, and of being held captive. She also told them of the energy stealing imps. Her eyes began to fill with tears as she explained what Elgarbam had said happened to Whistle. She told Ms. Cabot everything with great detail, leaving out the fact that she knew her mother was still alive though she hadn't really 'heard' her lately.

She felt this was not a time to have the entire magikal world thinking she was crazy, as the human world did. She completed her report to the old woman with how the fairies had fallen from the sky in their attempt to rescue her. When she had finished, Arthur, the chair, stifled a sob and handed her a handkerchief.

Where does a chair keep a handkerchief?

Wiping her eyes, she sniffled, blew her nose, and cleared her throat.

"I just wish I could have done something. I mean, what good is all this power if you can't use it to help someone?"

Sadie sobbed a little more thinking of Whistle and of Elgarbam still chained up and most likely being tortured as they spoke.

Miss Bruja softly laughed.

"Sadie, love, you don't have all your power yet so there was nothing you could do. Besides, little *señorita*, you didn't know who you were fighting or why, what could you, what could you have possibly done?" Miss Bruja uttered, her Spanish accent thick.

"I know enough. Elgarbam and Whistle filled me in...." Sadie's voice choked.

She really did love those little guys and was deeply sad that her first two real live friends were now either dead or close to it. She also felt very responsible for the fairies' deaths as well.

"It's okay to be sad, Sadie, but there is a time and a place for everything. You've no doubt dealt with sadness before, when your mom died, so get a handle on it. Mourn your friends later. Right now, we're in the midst of a great battle that may change things forever," Ms. Cabot said. "What you said about Tara and a bubble containing her and a goblin…we found no such thing when we went to her cottage. Not to mention, I've never heard of such a thing. You must have hallucinated some of this as your mind is trying to adjust to all that you've seen.

"Plus, you've been hit with several different potions. And who knows what those imps gave to you. Allroy, he was gone as well. No signs of him, a struggle or anything. We've got tracers out on the magik used there so we should have some answers soon."

"What 'bout the Ataraxia Heart? We must find it immediately, or I'll not 'ave me tea in peace and quiet 'gain, Moriganna," said Mrs. Teak.

The room became silent. All eyes were on Sadie. She began to feel a little uncomfortable and shifted in her chair, kicking a leg. Arthur grunted. Sadie stiffened.

"Sadie, I want you to think really hard about the question I'm going to ask you. Its importance is extreme. Do you remember where the heart is? Where did your mother hide it?" asked Ms. Cabot.

Genuinely confused, Sadie replied, "I have no idea what you're talking about."

She searched her mind and could not recollect her mother ever giving her such a thing as the Ataraxia Heart. She couldn't even imagine her mother owning such an object. It sounded so…intense. Sadie remembered her mother to be a nervous, cautious person with little personal effects about the house.

"My mother and I never spoke of…she never told me she was a witch." *Heck, I didn't even know I was a witch 'til about a week ago.*

The room was as silent as the air before a tornado. Mrs. Teak picked at the strands of plaster and string on her black cast. Miss Bruja adjusted and wiggled in her very short skirt. Arthur cleared his throat quite loudly, and Ms. Cabot hung her head as her fists clenched on top of the desk.

"Sadie, I don't think you realize how important this is. I know all of this," she spread her arms to encompass the room, "is a quite much to accept, being a newly turned witchling, accepting who you really are, the magikal world, all it's extraordinary creatures, and well, just about everything. But this heart, the Ataraxia Heart, can save us from the Syndicate."

Her voice lowered and became very serious. "It can save us from extinction."

Sadie stared into Ms. Cabot's eyes. She seemed a little frightened which made Sadie a bit uneasy.

How can someone be in charge and look to a mixed-up girl like me for an object that can save their world?

She twisted her hair between her fingers. She almost kicked her feet again, but thought better of it remembering she was sitting in, on, Arthur.

"Ms. Cabot, Miss Bruja, Mrs. Teak, my mother never even let me have a pet. Why would she give me a dried up old heart or whatever it is? She obviously kept me in the dark about her heritage, my heritage, so I'm sure you understand, I have no idea what you're talking about.

"I would love to help you, but I honestly can't. You see all I ever wanted was to be a normal kid with a family and friends. I wanted to hang out, eat pizza, play video games, and make it through high school quite possibly with a date or two. I wanted people to like me, to listen to me, to believe me. That's improbable now so I'd like to get on with my new life and try to do the same with it.

"I'm angry that this one isn't starting out so well, and as usual I'm in the middle of or the cause of lots of trouble, but I can't help you. Please, just send me wherever it is you send new witchlings, to witch school or whatever, and you can get back to your work. I just want to fit in, and so far in this new life I can't even do that. I am not extraordinary; I'm just a below average girl with issues of her own to handle. I don't know why everyone is so interested in me. There is nothing great about me. There never has been, probably never will be. I don't want all this insanity. I can't help you."

The air in the room was thick with silence. No one spoke; no one moved. Sadie watched the dust settling in the rays of light from the window. Finally, after what seemed a decade, Ms. Cabot stood up, put her hands above her head, and snapped her fingers. Hannah appeared, looking like she had been snatched away in the middle of making lunch because she held a grilled cheese sandwich in one hand and a spatula in the other. She looked a bit put off which Sadie thought she herself would be as well had she been zapped out of a good sandwich. Her stomach growled loudly.

"Hannah, you take Sadie, feed her, let her clean herself up, give her new clothes, and then show her around. Explain to her a little about her new life. After that little tirade, it's obvious she's in need of attention." She turned to face Sadie. "I'm sorry not to have put your needs first. You've been through much. As you don't really know us yet, you don't even really know yourself, your new self, so why would you even want to help strangers?

"I know you probably swore secrecy to your mother about the Heart's whereabouts. I mean, really, why else would she take you to live solely in the human world. I'm sure you probably need some time to adjust. Unfortunately, time is not what we have, but we can spare a little to let you think things through. Though you've told us nothing, it's obvious that the Syndicate hasn't found the Heart yet either.

"And witchling or not, I know when a child's stomach growls like that, they need food or they can be as unruly as a teething dwarf child. Rest, regroup, and we'll talk later. Right now, Miss Bruja and Mrs. Teak and I have much work to do."

She dismissed Sadie and Hannah with a wave of her hand. Sadie almost ducked; you never know what's going to happen when a witch waves her hands, especially when she's aggravated.

* * *

Sadie woke from her nap with a slight smile on her face despite her current situation.

It's amazing what a full belly and some sleep will do for a person.

She stretched and looked at her surroundings. Hannah had shown her the house, the offices. The glamour on the house hid well the intricate workings on the inside. From human eyes, it was a simple funeral parlor. In reality, it was chock full of magikal creatures and workings--unlimited rooms, hallways, and floors.

Hannah explained to her that every town had magikal beings, had offices for the Guild, as well as elements of the Syndicate. Magikal beings of all kinds worked and lived right alongside humans since time immemorial. It had amazed her that all these things happened right under the noses of unsuspecting humans, every day, and all the time.

But she also knew humans wouldn't be so accepting in this day and age. Hannah had told her that once, long ago, before the publishing of the Malleus Maleficarum, it had been so. Humans knew, accepted, and lived alongside the magikal beings. Many humans visited witches, or wise women as they were called back then, for healing and help in other matters. Kings had sought their advice, keeping them well cared for in courtly fashion, and let them counsel alongside the governing body.

Hannah also explained that witches earned their power with age. The older you got, the more power you had. The wiser you were, the more magik you could do. Sort of like the practice makes perfect motto. But none of this would happen without your talisman. A talisman was the center of your power. After all, magik didn't just happen; it had to come from somewhere. The witch's talisman was an enchanted object from within the magikal realm that held all the magikal energy one needed to enhance the natural powers. All witches had one; all witches needed one. Hannah also warned Sadie that if her talisman was destroyed, she would be destroyed. Sadie had felt relief at this fact; she still didn't have a talisman.

Hannah told Sadie how once you turn you're assigned an older witch, a guide if you will, to help your change progress smoothly. They also helped you learn to control your powers and taught you simple spells and magik. Sadie wasn't sure how she was going to progress. Everyone kept trying to kill her and Tara, who she assumed to be her guide, was stuck in a bubble with a goblin and no one believed her--just like they didn't believe her about her mother. Even though she had been given this new life, things were still the same. She was still the outcast, still not taken seriously by adults, and still not happy. Plus, now, she had to learn things all over again.

Hannah tried to explain how the magikal realm existed on another plane, like a parallel universe, but that was where Sadie started to become confused. Hannah said it was similar to layers of baklava--one on top of the other and there were many of them. Only beings from the magikal realm ever came to the human world because they used to live together so long ago. Some just couldn't let go while others love the technology.

No technology was allowed in the magikal realm. The other worlds all stayed to themselves. She also told Sadie that once you're a full witch at sixteen, you can travel to these other dimensions, these other worlds. Sadie had begun to think of the endless possibilities for her to fit in; she was daydreaming of a happy life and didn't catch the rest of what Hannah had told her.

A clamor outside her door brought her back from her thoughts. A commotion was going on, and the last thing Sadie wanted was to end up in the middle of another mess. She sighed and thought of her mother. All the things she hadn't told her about herself, about Sadie's birthright, and about this 'other world' that had been here all along. If only she had known, maybe things could have been different. Maybe her mom would still be with her and she could have guided Sadie through her witchling years. Sadie laughed at the thought of her mother doing magik. It seemed so weird to her.

The door flew open, hitting the wall, and Hannah popped her head in from around the corner.

"Sadie, come quick. There's something you must see," she said.

Sadie got out of her bed, smoothed her hair, and went out into the hall. Elves, imps, and fairies were all moving towards the courtyard in back of the house. As Sadie walked the hallway with the other creatures, none seemed to pay her any attention. In fact, they all seemed to be ignoring her, keeping their distance. As she approached the French doors leading outside, she saw a huge crowd amassed in a circle with Ms. Cabot in front. They parted for her to join.

Sadie gasped. Lying on the cobblestones in a small sad little pile was Whistle, or what was left of him. His little body had been branded from head to toe with a strange S-shaped insignia. He was missing his right arm and his clothes looked like they had been run through a wood chipper. Nailed to his head, right in the middle of his forehead with a nail the size of a railroad spike, was a note. It was written in red, and Sadie assumed it to be the poor wee man's blood. It read:

> Let this stand as a warning. This shall be the fate of all abominations in the human world. Our supremacy is rising, our powers are rising, and soon, all shall be restored; and the Syndicate will save humanity from your atrocities. We will rule both here and beyond, protecting humankind from your wicked breed.

When Sadie finally looked up from the body of her dead friend, everyone was staring at her with malice. Dwarves were growling low, fairies were shaking their heads, and two water sprites spit at her before disappearing into the fish pond's waters. Sadie could feel the animosity coming off of all of them in waves and hitting her person. Her stomach began to gurgle and not from hunger. She looked down at the ground, trying to hide her tears.

What now?

"It all be the fault of that girl, that witchling traitor," said a dwarf pointing a knobby finger.

"She's going to be our ruin. Give her to the Syndicate. Be rid of her," shouted an undine from the fountain at the center of the courtyard.

"I say we kill her ourselves, behead her, and make an example out of her, throw her body at the Syndicate's stronghold," hissed a gnome closest to Whistle's body.

Sadie went cold with anxiety and terror.

How could they blame me?

"It's not my fault. I don't know what's going on. I'm as angry as you and I...." But she was cut off by a loud rumble of the now angry mob.

"QUIET!" shouted Ms. Cabot. "We need to assess our situation. *WE* need to find out just how much power the Syndicate has gained. We also need to send spies to find out where all this new power is coming from, obviously they have more magikal objects." She turned slowly, deliberately, to look at Sadie. "And take her and lock her up in the Quiet Chamber...and keep close watch on her. For all we know she *IS* working with them. Maybe after a few days in the Chamber she'll remember where that heart is...or she'll confess to her conspiratorial ways, whichever comes first. Now is not the time for blind trust."

Before Sadie could defend herself, she was grabbed by two Minotaurs that were at least eight feet tall. The smell of animal hit Sadie's nose as their hooves clacked on the cobblestones. They picked her up by the arms so her feet were dangling and spun around in militant fashion.

"Please, I didn't do anything. I don't even know what's going on. Please, listen to me."

Sadie tried to plead with anyone, but the looks of contempt from everyone around quickly quieted her. She wished she was invisible.

"Lock her up now before I do something drastic. Whistle was a good ally and supporter of the cause. To die this way is appalling and someone will pay," Ms. Cabot said. There was wickedness in her voice and rage in her body language. "Send this body back to its family."

Sadie gave up trying to fight. The Minotaurs took her back inside and down a different hallway. She felt sick with sadness at the loss of Whistle. Small bursts of crackling light popped above her head as the anger began to build.

Once again, everyone hates me and won't believe me. Heck, they won't even listen to me.

Realization caused her body to go limp in the Minotaurs' grasp.

They reached the end of the hallway; when it looked like they could go no more, one of the Minotaurs took his hoof and touched a panel on the wall. It began to ripple a little and folded back into itself to reveal a chair inside a chamber no larger than four feet by four feet.

They threw Sadie into the chair and she landed hard, hurting her knee in the process. They didn't care about her well-being; no one did anymore. Not in the human world, and now, not in this magikal one either. Sadie wanted to curl up into herself as they shut the door, and she sat in total darkness.

Everyone hates me--again.

The darkness inside the box was deeper than any in the human world she had ever seen.

I wish I weren't a witch.

Sadie could hear her own heartbeat and feel the deep, empty blackness of her prison closing in on her.

All I ever wanted was friends and family.

She began to hear her heartbeat in her ears, and the silence seemed saturated with it.

Everyone I care about dies.

She pulled her knees up to her chest, but didn't cry. There weren't enough tears for all the sadness she felt at this moment.

$\mathcal{D}uped$

As she opened her eyes, Sadie tried remembering what day it was.

I feel like I've been here in the darkness for weeks.

She felt around in the blackness to see if anything might have changed, but the four walls and the confining dark remained. The rough wooden chair she was sitting in held no comfort, nor did her thoughts.

Everyone in the world hates me--again, and I can't do a thing about it.

The silence thumped in her ears to the rhythm of her heartbeat. It was only broken by a stifled sob. Sadie, once again, felt that empty hole inside of her beginning to envelop her. She wished for the sleeping potion she had been given so many times before so that this punishment would not seem so horrific. Images from her life began to torment her as she sat alone.

I'm only thirteen, and I've got not only one, but also two worlds that hate me now. I wonder if I'll ever get a chance at happiness. If I get out of here, I'm going to find a way to get to those other worlds. I'll stay there in one of the other worlds and leave all of this behind.

A small crackle of unrefined magik popped above her head.

As Sadie sat alone in the tiny, depressing room with her tormented thoughts as company, she began to wonder how long it would take for her to go crazy.

At least I'll have Crazy Mary to hang out with if that happens.

A scraping sound came from the black hole in front of her. Then small trickles of light began to appear. Sadie blinked her eyes. The wall in front of her began to ripple like an ocean of black oil. The pin pricks of light became brighter, and Sadie's eyes began to water. She rubbed them hard. Then, abruptly, it was as if the wall had never been there.

Standing in the bright white of the doorway was a figure.

I guess they've come to do to me what was done to Whistle.

As her eyes attuned, she recognized the figure as Hannah.

"Quick, Sadie, come with me," said Hannah, grabbing Sadie's hand.

The two girls ran down the hall away from the confining box of a room. Sadie's legs felt wobbly, and she had a hard time keeping up. As they ran, she noticed the funeral home was disturbingly empty. There was not one person or magikal being around. Hannah led her to a room at the opposite end of the house. Shutting the door behind her, Hannah turned to face Sadie.

"The Syndicate has attacked again, one of our offices in the next town over. No one knows how they're getting all their information about where we all are, not even Ms. Cabot. They want you, Sadie. The Society just might give you to them, I'm afraid. I let you out so you may have a fighting chance.

"They'll probably hit here next, and everyone is in the great room planning strategy. Ms. Cabot thinks you may be working with them, and she's telling the entire magikal world. She's furious you won't tell her where the Ataraxia Heart is; let me tell you, she's a bad enemy to have, as bad as having the Syndicate after you," said Hannah.

"But I don't even know what the Ataraxia Heart is. I don't have it and I've never seen it," replied Sadie. "I don't know anything about anything." Sadie's heart sunk as she felt the weight of the reality settling on her shoulders.

"C'mon, Sadie, I'm like you, not like them. You can talk to me, trust me. I'm on your side. I let you out, didn't I? Tell me where the Heart is, and I'll help straighten things out with Ms. Cabot. C'mon, we don't have much time," pleaded Hannah.

Sadie looked at the girl in front of her. She didn't know what to say. She wished she did have the stupid Heart. Then she'd give it to Ms. Cabot and all of this mess would be over. They can go fight their battles with the Syndicate, and she could try to form some sort of a normal life. She closed her eyes. Her stomach had that queasy, something-bad-is-about-to-happen feeling.

Of course I feel like this; I've been in a box for I don't know how long, and my whole world has fallen apart--again.

Hannah was staring at Sadie with an insistent look on her face.

"Hannah, I really don't know anything about a Heart," said Sadie.

Hannah let out a long, irritated sigh and looked at the floor. Looking up again at Sadie, she seemed as if she were choosing her words carefully.

"Okay, I understand. Look, everyone thinks Ms. Cabot is losing control. There's talk that the Syndicate will soon take over, and all magikal beings will no longer be allowed to exist on the human plane. We want to live here, the magikal world is so…well, it doesn't matter. I've got your backpack; you'll need it, and…are your ears pierced?"

Sadie just looked at the girl.

What a strange question to ask at a time like this.

"Yes," she replied. There was a noise somewhere in the house.

"Quick, put these on," said Hannah as she handed her a pair of small ruby stud earrings encircled with glittering diamonds. "They'll render you invisible, and you'll need that to get past Gur at the gates."

"Where am I to go?" asked Sadie. She was beginning to feel the tightness in her chest and her stomach was roiling at this point.

"There's a guide waiting to take you to a safe house. You can meet him at the diner on Main Street. You'll know him when you see him. Just stay at the safe house 'til all this is over. Oh, and Tara's there as well. I've told her all about Ms. Cabot locking you up, and she's madder than a wet cat. She'll fill you in on what's been happening. Now hurry, put on the earrings and go," said Hannah desperately.

Sadie quickly put the studs into her ears. She was immediately startled when she reached for her backpack and couldn't see her hand. It was strange and a bit disturbing to be invisible for real. She smirked at the irony of finally getting her wish to be invisible. Sliding her arms into her bags straps, she almost doubled over from the wave of nausea that hit her.

Something dreadful is going on.

"I'm ready," Sadie said. She said the words, but didn't really believe them.

Hannah giggled a little. "Sorry, Sadie, I'm not laughing, really, it's just…weird to hear you, but not see you. Our plan should work; now let's go."

Hannah led Sadie back down the hall, and they turned up another that ended in the front parlor doors. Hannah quickly opened the door and acted as though she was just stepping outside for a breath of fresh air. Sadie whispered a thank you and walked down the front steps to the cobblestone walkway leading to the front gates. She could see Gur sitting at his post and really hoped her new earrings worked. She had seen firsthand what trolls could do when they were mad.

I wonder what Mom would do?

Though it was not as much comfort as the real thing, not hearing her mother's voice for the last few days was weighing heavily on her. It had been both calming and helpful in times of stress.

She slowed her pace as she drew closer to the troll. He began to sniff the air, and she froze.

Oh, no, he knows I'm here.

She walked carefully forward, choosing her steps warily. Gur looked around. Sadie stepped lightly towards the gates. Gur sniffed the air frantically. Sadie touched her ears making sure the earrings were still in place, just in case, not that she was *really* worried. She wasn't quite sure what would happen to her if they found out she was not only out of the box, but trying to escape. And Hannah, what would happen to her if they knew she had helped Sadie.

Holding her breath, she stepped through the wrought iron gates and warily moved forward. Gur began to turn in circles, as if searching frantically for something lost. He grunted while he scratched his head and sniffed the air around him. Sadie took a step off the path and the frost covered ground crunched underfoot. Gur turned and looked directly at her. Cold fear swept through her stationary body.

After a few minutes the troll looked away and started sniffing the air once again. She stepped back onto the cobblestone drive and began walking quickly while constantly looking back over her shoulder at the giant beast.

When she reached the road leading to town, Sadie realized she had been holding her breath.

Shew, I made it, she thought, as she let out a long, measured lungful of air.

Sadie pulled on her backpack straps like a hiker and continued down the road a little easier.

I wonder what is really going on.

She thought about what Hannah had told her, that Ms. Cabot didn't trust her and wondered what to do. Weighing her options, she knew she had to listen to Hannah. At least Tara wasn't mad at her; maybe she could straighten all this out.

As she approached Main Street, lost in thought, once again the sound of her stomach growling brought her back to reality. The town clock struck three and caused her to look up. The parking meters appeared to be parking meters.

What is going on?

They in no way resembled the eloquently dressed sentries she had seen when being taken to the warehouse.

This is so...confusing.

Her stomach growled again, louder. Sadie saw Fulton's Main Street Grocery just up ahead, not twenty yards in front of her. The bins of apples, oranges, and bananas in the front window made her mouth water. She knew she didn't have any money and hatched a plan in her head.

I'll just borrow something to eat 'til I can pay them back.

Waiting for someone to open the door only took a matter of minutes. Mrs. Gallagher, her former Biology teacher, was heading right for the store.

It must be a weekend, otherwise she'd be in school making us cut up frogs or something.

The woman approached and opened the door wide, but when Sadie tried to enter behind her, the cold November wind whipped the door closed, almost hitting her in the process.

Sadie shivered and sneezed. A woman passing by said, "Bless you," to her companion who looked truly befuddled. Sadie muffled a chuckle.

With all the commotion, she hadn't realized just how cold it was outside. She knelt down in the alleyway next to the store. She wanted to check her backpack for that sweater Mrs. Teak had given her. Hopefully, it was inside. When she untied the drawstrings and started to look, what she found surprised her. All her magikal gifts were gone, there were two books, both titled something about human behavior, and the only other thing in her backpack was a bleached white bird skull, a little smaller than her fist. It had perfect emeralds for eyes and a sharp beak the color of faded buttercups.

She was drawn to those eyes the way a salmon is drawn upstream during spawning season. She ran her hand across the beak and felt tingles run down her spine. She petted the thing, lovingly, and smiled down at it. A warm, cozy feeling rushed through her body like it was summer and not fall.

She felt safe in its presence, like everything was going to be okay. She fell further into its eyes and let the world go away.

She heard the clock in the center of town chime four times and shook her head.

I've been staring at this thing for an hour?

She shivered and stood up on legs that were full of pins and needles. She drew the drawstrings of her bag tightly again and put it on.

Why do I feel like this thing is trying to tell me something?

Ignoring the cold and her hunger, she walked down Main Street towards Mable's diner.

I'll save the questions for Tara.

Crossing the street, Sadie caught sight of The Book Nook where she used to meet with her only friend, Mrs. Felis, for tea and company. It seemed so long ago to her.

Boy, things have changed.

The shop was still open; as she approached, she noticed the window she and Zeno had jumped through to escape looked as though nothing had ever happened. She peered inside as she passed. Behind the counter, sitting on a stool, was the old gray cat wearing glasses, which the humans saw as elderly Mrs. Felis.

How come I can see her, but not the parking meter sentries?

She wanted to go inside, to have a cup of tea, and sit with the old woman, but she thought better of it when Ms. Cabot's angry face flashed through her mind. Who knew if Mrs. Felis was against her now as well? Bitter nostalgia was soon replaced by fear as she saw a man-vulture fly overhead.

And I can see them?

It was headed to that same warehouse on the outskirts of town she had been taken to not so long ago.

Moments later she stood in front of the glass door to the diner, examining its occupants for magikal qualities. It only took a second to spot the gnome wearing an I LOVE THE GUILD tee shirt tucked neatly into his little trousers. He was sitting at the counter; as if he knew she were there, he turned and looked directly at her and smiled. The gnome threw some money on the counter, hopped off the stool, and made his way out the door. Once outside he motioned for Sadie to follow him.

They walked down Main Street and turned off onto the block where she used to live with the Argyle family. As they turned, Sadie caught sight of David's father sweeping his front walk and shuddered. He looked up and caught her eyes, his own seemed surprised. Sadie's stomach lurched a little, but then she remembered and felt safe in the knowledge that he couldn't see her because she was still wearing the invisibility earrings. She shivered again; she didn't like that man.

Though she wasn't that attached to the Argyle family, she still didn't like the idea of evil being so close to them. They were good people and had always been nice to her. Sadie looked again. David's father still stood there not sweeping, but staring at Sadie as she turned the corner away from him.

Why does it seem like he can see me?

She looked one last time, still a little unsure, to be positive he really didn't see her. David's father had returned to his sweeping. What she didn't see was his reaching into his pocket and retrieving his cell phone the moment she disappeared around the corner. She also didn't see how he very quickly began dialing a number while running to the same corner she just turned down.

Passing her former foster home, she saw into the big bay window of the kitchen where Mrs. Argyle was moving about, most likely preparing dinner for Mr. Argyle.

What I wouldn't give for a nice, calm, normal sit-down dinner with them right now.

But she knew that would never happen again and set her jaw as she pushed her hair behind her ears.

The curious pair, invisible witchling and stout little glamoured gnome, walked on to the end of the block and turned left. They approached a set of street side basement steps, and the gnome began to descend, looking over his shoulder at Sadie.

How can he see me?

She followed, wanting to get out of the cold more than anything at this point. The stairs led to a brick hallway under the house above. It was dark and all Sadie could make out was the light at the other end.

Ah, the proverbial light at the end of the tunnel.

She laughed to herself and gripped her backpack tighter. She followed, not really seeing the gnome, but hearing his feet scuff on the dirty brick ground. As they drew closer to the light, Sadie relaxed at the thought of spending time with Tara again. Stepping through the entryway, into a large brick anteroom, she heard the gnome shout, "NOW!"

Her arms were grabbed by two huge imps--the biggest imps she had ever seen, with the same sickly grey warty skin as the one at Tara's the last night she had seen her. Sadie was shocked; she thought imps were only small, child-sized creatures. Two more imps snatched the earrings from her ears and danced away from her laughing. The gnome stood staring at her expressionless.

"What's going on?" asked Sadie. Utterly confused and now becoming angry, she wanted answers.

The gnome who had been her guide began to transform into the hideous imp that had been in the bubble with Tara. He laughed and drool hung from his jowls, swinging with each evil snigger. He looked as immoral and menacing as he did that night at Tara's, only there was a new scar across the top of his boil infested skull. Grey ooze and yellow pus crusted and stuck to it in places, and Sadie felt queasy. She scrunched her eyes as a newfound headache settled in; she went a bit limp in the hands of the imps that held her. It moved closer, its breath reeking of rotting fish.

"You will make a trophy addition to my collection, my collection," it said as it stroked the scalps that hung sash-like from its putrid body. Sadie eyes fixed on the red felt that hung from a string around its neck. "Oh, you like this? It was a gift from that stinking gnome friend of yours. He did put up quite the fight, quite the fight."

Sadie now recognized the red felt as Whistle's little hat, and she choked back sickness. The imp had turned it into a purse of some sorts; as he reached into it, crackles of colored light popped and fizzled out over top of Sadie's head.

"HA! You can't do a thing can you, Sadie? Your magik is useless, a waste of time, as is keeping you alive, keeping you alive. Take her to the dungeon, to the dungeon," it said. "But first, we'll not lock her up with this. We'll not make the same stupid mistakes as before, as before."

It grabbed her backpack, ripping the straps right off the bag, leaving them dangling from her shoulders. Though it did hurt a little, Sadie did not cry out. She was resolute in the fact that she would not show these disgusting creatures who either had a hand in or did kill Whistle, any signs of pain or sadness.

The two foul-smelling imps dragged a fighting and kicking Sadie down a dark passage off to the left of the original entry. It was lit by sconces sporadically placed along the brick walls. The more she fought, the tighter their grip. She eventually gave up, letting them drag her limp body the rest of the way.   *No way am I going to walk to my imprisonment and death; they can carry me.*

They stopped in front of an iron barred door and pulled on it to open, the creaking and groaning of the hinges filling the silence. They threw her in and slammed the door hard, the noise echoing in the grimy, damp, dimly lit cell. For the second time that day Sadie sat alone in the dark, wondering how she ended up where she was, as the imps slouched off down the corridor.

Listening to their footsteps and grunting fading away, Sadie slumped down along the only dry spot in the cell and rubbed her temples. She could smell the imp's foul stench on her skin and clothes and tried not to be sick. She threw the remaining backpack strap to the ground in disgust and punched the floor, skinning her knuckles. Sparks of unrefined magik fizzled out around her.

"Sadie, is that you?"

A smile spread across Sadie's face and she scrambled to the barred cell door. Straining to see in the dimly lit dungeon, she did make out several other cells similar to her own. The voice seemed to have come from the cell directly across from hers, and she trembled with excitement and joy.

"Elgarbam? You're still alive! I am so glad to hear your voice," said Sadie.

A brief flash of guilt surged through her body as she realized that in all the commotion she had just been through, she had not thought of her friend that much. She clung to the bars of her cell desperately and spoke again.

"Everything is a mess, Elgarbam. Everyone thinks I'm a traitor, that I have this Heart thing they're all looking for. They all hate me. Except Hannah, she tried to help me, but it all went wrong. An imp, the same imp that came to Tara's tricked me. He saw me when I was invisible, tricked me into thinking he was a gnome, one of us, and he led me here. And I don't understand, it seems like all the magik is working...differently. And Ms. Cabot even thinks I'm working with the Syndicate; she put me in some sort of walled-in room in the dark. Whistle's dead, it's all falling apart, and I haven't even cast my first spell and I'm...."

"Ssshhhh. Not so loud, they're probably listening. Even though they're probably off roasting kittens on a spit by now, I don't trust them not to somehow be listening. And you're babbling again. One thing at a time, witchling," said the gnome.

Elgarbam scuffled his way to the front of his cell, his little knobby fingers trying to wrap around the bars as his pale little face peered out.

"I'm so glad to see you. Things are such a mess," cried Sadie.

"First things first, witchling-friend. How did you not see the imp for what he was? Witchlings, witches, and well, just about all creatures with magik can see through glamours. Why didn't you? This can only mean they've unlocked some sort of stronger magik than we have. Or something about the laws of magik is changing. That is bad, very bad indeed."

Shuddering

Seamus

After what seemed like an eternal night of listening to the screams, moans, and groans of other prisoners, the very same gnarled imp who had been the cause of all Sadie's troubles to date was standing in front of her cell. She didn't know how long he had been there--staring, glaring-- but when she awoke, he was there, nonetheless, in all his smelly, warty, evil, pus-covered glory.

She pretended to still be asleep.

How long have I been out this time?

He continued staring at her as if he were looking for something.

I don't even remember finishing my talk with Elgarbam.

The imp shuffled a little to his right, scratching his boil covered head and licking the pus from his fingers. Sadie stifled her gag reflex and continued peeking out from one barely opened eye.

"I can see the gas we pump in here keeps them knocked out for quite some time, Master, quite some time," it said to a dark figure that had appeared in the gloom. "I didn't find any sign of the Ataraxia Heart in her bag, but I did find her talisman--a very powerful one I might add. She's from the Raven Skull Clan, Master, but you already knew that, already knew that."

So that was my talisman, and now I've lost it. And, they can destroy a part of me if they destroy it. Great, I've screwed up again.

The imp crouched down to her level and tried to peer closer at Sadie. She squished her eyes shut even tighter and tried to control her breathing.

"It could be hidden somewhere on her person; we just threw her in here, ya know," it almost whispered in its raspy breath.

A rat scampered past Sadie's head and crawled through the cell door as she lay on the cold dungeon floor. The tall, dark figure squashed it with his boot-clad foot, and the imp grabbed up the oozing remains and gobbled them down with no regard for couth, or even what he was eating.

"Never mind the girl...for now, Gok. We'll get what we need from her later. I need you to send another message to the Guild. Use that other gnome; the one I think they call Elgarbam. Remove more body parts this time and come see me for the parchment; we'll deposit this message within an organ. Maybe then they'll begin to listen, just give us what we want, and stop trying to fight us. It's become so...annoying," said the tall, dark figure.

"Yes, Master, but if I may, what about the girl, what about the girl? Can I at least perform some torture on her to see if she'll reveal anything? I've got some great new toenail pulling techniques, and I haven't used my pus juicer in a while. I'd love to force her to drink, to drink," suggested the nasty imp.

Sadie could hear excitement in his voice which made her slightly tremble.

The figure in the shadows laughed a little. It sounded familiar to her, like she had heard that voice before.

I'll bet its David's father. He must have seen me and was just making sure the imp took me where he was supposed to.

"Not yet. In due time, my faithful servant. You will be wearing her hide or her scalp or whatever it is you like to wear of your sufferers soon enough," the Master replied before disappearing into the blackness from whence he came. As he departed, he barked more orders. "Mutilate the gnome, and bring the remains to me; I have a message to adhere to its goody-goody insides."

Sadie trembled at the thought and bit her lip. She didn't want to lose yet another friend in such hideous and horrible ways. Panic began to set in and roll through her in waves of nausea.

I have to do something.

She thought about her options, if any, as her anger built. Little sparkles of crackling red magik appeared in the darkness above her head and fizzled out before hitting the ground. The imp stood up from his squat quickly and backed away from her cell.

"Little deceiver. Nasty little liar. Pretending to be asleep, to be asleep. No doubt you've heard our next move, but it matters not, witchling. The Master has spoken, and it shall be done, shall be done. There's nothing you can do about it either. So give up now. Your friend is going to die, going to die. But you, if you beg forgiveness and hand over the Ataraxia Heart, maybe the Master will show leniency before killing you and forgo the torture.

"You shake your head no? Well, then, I'm off to get my implements of agony to take care of your short friend across the way. Think on your options, tricksy traitor, tricksy traitor and run your fingers through that hair to get the knots out. I want it perfect when I wear it on my sash, on my sash."

The imp slithered away down the dark hallway. Sadie waited to hear a door shut before she moved. Though none came, she was sure he was gone as his smell no longer disturbed her senses.

"Elgarbam, wake up. WAKE UP! We've got to do something and fast," Sadie called to her friend.

A slight shuffling was heard, and Elgarbam appeared at the bars of his cell door. He looked bleary eyed and tired, worse for the wear, and a bit put off.

"I have to accept my fate, Sadie. I'm but one little gnome held prisoner by iron bars. What little magik I do know is of no use to me now. Maybe you can save yourself…."

"I don't even have my magik, but I'm willing to try. Sometimes magik isn't always the answer, Elgarbam." Sadie was getting angrier. "We've got to at least put up a fight, if not to live then to try and save…well, just about the entire magikal world!"

Fizzles of light showered down from above her head. Though she was getting used to it, she was still amazed that she created these showers of radiance.

As Elgarbam and Sadie stood facing each other, holding on to their cell-door bars, a dark figure appeared further down the hall. It was black as night, hooded, and carried a sickle in its left hand. It appeared to be about eight feet tall, and the closer it got the less air they seemed able to breathe. They watched as it floated slowly past them and continued on down the dark corridor until they could see it no more.

A chill ran down Sadie's back as she realized what they had just seen. It was Death. Sadie was no expert, but she knew enough to know that if Death were that close to them, things weren't good.

As Sadie ramped up for another inspirational fight speech to deliver to Elgarbam, she was suddenly startled by soft fur rubbing against her bare arm. Shocked, she unconsciously began touching the spot and scanning the dark cell for its source. Looking down, she let out her breath as she recognized the feline in front of her.

"Grimm! Oh, my gosh! How did you get here? We've got to do something; they're going to kill Elgarbam! We've got to…."

"Sssshhhhh! It doesn't matter right now *how* I got here, just that I *am* here. Stand back from the cell doors," he ordered.

Sadie moved to the back wall of her cell and heard Elgarbam do the same. The cat stood in the middle of the dungeon corridor and turned three times widdershins. As he did so, a blinding white light exploded into the area, lighting up and then eventually blinding everything from sight. When Sadie could see again, the cell doors were gone, and Grimm sat perfectly still admiring his work.

"You can come out now," he said to the girl and the gnome.

Cautiously, Sadie and Elgarbam each came forward to meet in the middle with Grimm. Sadie hugged the gnome tightly with tears in her eyes and reached for Grimm to give some good scratches.

"Oooch, girl, you're crushin' me wee bones," garbled Elgarbam.

"Sorry, sorry, I'm just so glad we're free and you're alive. But we've got to get out of here and fast. Grimm, what do we do?"

The cat rubbed his head on Sadie's leg, causing that same old feeling of calm in her, and licked his paw before speaking.

"I've caused a…distraction, if you will, that has cleared the back entrance. All you have to do is follow this hall to the end (he pointed with his paw), and you'll be on Main Street. Elgarbam, don't use a glamour; put a spell on yourself to change into a…a backpack…and let Sadie carry you…."

"I'll not have a weak girl carry me. I'm a proud and strong gnome who…."

"Do you want to be eviscerated?" The gnome shook his head emphatically.

"Then do as I say. And once you're in town, head out on the north road to Tara's. You'll know where to turn off when you reach Shuddering Seamus," Grimm stated. "Now go, there's a war on, and it seems the Guild is losing."

Sadie and Elgarbam began to move quickly, with catlike stealth, down the corridor to the exit. Sadie quickly spun back for one more question. "Grimm, how did your magik work with all those iron bars, and who is Shuddering Seamus?" But the cat was nowhere to be seen.

"Come on, Sadie, that's not important right now. We've got to get to Tara's. Don't worry so much, girl-child," said Elgarbam. He waddled towards the light with Sadie following close at his heels. When they reached the brick alcove that would put them out on the street, the gnome stopped.

He began to mumble some words; as he did so, his little body began to sparkle and pop. From his feet the crackling bursts of light began and traveled up his body towards his little head. When the light show was over, in his place lay a burlap bag somewhat resembling Sadie's old backpack the imps had taken.

"Well, don't just stand there staring, put me on your back," said the Elgarbam bag.

Sadie giggled, picked him up, and swung him onto her back. "You're a bit heavy for a backpack," she said.

"I'm not a backpack, I'm a gnome, remember? And my weight is none of your concern," he quipped back.

"El, can you tell me how our, well, *your* magik didn't work in the dungeons of iron, but Grimm's did?"

Unbeknownst to Sadie, the gnome smiled at her shortening his name to El. No one had ever called him that before--and he liked it.

"Cats are inexplicable creatures. They have nine lives and can do many mysterious things. They've had much time to learn lots of magik. They've been witches' familiars for many moons, far too many for us to count, but at least five thousand human years. And even though they serve the witch or human they live with, they always have their own agenda.

"They always worry about cat politics first and ours second. Who knows for sure, but I'd reckon a guess that it was 'cause he wasn't in the cells, behind the bars like we were. Though to tell you the truth, little witchling, I really have no idea, and I wouldn't admit that to just anyone. Now, c'mon, let's get to Tara's house."

"Makes sense I guess," Sadie said as she began to walk Main Street. "I don't know anything about anything--yet, as far as magik goes. I'm just glad he came to help."

* * *

After following the dirt road north out of Cranberry Grove for about an hour, it soon became an even more choppy and unkempt dirt road. This dirt road wound on for another two hours before they came to a Y. At the head of the Y was a giant, twisty, knotted, and bent old oak.

"Well, now, what do we do?" asked Sadie. "We don't know which direction to take, and I see no signs of someone called Shuddering Seamus."

"That's because you're not really looking," said a voice from nowhere, but obviously near. "Oh, I shudder at the thought of not being recognized."

Sadie looked around and saw no one. Elgarbam began to pop and crackle, changing back to his gnome self, and slid off Sadie's back. He shuffled over to the giant oak and laid his knobby little fingers on its trunk.

"Good to see you again, Seamus. How's this November weather treating you? Not too cold is it?"

"Oh, it makes me shudder; it's so chilly. I can't wait for summer. 'Course, I shudder to think of all those birds making nests in my branches come spring. The babies' squawking all the time, the mess; oh, I shudder to think of it," said the tree.

Sadie walked closer to the oak; as she did, she looked for some sort of face. When she reached Elgarbam, she saw two eyes slowly open that had previously been camouflaged within the folds of the bark. Then she recognized a knot in the tree to be a nose and just under that a mouth opened to speak.

"I had some of those tree rats with the bushy tails, the ones you call squirrels, taking the rest of my acorns. Now I'll never have one grow near enough to talk to. Oh, I shudder at the thought of being alone for all of my time," said the giant old oak.

And, indeed, the tree seemed to shudder in the chilly breeze.

"Which way to Tara's?" asked Elgarbam.

"Oh, you don't have to go yet. I shudder at the thought of your leaving so soon. Can't you stay for a couple of years, just enough time to get to know each other again," begged the tree.

For a tree, a couple of years is the equivalent to a blink of an eye to a human, so his request wasn't that out of line though Sadie was a bit taken aback by it.

"We must get to Tara immediately. It's of the utmost Guild importance. This witchling and I are on important business," Elgarbam replied.

His little chest puffed out, and he held his head high, looking very much like a tiny general in a tiny position of command.

"I haven't met this one before though I did see her pass in the night with that centaur Zeno. I shudder to think I haven't been properly introduced. Maybe she could stay for awhile?" the tree asked.

"Tell you what, my woody friend, I'll bring back a birch and plant it for company if you give us the right way to take," Elgarbam replied.

"Oh, I shudder at spending time with a birch; they shed and peel and I don't like messes. Bring me a cherry tree; they're so pretty in the spring time. I shudder to think of the beauty," the oak said with a tremble.

"It's as good as done," responded Elgarbam. He pounded his little fist against his chest in a firm, oath-assuring thump.

"Then take the road leading east, I think. Wait, no, west. No, it's east. Sorry, I shudder at how many times we've had to change directions lately, what with all the fighting and treachery about. And I'll see you again soon, with my cherry tree friend in tow. Oh, how I shudder to think of the conversations we'll have. See you soon, gnome; goodbye, witchling with no name," the tree said.

"My name is Sadie, and we'll see you again soon Shuddering Seamus."

The tree became stock still, frozen, and far from his recent stature. Not a branch moved. His face disappeared back into the camouflage of the bark. Elgarbam smacked his hand on his head.

"What's wrong?" asked Sadie. Elgarbam just shook his head and motioned for them to walk the east road.

"We don't call him that to his face. That would be rude and hurt his feelings. Now he's not going to help travelers like us for quite some time," said Elgarbam. "Maybe that's why you had so much trouble in your world. They didn't think you were crazy; they thought you were rude."

Sadie blushed and yelled back over her shoulder, "I'm sorry, Seamus." But the tree did not respond.

"Great, now the next time we see him, we'll have to stay and talk to him for more time than I'd like to, and we'll have to bring a pretty special cherry tree," Elgarbam complained. "We can't worry about that now though; we've got at least a good country mile to get to Tara's."

"You seem to know the way," Sadie responded somewhat curtly. She had never, ever been called rude before, and her mistake was just that, a mistake. "Why did we have to ask Shuddering Seamus in the first place?"

"Cause Tara's is a magikal house. It changes direction, changes its placement all the time for safety reasons. I'm sure it's moved quite a bit since that little disaster the last time you were there. You heard Seamus; the path has been changing even more because of the war. Now c'mon; let's make time."

* * *

The pair walked on in silence except for Elgarbam's whistling. Whistling reminded her of Whistle, and Sadie wondered how many more good people and creatures would die before all of this was over and done. She pondered what to do next, to take her mind off Whistle. Her mood was still somewhat tainted by the dungeon stay, but she wasn't that worried. Tara would, should, have all answers.

She rubbed her temples to ward off the oncoming headache while her stomach began gurgling its own discontent as well. Elgarbam stopped along the way to gather the last vestiges of raspberries in the thicket alongside the road. Sadie gobbled down what she could find, at least the ones that had not been frost bitten.

When they reached a curve in the road that hugged the ridge of a valley, Sadie could see the tiny little cottage she remembered to be Tara's. It looked as though no imps had ever invaded. Alroy was at his usual spot in the pumpkin patch, chowing down on the gourd-like squashes and throwing the stems and attached vines over his shoulder into a heap.

Smoke came from the little chimney and all looked well. Sadie sighed and her mood lightened. They plugged on, leaving the road, and walking down into the valley towards what they hoped was a good meal, some good news about the war between the Guild and the Syndicate, and some good answers about what to do next.

Upon reaching the far edge of the pumpkin patch, Alroy looked up and sniffed the air. His eyes finally found Elgarbam and Sadie, and a huge smile spread across his face. The troll lumbered to his feet and ran to the pair with the ground trembling in the process. He reached them and held out his hand. "Any good food, tired of pumpkins and gourds?" he asked.

Sadie giggled, remembering the amount of food Alroy could eat. Elgarbam replied, "Not this time, Alroy; we've come unprepared for you, my large gray friend. I apologize for any inconvenience. Is Tara at home?"

The troll looked sad for a moment and nodded his head 'yes' before grabbing a huge pumpkin and shoving the whole thing into his mouth. Juice and seeds rained down on Sadie and Elgarbam, since trolls don't eat with their mouths shut. They moved quickly from under the gorging Alroy and towards the promising safety and comfort of Tara's home.

Approaching the door Sadie heard beautiful singing coming from inside. It reminded her of her mother.

SAAAADDDDIIIIEEEEEEEEEEEEE!

She stopped, still as stone. "Did you hear that? It was my mother," she asked the gnome.

"Still holding on to thinking your mother be alive, eh? They told me you were a bit crazy, but c'mon now, child, she's been dead and gone for over three years. You've got to accept it and move on," Elgarbam replied.

"She IS still alive and I KNOW it!" shouted Sadie.

The door to the cottage opened suddenly and the smell of cinnamon wafted out as Tara appeared before them.

"Tara!" shouted Sadie as she ran to hug the woman. "How did you get out of the bubble? And what exactly happened? How did the imps get in? I'm so glad you're alive; what's going on? Ms. Cabot thinks I'm a traitor. And what's the Ataraxia Heart? I don't have it I swear! Whistle's dead! How are we going to fix this mess? And I …."

"Ssshhh now child, so many questions to come rambling from one little lass." She hugged Sadie tightly. "Oh, I be glad to see you too after the mess that be goin' on. Come inside and we'll begin to try and make things right," Tara said, releasing Sadie from her tight grasp.

The three passed through the small door and into the large cottage as Tara ushered them towards the warming fire. Sadie hadn't realized just how cold it was outside and was glad to be indoors. As Tara brought them steaming mugs of cider with cinnamon sticks, she began to speak.

"First, let me offer many apologies at the loss of Whistle; he was a good gnome and a good friend. I'll miss him terribly," she said, placing a hand on Elgarbam's shoulder.

The little gnome bowed his head, but said nothing in return.

"Now, to answer a few questions. Ms. Cabot and some others from the Guild came to do damage control, but they didn't seem to see me in the bubble, nor did they see Alroy tied up and all staked out in the field. 'Course I couldn't get that nasty imp Gok to tell me anything about why, and he soon disappeared. And his repetitive speech can be so annoying. Grimm let me out of the bubble.

"I didn't think that old cat had it in him, but he freed me nonetheless. I hear the imp caught up with you in town, Sadie, and you were still being held by him, them, whoever the pesky devils be. I also hear you've lost your talisman in the process. 'Tis a shame. You'll need it to have full control of your magik, Sadie, love, especially since you're but a mere witchling.

"You do know that even though everyone has magik in them, it must draw from somewhere, and your talisman helps to gather the energy for you to harness. Magikal objects and talismans all come from the Source, not that we be knowin' who, where, or what that is, but that's not important right now.

"That's a whole other story. What is important is that we figure out where to go from here."

Though Sadie had already heard a little bit about talismans and the source from Hannah, Sadie didn't dare interrupt Tara as she spoke. She didn't want to be called rude yet again, and she had decided it would be best if she learned all that she could. Her plan was to *try* and keep her mouth shut and take everything in. With her new resolution in mind, Sadie watched Tara get up to cross the room. Her always-beautiful velvet skirts rustled as she went to get a book from one of her shelves. On her way back, she began to speak again.

"There's something amiss in our magikal world. There's something amiss in this human world as well. Something that shouldn't be. I've been trying to figure it out, been looking through the histories here, but I haven't reached any conclusions yet. I do know there has to be a traitor in the Guild. What I did find out for sure was that someone or something has...."

Tara's words were cut off by a boom of thunder that shook the house and rattled the windows like an earthquake. A roar like a freight train bellowed in their ears while a wind began to blow inside the house, disturbing all of Tara's neatness and order.

"SAAAAADDDDDIIIIEEEEEE!!!!!"

It was her mother's voice again. This time louder, clearer and Sadie was sure that Tara and Elgarbam had heard it, too. When she looked to them for some sort of acknowledgment, their faces began to blur; she felt as though she were being pulled apart at the seams--again. In an instant, all went black then changed again in a burst of green light. Sadie was sitting in an empty, grey stone-walled room with no windows or door.

Adrienne MacDougal, Transportation Spells, and the North Wind

Sadie checked herself in case some parts went missing in this transportation. She assumed this must be another one of Hannah's doomed transportation spells and was just glad she made it through in one piece.

When she saw that all was right, she stood up to survey her surroundings and prepared to be hassled by Ms. Cabot, the rest of the three, and whoever else was against her as well. What she found was not what she expected. She was in a room very unlike any that were at the Guild headquarters. Walking around, she saw no signs of a door, much less a window, and she guessed the room to be about ten feet by ten feet.

The faint smell of something burning lingered in the air, and the temperature began to drop. Wrapping her arms around herself, Sadie put her back to the wall and waited. She didn't know what she waited for, but she didn't have to do it very long.

A mist began forming in the far corner. It was inky and contorted and swirled with jerky motions until it converged in the shape of a man. He stood over six feet tall and was wearing a black suit with an unusual bunch of purple flowers in the lapel. His arms were crossed behind his back, and his face wore a familiar smile.

Why do I feel like I know him?

He snickered a little and began to speak in a deep and condescending tone.

"I am THE MASTER, soon to be the Master of All, this world, the magikal realm, and all the realms if I feel the need. A measly little girl such as the likes of you will never best me. You will give me the Ataraxia Heart, or I will do to you what I did to your mother."

(The mention of her mother made Sadie's stomach lurch.)

"I see that manipulating from behind the scenes is not working-- sending an imp to do a man's job and so on. So here we are, face to face; let's see if we can come to some sort of arrangement. It's either that or I destroy you now!" he bellowed, and to Sadie it was an obvious show of force.

A flurry of bursting sickly green light sizzles and pops rained over his head though he hadn't moved a muscle. The burning smoke scent filled the room again, infecting Sadie's already sickened stomach.

Sadie hesitated not knowing what to do or say, and she focused on the man's face. He seemed to have a grey sheen to his skin. She knew she didn't know him, yet still she couldn't shake the feeling of familiarity.

"I don't have the Ataraxia Heart, and I don't even know what it is," said Sadie.

She was disheartened and getting a little aggravated that everyone expected her to know where this Heart was. She didn't even know what it was.

"Don't play stupid with me. You're a MacDougall, eternal keepers of the Heart. After much torture, your mother still held tight to her silence so I KNOW you must have it. Now tell me where it is, and I'll make your death quick and painless," the man replied matter-of-factly.

Sadie thought for a moment--either way she was going to die, so why not lie about it?

"I can give you the Heart if you let me go to get it," she said.

"Do you think I'm stupid? Do you think you can get the better of me? You tell me where it is, girl…no, wait."

The man called the Master smiled and ran his fingers through his hair. He sniffed his lapel and continued.

"I wouldn't usually do this so abruptly, but I'm running out of options. Your stubbornness in not telling me where the Heart is…is admirable. Maybe you can work for me once this is all said and done. No, I could never trust you completely."

(Sadie hated that it was like he was having a conversation with himself and not her.)

"I think it's time to just pull out 'the big guns' as they say. I think, no, I know, I have something that will make you talk," he replied.

The man raised his arms and snapped his fingers. In a moment's time and with a burst of green light, Sadie was transported yet again. This time she landed in a dark, dank dungeon. The smell of burning permeated the air and distant moans of agony broke the silence.

"Sadie," said a breathy, timid voice that she was used to hearing only in her head.

As Sadie turned, she nearly fainted with shock. With her heart racing and an unknown feeling coursing through her body, she ran to the far side of the dungeon.

This must be a trick.

"Sadie, I love you so much; it's so good to see you again. I never thought I would," said the voice. "Please, come to me." And then this voice said something to confirm Sadie's deepest desires. "Come give me a ladybug hug, my little beguiled child."

Sadie felt like weeping. When she was a tiny thing, her mother used to say that Sadie gave ladybug hugs, wrapping her in fluttery arms like wings. She also used to call her Ladybug. She used to call her "my little beguiled child" because life was so full of wonder and excitement back then that Sadie had trouble containing herself most of the time. This was all long before her mother had died, well, before everyone but Sadie thought she had died.

It had been three years since her mother's supposed death. Sadie KNEW she was still alive. She still didn't know how, but she knew. Everyone thought she was crazy and now, with her mother standing before her, she felt a validation to her claims that had caused her so much grief.

Those who jeered her, those who teased and tormented her for not accepting her mother's death, would soon be called out. Her heart was filled to the brink of bursting from sheer joy and happiness. But she was also afraid. Afraid this was yet another trick--that somehow the Master had found out her mother's pet name for her.

Sadie remembered that awful dream and wanted to believe so much that this was, in fact, her mother. Trusting her instincts, she decided it had to be. No strange feelings in her stomach or head argued the fact.

She ran to her mother, wrapping her arms so tightly around her it made her gasp for breath. Sadie heaved and shook with years of built up sorrow. Sadie's mother laid her head on Sadie's, her arms shackled in iron chains. The two sobbed together for several minutes before her mother finally broke the silence.

"Shhhh. It's okay now, Sadie. We're together. We'll find a way to get out of this, I hope; when we do, we'll set things right," her mother said through her own sobs.

Sadie hesitated for a moment and tensed, remembering once again the horrid witch-thing in her dream that had tricked her into thinking it was her mother. She thought for a brief moment this was history repeating itself. She relaxed when she also remembered her mother's ladybug reference and realized that was something only she and her mother shared.

I will trust my inner feelings; I will trust my heart, and my heart says this IS my mother.

"Mom, why didn't you tell me I was a witch, how did all of this happen, why is all of this happening, and what is the Ataraxia Heart?" begged Sadie through her subsiding tears.

Inhaling a deep, long breath, Sadie's mother looked at her daughter and began.

"I used to work closely with the Guild, fighting the Syndicate. Certain 'qualities' came easier to me than others because I held the Ataraxia Heart. Our family always has. But the troubles only seemed to be getting worse. When you were born, your father and I tried to hide you away from that world. We traveled through many realms trying to find a safe place to rear you.

"We eventually settled on the human world since magik is no longer commonly practiced there--no longer under the eyes of humans. We had planned on telling you everything when you came into your powers at age thirteen. I loved you so much I didn't want any harm to come to you. I see now that doing so only brought more harm and trouble your way and that I was wrong.

"Your father died when you were almost one, when the Syndicate held one of their many attacks. That's when I knew I had to pass the Heart to you because they would be coming for me next. As long as they didn't know what the Heart really was, I thought you'd be safe at home with me, with powerful magik all around you and the house.... Everything went well until the Syndicate found me, and that left you all alone, not knowing anything...."

Her words were broken off by more tears of grief.

Sadie's arms had begun to ache, and she reluctantly released her hold on her mother. Looking into her eyes, Sadie no longer felt any anger at her for not telling her the truth. She was even letting go of all the unkind and hurtful things that had happened to her for insisting her mother was still alive. At least for the moment.

"I knew you were still alive. I felt you…I even heard you," whispered Sadie.

"I tried to reach you telepathically, but guessed you weren't getting it because you didn't know you could do these things or because these iron chains had more effect than I thought. You were never taught like I should have taught you. Plus, what could you have done? You don't even have your talisman yet."

"I had it; Hannah gave it to me, but the imp they call Gok took it when he captured me."

"I thought I heard my name," said Hannah, appearing from nowhere in waves of rippling magik.

"HANNAH! Boy, am I glad to see you!" shouted Sadie as she rushed to give out more hugs. As she wrapped her arms around her, Sadie felt the girl stiffen, and she smelled something burning on her clothes. She backed away, looking up into the girl's eyes for clarity.

"It was so much fun manipulating you, Sadie, and almost too easy. Coming to you in your dreams, well, that was just fun, especially seeing your face when I changed from your mother to that wretched-looking witchy-thing. Not my best look, but it served its purpose.

"And then you didn't eat the To Die for Cake. I was a little worried, but that's a good thing 'cause the Master wanted you alive. Boy, I woulda been in trouble. Again, things worked in my favor. You believed I really liked you; you believed I was on your side. It's so easy to manipulate someone who is in desperate need of friends. So then, you took your talisman directly to the Master."

(She pulled the raven skull from a pocket in her dress.)

"You made it easy to plant the seed of your alleged deception by not knowing about the Ataraxia Heart. I guess we can thank your mother for that. And you know absolutely nothing of magik. All I needed was a little help which I got from my brother."

David magikally appeared beside her, and Gok appeared on the other side.

Sadie backed away when the stench coming off the imp reached her nostrils. David stood with a smug smile on his face, and the imp drooled with delight while petting the scalps on his sash. Sadie looked back at her mother, helpless in iron chains, and began to shiver as emotions of all kinds ran through her body. She trembled as the feelings swelled inside her.

The raven skull in Hannah's hands began to shake, causing the emerald to glow slowly. It began to tremble more violently, and Hannah struggled to hold onto it. Suddenly, it flung itself into Sadie's hands.

"Hannah, the skull, now what are we going to do?" David asked this question with a hint of sarcasm thrown in.

"It's of no concern to us; she doesn't even know how to use her powers yet. And stop acting superior to me; the Master says we're equal. What we need to focus on is getting that Heart," said Hannah.

The imp had slowly begun to inch his way towards Sadie's mom while David and Hannah went for Sadie. No longer able to control her anger and pent up frustration, magik began snapping and crackling above Sadie's head.

"Look, the stupid girl can't even form complete magikal energy," said David.

"She's as dumb as they said and untalented to match, and I think everyone was right about one thing. She's certainly not like any other MacDougall."

Sparkles of light began to shower down on Sadie as the magikal energy became stronger and seemingly more focused. Crackles and fizzles of sparks changed into a rainbow of colors above her head.

"Sadie, come touch me," said her mother.

Sadie backed slowly towards her mother, leaning into her body when she reached her. As soon as they touched a burst of light came from the raven skull eyes, Sadie's chest felt oddly full and yet emptying at the same time.

The chains holding her mother disintegrated and the ashes fluttered to the ground. As soon as her hands were free, Adrienne MacDougall threw up her arms and a protective force field surrounded the pair. Gok, David, and Hannah ran towards them, but were knocked back by the invisible shield.

"Now what, Hannah? The Master isn't going to like this, and I must say that it doesn't look good," said David. "And I'm not being sarcastic; I'm being very serious."

"Don't count us out yet," said Hannah as she shot magik of her own out of her finger tips and at the shield.

It bounced off, showering Gok with sparks. The imp cowered, and for the first time, Sadie saw fear in his eyes.

"I'm going for the Master," shouted the imp. "And I'm gonna tell him just how bad you've screwed up now, screwed up now."

He disappeared in a cloud of thick oily smoke.

Hannah and David stood staring at Sadie and her mother. The four seemed at a standstill. Sadie began to wonder how they would ever get out of this one. If it were a chess game, they would be at a stalemate.

"Sadie, I want you to hold tightly to the raven skull in your left hand and put your right hand over your heart, holding three fingers up in the sign of a W. I'll be here, right behind you, with my left arm around you and my right doing the same as yours. When we do this, I want you to visualize a safe place, somewhere we can go that's far from here, somewhere…." But her words drifted from Sadie's ears because she had already begun doing what her mother said.

The world around her began to spin, not in an unpleasant way, but in a comforting and cozy kind of way that swept through her whole being. The spinning became a blinding rainbow of colors and sparkles, and flashes of crackling magik snapped and popped all around as the scene before them slowly changed. The last thing Sadie saw clearly was David punching his sister in the arm and the looks of surprise on their faces.

When the comforting spinning feeling subsided, along with the bursts of magikal sparkles, the scene that started to materialize was fire. The fire became a fireplace; the fireplace was in Tara's cottage. Sitting before it were Tara and Elgarbam with similar surprised expressions that the mother and daughter pair had seen on Hannah's and David's faces.

"Well, I know who the spy is," said Sadie. For the first time in a long time, she didn't babble on.

Tara jumped from her chair, put her hand over her mouth as if to stifle a scream, and ran to Adrienne. She stopped just short of her, looked at Sadie standing in front of her, and then grabbed them both in a hug to rival that of a grizzly.

"Well, if that ain't the darndest thing," said Elgarbam. The little gnome waddled over and, trying to hide the tears in his own eyes, joined the group hug.

"'Tis a good thing to know your daughter's not the crazy loon we once thought. You really are still alive, Adrienne. I mean, it's really you, right? I'm not trusting me eyes like I used to with all this 'new magik, new glamour stuff' going around," he said as Adrienne scooped him up.

"Ooch! Put me down, woman. I'm a proud gnome with dignity, and I'll not be tossed around like some child's toy," said the annoyed gnome.

Adrienne laughed and set him down. All the pain and suffering Sadie had been holding in for three years was released at hearing her mother's laughter once again. She cried silently to herself, but these were tears of joy.

"It's good to know I was missed. It's even better knowing my daughter never gave up hope on my still being alive, unlike some of you friends of mine."

(Adrienne winked at Tara and Elgarbam.)

"What I want to know is why no one listened to her. I mean, we're witches; it's not entirely inconceivable to imagine I had lived through the Syndicate's attack on me," said Adrienne as she hugged Sadie again.

"Adrienne, we sent out magikal tracers, we sent out spies, we did everything, but found no sign or you or source of your magik. What were we to think? Plus, Sadie didn't even know she was a witch. What were we supposed to think? We certainly didn't believe you'd go off and get yourself killed without telling her of her heritage. When we used to watch her, we just thought she was crazy, like the human world assumed, for thinking you still alive," Tara explained before turning to Sadie.

"You said you knew who the traitor was? Who is it?"

"It's Hannah," said Sadie.

"Hannah? But she's just a witchling in training--handpicked by the Three themselves. Are you sure? How do ya know, lass?" Tara seemed rather agitated at this news, and all the butterflies and birds that usually sat on her or encircled her immediately fluttered or flew away.

"Oh, she's right, Tara, no doubt about it. We've got to get word to the Guild, more specifically, the Three. Tell you what, take care of Sadie and get her to explain things to you while I'll pop over there and explain things to Ms. Cabot. We'll meet at North Wind's Cave when we're done here and there. I can't wait to see the look on ol' crotchety Cabot's face when I appear, apparently back from the dead," said Sadie's mother, but as she threw her arms up to magik herself away, Sadie ran to her and begged her not to leave.

"Sadie, it's okay Ladybug, nothing will separate us again if I can help it. Tara will keep you safe."

(Elgarbam cleared his throat.)

"Excuse me, Tara *and* Elgarbam will keep you safe 'til we meet up again. I won't be long, promise. I must go if we're to stop the Syndicate from destroying all we know."

Sadie reluctantly pulled away from her mother, knowing she was right and watched as she disappeared into thin air. Letting her go again so soon almost hurt as badly as losing her the first time. When she cleared the lump from her throat, she turned to face Tara and Elgarbam.

"I don't suppose a gnome could get something to eat before he's called to action?" asked Elgarbam. He held onto his stomach as though he were suffering great pain. "A great warrior such as I am has to stay full of nutrients and protein to be able to battle as I do."

Tara laughed and Sadie smiled as the gnome truly looked like he might faint from lack of sustenance.

"Elgarbam, we have to leave right now, lad. The Syndicate could whisk Sadie away again at any moment if they know where she is and my guess is--they do. You can eat at North Wind's. Now c'mon, folks."

She reached for Sadie's hand.

"We've got to…Sadie, what is that in your hand?"

With all the commotion, Sadie had forgotten about her talisman. With a sweaty fist, she slowly opened her balled fingers revealing the raven skull with the emerald eyes. The smooth bleach white surface sparkled in the glow from the fire, and the sharp beak had left a small bloody dot on her palm.

"If that don't beat all, you got it back. If I didn't know better, Sadie lass, I'd say your luck really turned around for you today. Not only do you get your mother back, but your talisman as well even though everyone's magik seems to be changing. Now, hold tight to it and the Ataraxia Heart, and all should be turnin' in our favor," said Tara.

"But I don't have the Heart, and I forgot to ask Mom where it is," said Sadie.

"No worries, lass, you two can work that out when we all meet up again. Now, are we ready to go?"

Tara swept her arms into the air and began to spin widdershins. Sadie felt tingly all over and got goose bumps on her arms, but she decided she would much rather feel this way when transporting than she had all the other times when bad magik had moved her places.

The room began to shift and spin, slowly melding from Tara's little cottage in the woods to a glistening snow field with giant mountains of ice jutting up here and there throughout the landscape. The wind blew fiercely down on the threesome, and Elgarbam had to hold on to Tara's skirts to keep from being whisked away.

"Hold on to me; the entrance is just over there beyond that lone pine tree," shouted Tara above the winds.

Sadie scanned the landscape and, sure enough, in this vast icy desert was a lone tree almost completely bare of any needles and bending with the airstream. They all held hands and trudged along on top of crusty, crunching ice and snow 'til they reached it. Sadie couldn't see anything resembling an entrance and hoped Tara wasn't mistaken. It was extremely cold, and she was beginning to feel as hungry as Elgarbam claimed to be.

A low, slow rumbling turned into a mountainous roar and a voice strong, loud, and mean enough to scare several evil trolls shouted, "Who goes there?"

Sadie felt Elgarbam tremble, and she gripped Tara's hand tighter herself.

"It is Tara of the Isle, North Wind. I've come for your help, and I have visitors with me. Let us in," replied Tara.

A small rip started in the ice behind the tree. It cracked, splintered, and grew to become an opening large enough for Gur or Alroy to fit through. Tara led them inside where they stood before a vast door carved from ice. It had intricate winter scenes impressed upon it; the door handles themselves were giant reindeer antlers. Sadie began to wonder if she really wanted to meet whoever lived here. If his voice were any hint at his presence, he must be fierce.

Slowly, with much creaking and groaning, the doors opened to reveal a huge inner sanctum. The floors were blue ice covered in polar bear skin rugs, and the walls seemed to be in perpetual motion with snowflakes raining down from nowhere to nowhere. The furniture was carved from thick dark wood, and stars seemed to twinkle in the ceiling like an endless sky. Rows of bookcases reaching into the sky-ceiling lined the left side of the room and, on the right, sitting areas arranged in orderly fashion.

From behind a particularly fat-large bookshelf, too wide for most regular sized people books, popped a tiny little man just a head smaller than Elgarbam. In a voice that sounded like someone had sucked all the helium out of a balloon, he said, "Welcome to my cave. Sorry about all the theatrics. You never know who's poking about out there; come in, come in, make yourselves at home."

Elgarbam snorted to himself. "All these legends of the fierce North Wind, all this fright about him and this is what he is--a little man with a little voice. He's no bigger than me one good leg."

Tara quieted him.

"Elgarbam, do not be rude to our host. North Wind must put on a show or else summer would never concede to winter, and the balance of nature would be upset.

"North, I apologize; you know how gnomes can be when they're hungry, especially Elgarbam here. Not to mention, he's got pride to boot. This is Sadie of the MacDougall clan and a new witchling at that. Things seem to be quite a mess for us right now, and I'm to meet Adrienne MacDougall, Sadie's mother, here at your cave. So might we have a bit to eat while we wait? I'll fill you in on what I know about our situation in the meantime."

A chair that had previously been facing backwards to them spun around, and a light blue skinned man wearing white clothing dropped the book he had apparently been reading, or at least pretending to.

"Adrienne MacDougall!" he exclaimed, "I haven't seen her in what must be ten years. She used to make me the prettiest flower garlands, and I would turn them all to ice, much to her delight." The blue skinned man crossed his arms over his chest as though he had said something very profound.

"Well, if it isn't Jack Frost. I thought you'd be busy down on earth what with winter comin' an' all. Your latest work ruined Gur's eastern pumpkin patch; let me tell you, it's not easy to feed that goliath. No, you know what? I know you were down there; the frost had been staying on the ground a little later in the day than is usual. You do relish gossip and scandal. As if I don't already know what brings you here," asked Tara.

"Just stopped in for a chat and some gossi…I mean, I heard through some elementals that you were having trouble again with the Syndicate, and since everything is carried on the wind, I thought I'd come to the source for my information," Jack replied. He stood with his arms crossed over his chest as if he were a man of great importance.

"Everyone have a seat, and I'll get you all something good to eat, something that'll warm your southerly bones. You can explain everything to me," Jack Frost cleared his throat, "to us I mean, while we feast and wait for Adrienne to show up," said the wee little man with the big reputation as the North Wind.

"Such a windbag, he is! I'll bet he used that deep, scary mountain troll voice to ward you off, didn't he? If this book about sea dragons weren't so interesting, I'd have listened more closely to his show. Come, sit with me and tell me everything," said Jack Frost.

So Many Magikal Beings, So Little Time

Jack Frost, North Wind, Sadie, Tara and Elgarbam sat around the large feasting table discussing all that had been going on. They ate, talked, and shared a few much needed laughs together while waiting for Adrienne to meet up with them. After several hours of this reveling, Sadie began to get a bit antsy, worrying about her mother and not enjoying herself anymore.

"Do you think she's okay? I mean, she should be here by now right? Maybe something's happened," Sadie said to all at the table.

"I'm sure she's fine, Sadie. You're mother is a very powerful witch, and I'm sure she'll not make the same mistakes as before. Being held by the Syndicate is enough to make anyone change their protection habits and spells. She's probably gathering up reinforcements, and I'm sure she's tormenting Ms. Cabot a bit. Who can resist teasing that old bat? She's got more wrinkles than a hundred-year-old forest brownie and her personality is lacking in…" started Jack Frost, but his musings were cut off by Tara.

"You stop it right now, Frost. 'Tis not nice to tease little girls no matter what or who it's about. Sadie can attest to that from personal experience," she gave Sadie a wink and a smile. "What we need to do is try and figure out what exactly we *can* do to help our situation. We need to figure out why our magik is not working properly and how it's come about. Oh, if only we knew what was going on! Our very lives depend on it. Plus, Sadie and Adrienne were able to use the magikal…problems…to their advantage and get away from the Syndicate, so maybe we can, too."

The five sat with newfound energy, bouncing ideas off of each other, proposing theories as to how the Syndicate was gaining power, guessing at why all of their magik wasn't working quite normally, and who was to blame. While they did, Sadie grew increasingly impatient. When she couldn't stand it anymore, she stood up and began to pace the vast room. All eyes were on her as she wandered the bookshelves, wringing her hands and twisting her hair between her fingers. Finally, Elgarbam could take it no more.

"If ye don't sit down, girl, I'm going to get indigestion. I hate to have me meal ruined by indigestion," he said. He had more of a twinkle in his eye than harshness in his voice.

"I'm sorry; I'm just so worried. I can't lose my mother again, not now. I just want…."

A loud rap at the door caused all in the room to jump slightly in their chairs. Sadie shot an anxious glance at Tara and ran to the wooden behemoths that stood between her and her mother. She just *knew* she was on the other side, not that she could open those heavy things by herself.

The North Wind hopped down off of his chair and waddled as fast as his two little legs could carry him to a table beside it. He stared into a snowball perched upon a stand of ice, glowing blues and greens of extraordinary brilliance. With his miniature little hands he rubbed it delicately, it began to glow stronger and even more brilliantly until it's radiance eventually encompassed the whole room.

"Answer the door! Please," she added, remembering herself, "I just know it's my mom."

And she really did just know.

"In due time, dear. I know she's out there, but there's someone…several someones…with her that I just can't, well, *see*, in my magik snowball," he replied. "This could be a trick. She could have been captured and the people or things with her could be Syndicate forces. I think this calls for some more of my 'enhanced voice' and a bit of magik."

He lowered his mouth to the glowing blue orb and began to speak.

"Who goes there?" Sadie giggled at the sight and sound of such a tiny man with a giant's voice. He shot her an annoyed look and continued. "…name thyself, all of you beings on the other side of my door, or be doomed to spend eternity encased in an ice crypt at the bottom of the coldest sea in the known world and beyond!"

"It's me, Adrienne MacDougall, and I've brought some friends. If you don't let me in, North, I'll make it so you spend your summers with the Heat Wave family and their numerous offspring who have pyromania tendencies. This is no time to play games, and I KNOW you're expecting us," replied Adrienne.

She sounded forceful, yet Sadie could detect a hint of play in her voice.

The North Wind conceded that it was no trick and waddled towards the doors. He waved a little wand he kept secreted in his trouser pocket, and the usual sparkles of light began to appear, except his dissipated in snowflakes. The vast doors began to creak and groan as they opened to the cold frigid air. The sky on the outside was a deep azure blue and matched the one inside. From the light of the moon behind them, several figures were outlined in the night. It looked more like a mob than some casual visitors.

In the middle, Sadie recognized her mother's normal sized stature, well, what she now believed to be normal, after all that she'd learned over the last few days. All around her and behind her were shapes and figures of creatures, some Sadie thought she recognized, most not. They all came into North Wind's abode with Adrienne leading the way and spread out in a semi-circle behind her. Sadie ran to her mother and flung her arms around her.

"I told you I'd be back, Ladybug; no need to worry about me anymore," she said, reciprocating the hug tightly.

"Did you tell mean old Ms. Cabot I'm not a traitor? Have you all come up with a plan? What are we gonna do? I'm not sure that...."

From behind Adrienne stepped the curvy and very fashionable Miss Bruja, the rotund and motherly Mrs. Teak, and slowly, from behind them, came old Ms. Cabot. The Three had come as well. Sadie's cheeks went hot.

"Dahling, everything has been explained. That is, once we recovered from the shock of seeing her," said Miss Bruja as she pointed to Adrienne.

"Oh, and I thought me eyes were deceivin' me. Nearly fell off old Arthur. And I must say, that chair sopped me skirts with all his tears o'joy. 'E always did 'ave a fondness for Adrienne, ever since she got 'im out from under 'enry the Eighth. Can't say I blame 'im, 'Enry was such a large King," said Mrs. Teak. "'Ave ya got any tea, North? 'Tis a bit chilly up 'ere."

She moved towards the table where Jack Frost, Elgarbam, and Tara still sat.

Ms. Cabot came to the forefront, staring at Sadie with her piercing raven eyes. She walked towards the child, making her nervous, and stopped just short of three inches to her face. She cupped Sadie's cheeks in both of her old wrinkly hands and bent to stand eye to eye.

"I am truly sorry for doubting you. You must understand we didn't yet know about Hannah, and were not sure exactly whom we could trust. I hope you can forgive me. I will make sure you and your mother spend an exorbitant amount of quality time together after this war and before you begin your training. Please, child, do not hold this against me or the Guild. Even though we are witches with great powers, we are truly human and make mistakes; we cannot and do not know everything."

Sadie smiled and without hesitation she hugged the old woman tightly. Ms. Cabot stifled a smile and laugh, but returned the hug awkwardly. It was obvious she wasn't used to such displays of physical contact.

"Enough, child, you may melt my icy exterior yet, plus, we've got work to do," Ms. Cabot said as she released Sadie, somewhat reluctantly it seemed to those watching.

"I'm the only one truly with an icy exterior, plus I've got...."

"Enough, Jack, we know all about your attributes," said Tara. "Let Ms. Cabot start the meeting."

Jack begrudgingly gave up the spotlight and settled back into his chair. Ms. Cabot cleared her throat and began.

"Now, some of you know each other; some of you don't. I'd say introductions are in order before we all sit to plan our strategy. I want each of you to step forward, state your name, and take a seat at the table."

(She turned to face the table.)

"Tara from the Isle I'm sure you all know."

(She motioned towards Tara as she said this and Tara nodded.)

"Elgarbam is a mountain gnome from the Scottish Highlands, Whistle was his long time companion and dear friend. I'm sure he'll give us all he's got in the way of fighting if not for Whistle's memory, then for our cause. Jack Frost, everyone knows; he makes sure of that. And shouldn't you be at work? I don't like the shirking of responsibility, but if you'd like to join our fight, you're more than welcome."

Jack Frost leapt from his chair and bowed deeply at the waist, flaring out his coat tails in the process.

As he slowly rose, he began to speak. "Ms. Cabot, I would love to join your ranks, but being aligned with the Elementals, I too have taken a vow not to get involved with the goings-on of you mortals. I apologize for my inquisitive nature, but my job can be so boring at times. Snow here, ice there, blizzard up north, freezing rain in the south, same thing, every year, all around the world.

"I do enjoy your drama, but as you say, I have work to do farther south. I think I'll be headed to Vermont, New Hampshire and, of course, Maine, if you would like to keep me posted on the war. If we can somehow keep it from Mother Nature, I will do what I can to help, should it be absolutely necessary. I've grown a weakness, I mean, fondness, for the MacDougall child. Such a sad little life she's had so far and I...."

"Enough, Jack. Thank you for the offer; if we REALLY need you, I'll call. I can't imagine your mother would be too mad at you, or us, knowing what rides on the outcome of this battle. Now, let the other introductions begin," said Ms. Cabot as she took a place at the head of the table.

Without a moment's hesitation, Sadie's mother came forward and introduced herself quickly, assuredly. Looking down at Sadie when she finished, the girl realized it was her turn and stated who she was. Though she sounded a bit uncertain of herself and her place amongst these magikal people and creatures, one reassuring look from her mother and all felt well with her again. Adrienne took Sadie by the hand and walked with her to the table. They both sat next to Tara and let the preamble continue.

Stepping from the crowd assembled at the door, a large bulky beast of a man carrying a battle axe came forward. It glinted and shone in the light, enough to make Elgarbam look down at his own little weapon and sigh. He wore a Viking helmet and leather garb. His beard touched his belly, which was very large, and a number of muscles bulged from under his clothes. The top button on his tunic looked as though much had been asked of it, as it strained to contain the hulking man's broad chest.

"I am Sven the Strong, from Valhalla, come to assist in the battle against Evil. I pledged my loyalty to the Guild my first time on earth and do the same this time as well. The gods of my world have seen fit to give me one more span of time on earth to assist in this battle, as I am such a noble warrior. I am and always shall be the strongest Viking to ever live in Valhalla and on this planet. Plus, my magik isn't too shabby either."

The giant man took a seat next to Elgarbam. The little gnome fidgeted in his chair and stroked his beard in apparent jealousy of this new, larger version of himself.

"I am Zeno and will bring my centaur brothers to arms with the Guild, as always, and vow to protect the MacDougall clan in the process," said the centaur. Sadie shot him a huge smile, and the centaur nodded before his clacking hooves took him to stand behind her and her mother.

Sadie turned and hugged him from her chair. The centaur smoothed her hair and looked down on her tenderly.

Gliding forward, as if floating on air, swept a woman holding a small harp. Her stunning looks caught the eye of every male in the room, and their breath as well. She was easily the most beautiful woman Sadie had ever seen. Even Tara seemed average in her presence. This woman's moves--fluid and graceful, her looks--timeless. She made modern day supermodels look pale in comparison. Everyone was captivated. Everyone's attention clung to this beauty, waiting for her to speak.

She opened her mouth, slowly, deliberately, but out came the most horrible-sounding string of notes Sadie had ever heard. She put her hands to her ears and scanned the table to see if the others reactions were nearly the same as hers. The other women in the room seemed a bit annoyed, as well, but the men seemed to gush even more at this strange, ethereal woman. Elgarbam grabbed his heart. The Viking had drool sliding from his slack jaw. Every man in the room was in awe.

"My song powers are obvious to the men here, as well as the women, I see."

(She looked at Sadie with a knowing smile.)

"I offer my song in bringing down the Syndicate, at least the men of that evil group. I will do what I can to protect the innocent from danger and destroy all wicked and malicious powers that be."

Elgarbam had unknowingly begun to stumble in her direction as she spoke. When she stopped, the little gnome shook his head and looked confused.

"Don't worry, Elgarbam; most men are entranced by my voice. I've brought many a battle ship to crash upon rocky shores, for I am the Lorelei. I promise not to speak anymore, lest my voice be needed in assistance. I do offer a spell that will protect you all from my charms if anyone is willing or in need. I can see the gnome will be the first in line."

A small round of laughter escaped from some of the room's inhabitants. Elgarbam blushed and returned to his seat. Sven smiled at the little guy and whispered in his ear. Whatever he said seemed to relax the gnome and a bond seemed to be forming.

There was a shuffling sound and from the very far reaches of the entrance came four very small, very cute, furry little creatures. They looked similar to hedgehogs, except smaller, and Sadie thought they'd make great pets. She wondered to herself what they could possibly do if anything, and she assumed they belonged to someone in the group, possibly the Lorelei. She fidgeted in her chair. The largest of the four little creatures stepped forward to speak, catching Sadie off guard.

"We're Blaze Bellowers from deep within the magikal realm. We don't oft' come here to the human world, but felt our services might be needed in a time like this. If the magikal realm itself were not threatened, we would have stayed put, but it seems as though our services could be a welcome addition."

Sadie seemed perplexed. Without thinking, she spoke up.

"What can you do? I mean, you're so little and cute," she said.

The four lined up again and turned to face the grouping of chairs by the far wall. The large, lead Bellower left the group and came to the table. He looked at Ms. Cabot, she nodded, and then he took a fizzy drink that she had magikked from thin air. Waddling back to his lineup, he passed the drink down the line after taking a large swig.

When the can was empty, the last one tossed it and the foursome began to rumble. The cute and tiny little creatures trembled and few small burps escaped. They seemed to be gearing up for something. In one mighty burst, they let loose a stream of fire and heat that burned one of the chair groupings to a pile of ash and cinder. And it also caused the room temperature to rise slightly. As the ash settled, they turned to face the group.

"Is that good enough, witchling?" the larger one asked Sadie.

Embarrassed yet again, she replied, "I'm sorry. I'll never question another magikal creature about their abilities, no matter how cute they are."

"If we may continue then?" asked Ms. Cabot.

The hair on the back of Sadie's neck rose as the next two participants came forward. They had been hiding behind the three trolls and five other people that were blocking the entrance. It was none other than two of those man-vulture things she had come into contact with during the several small battles with the Syndicate so far. They lumbered forward, as if it were awkward to walk instead of fly. Chained to their hideous legs was a surprise Sadie had not expected.

"HANNAH!" she exclaimed.

The distain in her voice was not hidden.

One of the man-vultures began speaking, uncomfortably, timidly, and he seemed in so much pain.

"We're an abomination created by the evil magik of the Syndicate. We have no name. We want no name. We want only to exist on some plane where we can live in peace--after all this war business is over. Ms. Cabot has promised us that, and we have promised allegiance to the Guild until it can be provided."

(His speech was labored as was his breathing.)

"Not all of our brothers have gained conscience or intelligence enough to think for themselves, but we have. That's why we're here. Use us as you wish."

It bowed deeply, completely, and stayed in that position for a bit before righting itself again.

Sadie lowered her head. She felt bad for the creatures and their lonely, depraved existence. A lump welled up in her throat, and she began to twist her hair. She made a mental note to try and talk to them, to try and make them feel better sometime soon. She knew from experience what it was like to be an outcast. As the creatures took their place at the table, she caught a whiff of the burning smell she had been witness to before when dealing with those of the Syndicate.

"Hannah, not knowing we knew her traitorous ways, came back to the Guild to make more trouble. We brought her here to you, North Wind, in the hope you could keep her in one of your 'Ice Boxes' 'til this war is over, and we can decide her fate," said Ms. Cabot.

"Would be my pleasure, One of Three," he said.

He then took Hannah away to parts of his palace unknown. Sadie didn't want to know.

One by one the rest of the group stepped forward. The three trolls were distant cousins of Gur and Alroy. They pledged their undying devotion to the Guild and promised to squash as many evil-doers as they possibly could. They also carried with them a magikal talisman from the magikal realm that gave them the power of invisibility. Sadie laughed to herself at the thought of these three giant and menacing looking trolls simply appearing before their foes. If there were ever a reason to soil your pants, they were it.

The next to come forward was a wizard who resided in Romania though you couldn't tell from his attire. He wore Bermuda shorts, sandals, and had on a Hawaiian shirt; nothing matched. His glasses kept sliding down his nose and were held together with tape at the middle. He had a pocket protector and wore a large ring on one finger that looked like a globe. His name was Martoose. He said he'd been practicing magik practically since birth. His powers were so strong that he claimed he didn't need a talisman or any magikal object to conjure anything. He also claimed to be a direct link to the Source. This interested Sadie, and she made a mental note to talk to him more once all the fighting was over.

The second was a beautiful woman who moved forward, only to change into a man before their very eyes. She/He said his name was Versipellis. It then changed into a teal blue snake that wrapped itself around Tara before slithering over to Miss Bruja. When it reached Miss Bruja it turned into a soft and cuddly kitten that purred against her neck.

The kitten leapt down from her lap and then jumped onto the table. When it reached Sven and Elgarbam, it-he-she spoke again.

"I can be of much service to the Guild as I can become whatever is needed of me," it said as it changed into an elegant maiden dressed in white.

As she lay on the table before the Viking and gnome, the two seemed as lost in her beauty as they were with the Lorelei.

"But my true form, the one that may be needed most is this."

As soon as the last syllable was uttered, the maiden quickly changed into an enormous, menacing werewolf, complete with fangs dripping with saliva. It let out a howl that caused Elgarbam to leap into Sven's arms. The bookcases rattled and crystal vases shattered. Some put their hands over their ears while others seemed to quake in their shoes.

"Enough of the theatrics, Versipellis," said Ms. Cabot.

The shape shifter returned to a human woman form and sat next to Elgarbam. The little gnome slid a bit closer to Sven and kept his eyes on the creature for the rest of the introductions.

Third to come forward, leaving two left, was a child of Asian descent. He carried before him a glass bowl that held three yellow octopuses.

"I am Niko from Japan. My family has offered the use of the Kyuusoku Chi. We've been their keepers for Millennia and, as always, are faithful to The Guild. Kyuusoku Chi, loosely translated, means Fast Energy. Would those here care for a demonstration?"

All in the room seemed fascinated and nodded "yes" simultaneously. Some leaned forward in their seats and others eyes grew wide with anticipation. As Niko waved his hand over the glass bowl, the octopuses gathered near the surface. One began to float from the water into the air above the table. Its tentacles spread out and beautiful sparks and flashes of light began to appear in the air.

Soon, a firework display, the likes that none had ever seen before, was bursting and exploding in the air above their heads. The octopus changed color and so did the fireworks. The crowd watched in awe. When it was finished, all seemed stunned.

"That's beautiful an' all, but 'ow will this 'elp us in..." started Mrs. Teak, but she stopped short when she realized that all of them were tied to their chairs, unable to move while the remaining two octopuses floated at the head of the table.

"Distraction can be a powerful weapon, as can this," said Niko. He waved his hand again in a circular motion; before he was finished, the octopus had untied everyone with faster than lightning speed, returning to the bowl, and all was as it were before.

"Very impressive, child, come to the table," said Ms. Cabot. She then turned to face the doors. "Now, you two, show yourselves and your powers."

The last two people walked forward, snapped their fingers, and one turned to fire and the other ice.

"I'm Charlotte O'Reilly, and this is my brother Duncan. I am in control of fire and he is in control of ice--makes for a tricky family dynamic, but great use in times of need. We come to assist in any way possible."

The O'Reilly's nodded recognition at Tara, and she smiled the same.

"Been a long time, how's the Isle fair these days? I haven't had much time to go back for a visit lately. I see you two fare well, and wish good tidings on your family," said Tara.

"The Isle misses you, Tara. It's in need of your charms. Mother sends her best; she'd be here, but is dealing with some very stubborn imps from the Cliffs of Mohr who refuse to stay put. They be terrorizing the local gentry and stealing their wares. If rounded up in time, she says she'll come to assist. You know her first loyalty is to the Isle."

Turning to the crowd around the table, Charlotte O'Reilly continued.   "Mother has control of water and father wind. Mother won't let father come without her...she's the boss."

"Good, we'll look forward to their arrival. And now that we're all properly introduced, let the strategizing begin," said Ms. Cabot. "Oh, and let me add, we have the sworn oath of all magikal creatures residing in the human world to fight alongside us for our future existence. Now, I, being One of Three, think we should begin with this...."

A Right

Beasty Foe

"Now that we're all agreed it's necessary to go to war to save our race, as well as humankind and the other worlds, and we're agreed at our plan of attack, I think we should separate and gather all those who couldn't be here. Oh, and all others, magikal and not, who will fight for the cause-- who will pledge to help destroy the Syndicate. Everyone is to meet at our offices at the Cranberry Grove Cemetery within one day's time," said Ms. Cabot.

She slammed a gavel down onto the table that had magikally (of course) appeared in her hand.

Sadie was relieved. They had been sitting around North Wind's table--arguing, discussing, and planning strategy to the point of her extreme frustration--for even more hours besides the ones they'd spent waiting for her mother to arrive. *How can adults sit still so long?*

Several times she had to stifle yawns, and she had realized several hours ago that one can only fidget for so long in the same chair without wanting to run screaming from the room. Ms. Cabot looked at everyone still sitting around the table and spoke once again in a more somber tone.

"This isn't going to be easy. Some of us will die; some will be forever changed. Who knows what dark magik the Syndicate has unleashed? All we can do is keep our purpose in heart, our minds on the end result, and our battle for good shall prevail. Now, if there are no further questions or comments, let's part ways and do what needs doing," she said.

Sadie sat upright, rather quickly, remembering a key factor in this war. "Um, Ms. Cabot? What about the Ataraxia Heart," she murmured.

The room went silent. Versipellis shifted into the form of a mouse while others looked away. One of the Blaze Bellowers let out a hiccup full of smoke and heat before slapping his little paw over his mouth. Some put their heads down, averting their eyes from Sadie and her mother, who sat beside her. Adrienne MacDougall put her arm around her daughter, cleared her throat, and gently turned Sadie's face to meet hers.

"Sadie, everyone here has been informed about the Heart. Not since its first appearance in our family millennia ago has anyone other than the bearer known about its whereabouts or how it's passed or even how it's used. I felt that since these are dire times, it was necessary to tell them all. No one can speak about it. We can't tell you a thing. Though all know you have it now. You must discover it and its powers on your own. I can only pass it to you, which I have."   Sadie tried to interject that she never gave her any such thing as a Heart, but her mother put her finger to her lips.

"That is the only way its great powers will work. You must discover it, and it must discover you; that way you'll each know the others true intentions.   Now, we speak no more of it 'til you find it and all its glory, *on your own*. Do you understand?"

Sadie nodded. Now more confused than ever, she felt as though everyone but she had been let in on some great secret, and she didn't like it. And in fact, that wasn't far from the truth.

"Let's depart," said Ms. Cabot, slamming a fist on the table.

The room became filled with muffled chatter as the magikal beings and creatures assembled began to mingle and form small groups. Some took off immediately, like the Lorelei and Sven, while others relayed where they were going and who they were bringing back. The desire not to sit still any longer had left Sadie, and she sat alone at the table, pondering the Ataraxia Heart. The centaur Zeno trotted over to her after leaving his conversation with Versipellis and the O'Reilly family who had congregated by the door.

"Girl, why the sad face? You trusted me before when we had to fight our way out of the bookstore. Do you trust me now when I say that you will find your path?" asked Zeno.

Sadie took a deep breath. "I never got to thank you for that, so, um, thank you. And yes, I trust you, Zeno; I'm just worried I'll let everyone down. I have no idea of the Heart's whereabouts, and I have no idea what to do with it once I find it.

"I'm not even a full witch yet; I'm just a witchling that was thrown into the middle of a giant mess. I'll bet other witchlings don't have this hard of a time when they turn. And another thing, that ring you gave me, what's it all about?" Sadie rambled out.

"Trust in yourself. I think you'll be surprised at what you can accomplish if you put your heart and mind into it. Sorry about the heart thing, no pun intended," said Zeno with a deep laugh. "And they say centaurs have no sense of humor. As for the gift I gave you, you'll know when and how to use it. I'm sorry to leave you with another riddle, but I really must go and gather my brothers in arms. You're a smart girl, Sadie, and a powerful little witchling. I believe you'll figure it all out when you need to. If not, I'm afraid I'll just have to become a cart horse for the mine gnomes."

He laughed a strong, deep laugh that made it quite clear their conversation was over.

Sadie laughed, too. What else could she do? As everyone else left, Zeno said his goodbyes to Adrienne who had come to stand by her daughter. Soon, only the North Wind, Sadie, her mother, and the Three were remaining.

"I best be getting' 'ome to me tea. I've not 'ad a decent cuppa since leaving the Guild 'eadquarters," said Mrs. Teak as she snapped her fingers. In a puff of smoke smelling like fresh baked bread, she disappeared.

"And I simply must get my nails done before all of this hoopla begins," said Miss Bruja. "I'll leave behind nothing less than a good looking corpse should I not make it through this battle."

With a swish of her hips and a whoosh of her arms, she too disappeared.

"I best get to work myself," said the North Wind. "There's a gale that needs happening off the coast of Massachusetts tonight, and I'm already four hours late. At least it'll keep those weathermen on their toes."

He, too, left the room by a side door, and all who remained in the massive hall were Sadie, her mother, and Ms. Cabot. The air seemed heavy to Sadie, and all she wanted to do was disappear with her mother, back to the life they once had. It all seemed like a distant dream.

"Sadie, you will get through this, and we are all right behind you, as one big extended family. Though you must discover…certain things…on your own, you are no ordinary witchling. We need you, Sadie; we need you to be strong and have faith in us, in yourself. I apologize once again for ever doubting you, and I hope we can work together in the future. You're going to make one heck of a witch, dear," said Ms. Cabot.

With a nod and a wink she vanished, leaving behind a rainbow assortment of sparkles of light that burned out as they hit the icy floor.

Sadie looked up at her mother. Her eyes welled with tears she could no longer hold back and the deluge began. Heaving with sobs and leaving a wet little puddle on North Wind's table, Sadie let it all out.

"Sssshhhhhh, it's okay, Ladybug. You and I, we'll get through this," said her mother as she held Sadie tightly.

"I just don't want to lose you again. It was hard the first time even though I KNEW you were still alive and nobody would listen to me. I also don't want to let anyone down, especially not now. I've never had anyone tell me the things Ms. Cabot did.

"I have friends now, people who are depending on me to discover something that I know nothing about. I never had anyone count on me or depend on me for anything. Can't you tell me anything, something to make it easier? I promise I won't tell anyone," cried Sadie.

"I can't say a thing; that's not how it works. There are some things in life, whether it be a witch's life or human's that one must find out for oneself. And when you do, that's what gives the discovery so much power, so much importance. This is one of them, Sadie. You'll understand what I'm saying, what it all means, when it happens. I believe in you, the others believe in you, now you must believe in yourself," said Mrs. MacDougall.

Sadie took some comfort in her mother's words, maybe just because her mother was with her, but it helped nonetheless. She stood up, wiped the remnants of tears from her eyes, and hugged her tightly.

I will not let my friends and family down, she thought to herself as her mother smoothed her hair and brushed it back over her shoulders.

"That's my girl. Now, are you ready to go? We've got a ton of wood nymphs to round up and some rather argumentative spirits to get past in order to do so. Hold on to my left hand with yours, put your right over your heart with three fingers in the sign of a W and...."

"I know, I remember," said Sadie with a smile.

The mother and daughter were off in a flash of light, as was everyone else, to begin their part in the battle between the Guild and the Syndicate. It was a battle that would decide the fate of everyone in every plane of existence.

* * *

Sadie and her mother materialized in a huge, rolling, and recently snow covered field of old cornstalks. Immediately in front of them was a vast, dark forest. The trees were so close together it seemed impossible for anyone to even attempt to enter--not to mention the foreboding look of all the trees bereft of leaves with their twisted, gnarled branches winding in and out of each other like so many angry arms. Sadie shivered at the sight; her mother stood tall.

"Are you ready to meet the wood nymphs? I think you'll like them. It's the spirits haunting the woods that'll probably give us some trouble."

Adrienne MacDougall smoothed her daughter's hair with her hand as she spoke to her. The comfort she brought to Sadie was obvious, and they stood side by side to face their latest challenge-- together.

Sadie nodded and the pair walked forward towards the imposing forest. Upon entering, Sadie's stomach began to knot and her chest felt a little tight. She was beginning to understand what this feeling was. She got it every time something was about to happen: sometimes for good, sometimes for something quite possibly not so nice. As they walked on, Sadie could swear someone or something was watching them. The hair on the back of her neck rose, and it wasn't from the chill in the November air.

The forest was indeed thick, and they had to maneuver carefully through the tangled and quite substantial undergrowth. Without speaking to one another, the pair moved forward and had made enough progress that Sadie thought they were probably about five hundred yards inward. There were no animals about, which Sadie thought odd, save for a large white owl that immediately and rather silently left the vicinity. Stepping into a clearing lined with a thicket of spiny brambles, Sadie spoke. "I haven't seen any spirits or ghosts or anything. There aren't even any animals, except that owl we saw. And where are all these wood nymphs supposed to be? I thought that...."

But her words were cut short by a distant moaning.

"That's the trees in the wind, right, Mom?" She asked this question more to comfort herself than to get an actual answer. She knew the answer; there was no wind.

The moaning grew louder and came towards them faster and faster until it seemed to be surrounding them in the clearing. Squinting her eyes, Sadie tried to see whom or what it was coming from. Several ethereal bodies could be seen ducking, dashing around, behind trees here and there. More moans came; more translucent shapes began to gather. Finally, they seemed to be surrounded by spirits on all sides, about four deep into the woods. It looked like an unearthly army had come to do battle. She looked at her mother and was somewhat surprised that she seemed calm and almost annoyed.

"Show yourself, wraiths. Come into the clearing; we are not afraid of you, and we know your purpose. No matter what, we are getting through this wood," said Adrienne in a tone Sadie remembered her using when she was in trouble for doing something bad.

She smiled at the memory and took her mother's hand, squeezing it, more for the love and admiration that rushed through her than from the fear that had been building.

A snapping branch behind them brought Sadie back from her memory, and the mother and daughter both turned to see the source of the noise. They saw nothing. In large groups the gathered spirits began to make a hasty retreat into the forest. The woods were unbearably silent. More ghosts left in a hurry. Another snapping branch. This time to their left. All the spirits were gone. Then another to their right, and the pair spun around to face the sound.

"Don't be afraid, Sadie; it's just the spirits playing tricks on us. They haunt these woods to keep others from finding the wood nymphs so that they may live in peace. Don't let them scare you; they can do no harm. At least not to us," said Adrienne.

"They can't, but I can."

Stepping from the tangle of briars, some embedded in its skin and raking blood trails across its flesh as it moved forward, came a creature so hideous it was hard for Sadie to look at.

Its black skin oozed yellow seepage in places where pustules seemed to burst from the briars scraping them. Greasy lips smacked and parted to reveal a long, blood-red, snakelike tongue. Its glowing orange eyes flashed threateningly, and its pupils turned to slits as it came to stand across the small clearing from Sadie and her mother.

Sadie trembled, never having seen something from a distance that was large enough for her to focus on the detail in its eyes. But the worst was yet to come. Beneath its two muscular arms, two more on each side tore from its flesh and formed and flexed, baring razor sharp claws. The creature dropped down on its arms as its legs retracted to match its arms length. The skin on its back began to bubble and then tear.

From the bloody rips came enormous black leathery wings lined with spikes. They were the length and height of a small truck. Spikes and spines began to rip through its flesh and protrude from any spot left available. The air was permeated with a burnt hair smell, though no fire was to be seen. Sadie almost gagged when the stench hit her nose.

"Sadie, take my hand. This is something new to me and utterly evil. Can you feel the evil? We'll have to fight this together," said her mother.

"Fools, you cannot fight me. I come from a place you can't even imagine in your nightmares. And how often does one win in her nightmares? I am going to eat you both alive, piece by tiny piece, so each can bear witness to the other's horrific and painful death," the creature said, taking a step forward.

"Who are you, who brought you here, and where do you come from?" Adrienne MacDougall stood her ground though Sadie had taken a step backwards.

"I don't have to tell you anything, but since you're going to die anyway, I see that it can do no harm. I am Sintar, a part of the Reaper Clan. I was brought from my world on the 15th plane of existence by the Master. He promised plenty to eat and, indeed, that has been true."

As he said this, he picked and then pulled a rotting, detached hand from between two of his enormous teeth, threw it into the air, and gobbled it down.   "We've never been able to travel to other planes of existence before; now that the Master has found a way and shall rule all, we can go where we want and will--until we are all that's left or for as long as he allows. I'm here to dispose of those who oppose him. You will be next," it said with a deep, ominous growl. "I can smell the goodness in you, and it makes me SICK!"

"Sadie, quick, W!" her mother shouted.

Sadie knew what she meant and threw up the sign over her heart while holding tight to her mother's hand. Instantly, a protective shield filled the air around them as the creature charged forward. Quicker than Gur on a cookie, it hit the shield and sparks flew, blinding all three of them. In the moments it took to regain their composure, the beast was up and charging again. This time it hit the force field in a different spot and once again was flung backwards as sparks burst into the air.

"Sadie, I don't know how much longer our shield will hold. This creature is very powerful. Our Magik can only do so much, and it doesn't seem to be working properly--again. See how the shield ripples in places? That's a tear in our magik. We can't transport or even materialize somewhere else while the shield is up so we'll have to try to disappear quickly as I let go of the force field. We have to time it just right so be ready. We'll aim for somewhere else in the forest, though I don't know how close to the nymphs I can get us. Are you ready? Can you do this with me?"

Sadie nodded, her mouth dry as the desert and her hands shaking with tremors. The beast charged again with the same results, except this time, when it hit the ground, Sadie's mother released the protective shield, and they both gave their signs of W over the heart.

The beast, realizing they were vulnerable, charged again. In a split second it was close enough for Sadie to see the dark, stinking inside of its throat, but in that same split second the mother and daughter materialized into a deeper, darker part of the woods. Back in the clearing, the beast seemed disoriented and then roared so loud the trees shook. At their new destination, both Sadie and her mother heard the roar and trembled a bit in their shoes.

"Come on; we've got to make time. We've got to get to the nymphs and then back to the Guild before that thing finds us," said Adrienne as she took off running with Sadie in tow.

They ran with the ever present sound of the bellowing beast in the distance. They stopped when the forest seemed to block any more movement from any creature, living or dead. The tree branches stuck out in awkward places that they shouldn't be growing. They grew from the sides of trees, from the ground, and even on strange looking bushes. It was as if the flora had built a wall.

Breaking through a particularly snarled and tangled batch of tree limbs, they stepped into a clearing that seemed untouched by the changing seasons. As they did so, a whizzing arrow flew past their heads and embedded itself in a tree behind them before turning into just another branch. Sadie had hit the ground; when she did, she realized that lush green grass carpeted the forest floor now and fruit tress of every kind hung heavy with their precious bounty. Butterflies flitted about from gorgeous flower to gorgeous flower. Birds sang and the air was warm and inviting.

Will this magik stuff ever stop amazing me?

"Is that you, Adrienne? Oh, my, we thought you were dead. I'm so sorry about almost killing you. We thought you to be that beast that's been tormenting and destroying us for the last few months. Oh, it comes from a dark place that one. Sorry again for almost killing you. Hey, everyone, it's Adrienne MacDougall," said a voice from within the trees.

"Yeah, I suppose I'll get that lots in the next few days. It's a funny thing, coming back from the…uh, I guess we'll call it--dead. This is my daughter Sadie, and we've come to ask for your assistance in our fight against the Syndicate. Will you come to aid in our fight?"

(The beast roared a little closer than all present would have liked.)

"That is, if we can get out of here before that beast comes back," said Adrienne.

"We've been hiding in these trees for months now, at least those of us who didn't fall prey to that monster. There's not many of us left. We don't know what that creature is or why it's here, but if you could get us out of here, we'd gladly help in your fight," said a pair of eyes peering out from the tree tops.

"Great, then come down from the trees to stand with us, and I'll do my best, along with my daughter's help, to get us to the safety of the Guild," replied Adrienne.

Slowly, one by one, several small elf-like creatures emerged from the trees. They were brown skinned, nimble, and graceful. Sadie thought they were absolutely stunning. They had large doe-like eyes framed with extraordinarily long eyelashes, long thick black hair, and wore shifts made of something paper thin that moved like silk.

Some had mistletoe wreaths worn as crowns while others had flowers around their ankles and wrists. They smelled divine, like honeysuckle on a summer's day; when one brushed past Sadie, it felt like a warm wind had blown past her arm. She sighed and inhaled the rich scent while they all gathered around.

"We're all that's left, Adrienne. All that haven't been eaten by the beasty from Hell," said one who stood apart from the rest.

"It's okay. We'll sort this mess out once back at the Guild," replied Adrienne. "All of those already consigned to the battle are out gathering forces as we are; when we meet up again, I'm sure all of us will have much to discuss."

The beast roared somewhere near, and all the nymphs drew arrows. Sadie wondered how she had not seen them before, but now these beautiful little creatures all sported carved wooden bows and quivers full of arrows with brightly colored feathers.

"Stand close, all hold hands; those closest hold onto Sadie and me. Steady now, are you ready, Sadie? Okay, let's give it a try," said Adrienne.

As she spoke her last word, the beast broke through the tangle of vines and branches and flashed his tongue. He began his charge just as Sadie felt herself begin to dissipate.

What's taking so long? Sadie thought, as the beast came closer in a stalking like prowl. Some of the nymphs began to squeak and squeal. One broke loose and tried to run for the trees, but the beast soon devoured it in one large bite. As they all watched in horror, the two nymphs that had been holding the recently deceased one's hand joined their own hands, and the scene in the forest began to fade.

Soon, in a heap of relief and some cries of grief for their friend, the remaining nymphs, Sadie, and her mother were standing in the foyer of the Cranberry Grove Funeral Parlor. Adrienne MacDougall collapsed on the ground. Sadie quickly dropped to her knees beside her.

"Mom, what's wrong? Are you okay?" asked Sadie in a panic.

"Yes, dear, I just need some rest, desperately. It took much out of me transporting all those nymphs. You'll soon learn all about the woes of transporting. Get Ms. Cabot to come to me as you take the nymphs out back; they feel safer in trees…oh, and Sadie, you did marvelously back there," she said before closing her eyes and falling fast asleep.

Let the

Battle Begin

Sadie was sitting next to a very grand fireplace in one of the many rooms at Cranberry Grove Funeral Parlor. She was watching the nymphs play in the trees of the barren garden out back. At least, it had been barren when she took them out there the prior evening. Now, it was coming back to life regardless of the snow falling all around. She watched two of the nymphs carefully grasp some of the reeds from within the center fountain, which had been frozen over, and gently blow on them.

Suddenly, they burst to life, sending ripples around the fountain and green replacing brown all the way around. Two beautiful blue undines leapt from the water, doing flips in the air, and only splashing back down once they had kissed the wood nymphs on both cheeks. Sadie sighed and wondered when she too could do such wonderful magik, that is, without it fizzling out over the top of her head.

"In time, lass, in due time," said Tara as she strode into the room full of purpose.

Sadie was delighted to see Tara again and ran to her, arms wide, despite the fact she had read her mind, again. Even though Sadie had asked her not to, it didn't seem to bother her. She was just glad to see Tara.

"I'm so glad you're back. Mom's still sleeping. I think it took much out of her to transport all those nymphs. And we ran into a creature from another realm, and...."

Tara laughed. "Sadie, Lass, you're such an excitable child. And you do ramble on. I've already spoken with Ms. Cabot, and she filled me in on what happened in the nymphs' wood.

"The fifteenth plane had been blocked from all visitations for as long as I can remember and for good reason, as you saw. Any removal of creatures from any plane has always been banned for millennia. Obviously, the Syndicate has found a way to overcome our magik. They've found a way to overcome all magikal laws and regulations.

"This is both dangerous and a horrible mistake. This leader of theirs, what's he called, the Master? Well, he obviously thinks he can control these creatures, but he or she, or whatever it may be, will soon find out what an evil den of awful he's opened the door to. We're now trying to figure out how he did it, and what other creatures he's brought here that shouldn't be. Oh, lass, if only things were the way they used to be...."

Tara seemed to drift off, her eyes were distant and little glassy. Sadie wished she could read her mind like Tara could read hers and others. Actually, Sadie just wished she understood all this magik, the rules that applied, why certain people had certain gifts and others had different ones. She wanted to know why some people could transport, some could read minds, while others couldn't and some had gifts within them while others needed talismans and magikal objects. She just wanted to know how it all worked, how her magik worked, and how she fit into the grand scheme of things.

If only she weren't stuck in the middle of this horrible war, she could well be on with her learning. There were so many things she wished to do, so many things she needed to learn. And she was so confused about everything.

"Well, you two look like statues. If I didn't know better, I'd think you were under some sort of spell," said Adrienne MacDougall as she strode into the room, smiling and refreshed.

Her voice broke both Sadie's and Tara's trains of thought and snapped them back to the reality of their present situation.

Tara smiled and went to sit in one of the big, comfy upholstered chairs by the roaring fire. Sadie hugged her mom; she couldn't get in enough hugs these days. She had vowed to herself to hug her mother even more, now that she had her back. Her mother smiled and reciprocated before ushering Sadie with her to fill the remaining seats by the fire.

"Sadie, there are some things you need to know, and some things I need to tell you, as your mother, before we leap headfirst into this nasty battle between the Guild and the Syndicate," her mother started.

"How can I possibly learn all of my magik before then," asked Sadie, "there's too much. It's so complicated, and I've only just become a witchling. Am I not supposed to have at least three years of training or something?"

Her mother smiled at her and reached out to stroke her long, brown hair. Sadie brushed it away from her eyes before beginning to twist it between her fingers.

"If truth and righteousness be with us, you'll have ample time to learn all that you need about magik, but for now, I need you to know several important facts that will affect the outcome of your magik and, quite possibly, this war," said her mother.

"And what your mother is going to tell you, you need to take to heart, lass. It's of the utmost importance," added Tara.

"Sadie, my Ladybug, as a witch or witchling or any magikal being, for that matter, you are no longer bound by space and time, nor any of the laws of nature that apply here on this earth in this human realm. With that power and knowledge comes great responsibility. All magikal creatures discover this, and you will soon as well." Adrienne cleared her throat. "Some magikal beings use their powers for good, some for bad, just as men do in the human world. You must remember that whichever path you choose affects everything, and everything you do returns to you-- threefold."

Sadie was a little offended. How could her own mother think she would possibly choose evil over good?

There are some old classmates of mine that I would like to shock into reality, the ones who teased me so relentlessly in school, but I would NEVER be a bad person or witch, she thought to herself.

"Mom, I...."

"Please, Sadie, let me finish. Now, some of us, including myself, Tara or even you may not make it back from this clash. If you do survive, you must go on with or without me. For you hold the Ataraxia Heart in your possession, and its powers can help every world, always, 'til you pass it on to your daughter." (The thought of losing her mother again made her stomach lurch, and who said she wanted to have kids?)

"And I want you to be the best and kindest witch this side of the magikal realm. You have a great power and responsibility by being the Keeper of the Ataraxia Heart. Use it well and wisely. For it's hard to correct all the evil or bad you've done once it's put out there in the universe. The reason being is that since it revisits you threefold, it's just hard to catch up to it all.

"I'm telling you all of this because I am your mother and I love you. I want you to succeed in all your endeavors. I want, I need...we all need for you to discover the Heart and all that comes with its possession," her mother finished as she looked Sadie right in the eye.

"Are you trying to read my mind? 'Cause I hate that, and I'm teaching myself how to block any unwanted mind visitors," said Sadie.

Her mother laughed and so did Tara, their combined voices sounding like music hanging in the air.

"No, Sadie, I was just admiring what a beautiful young woman you are becoming. You look so much like your father, and I miss him almost as much as I've missed you these last three years," she said.

A single tear slid down her cheek, making a dark spot on the deep blue velvet dress she was wearing. Sadie didn't know what to say; she never really thought of her father. She KNEW he was dead. At the same time, she had never seen her mother cry for him; she always seemed so, well...together.

Sadie guessed that if she had known him, her feelings would be different and she might cry, as well. She made a mental note to talk to her mother more about her father when all of this was over, if they lived through it.

Wiping her cheek and smoothing her hair, she stood and spoke. "Well, I didn't expect to get so emotional about everything. Now, we've got to get ready for our mission and this battle. Shall we go to the meeting chamber? I think the Three are waiting for us there."

Tara stood, as did Sadie, and they followed Adrienne out of the room. They made their way to the office of Ms. Cabot, One of Three, and the witch that Sadie thought to be the most powerful out of everyone she had met. And the most intimidating, she didn't mind admitting to herself. She also didn't mind admitting to herself once again, of course, that she felt she was in no way ready to really do magik let alone fight in a battle that could affect life on several plains of existence. Sadie wondered what a thirteen-year-old girl could do in the face of such evil, even if she were a witch or witchling.

"'ello Dearies, would you care for a cuppa?" Mrs. Teak questioned.

Grimm lay curled up on her lap, and he purred while she stroked him. Mrs. Teak looked down at him with a smile.

"'e's been staying with us while Abigail Felis 'as been off on some mission collecting artifacts and talismans that may 'elp in this endeavor. I personally think 'e's more content 'ere. I give 'im as many biscuits as 'e wants. Abigail always monitored his consumption, saying she didn't want a fat cat. Cats are supposed to be a bit fat, don't ya think? Would you care for a biscuit, Sadie?"

"There will be time for that later, you English twit. We've got work to do," responded Miss Bruja in a rather nasty tone. "I swear that woman has the personality of eighty grit sandpaper and the brains of a mentally impaired troll. How could she possibly lead the Guild, much less the Three?"

"I apologize for these two; they've been arguing for the entire day about who should become number one should I meet my demise. You see what power does to people; all they want is more, even within our ranks.

And it's not like they get a pay raise with the position. Don't let them get to you. As I told them, nothing will bring me down save for the constant bickering from these two that I can't escape. I was about to put a deaf spell on myself to avoid any more of this squabble," she said.

"And I would pray thee give me some relief as well, but who listens to a meager chair, even one who breaks his back giving seat and service to some rather large guests that you have--most all the time I might add," said Arthur.

Sadie smiled, remembering her initial shock at her first encounter with the talking chair; it was yet another part of her here and now that seemed like centuries ago.

"The three of you, along with a small army that was not conscripted, but volunteered to go with you, are to infiltrate the Syndicate's main offices while the legions we have amassed will begin our attack on every Syndicate stronghold around the world slightly before you enter your target. This should give you ample room to move about. I'm assuming most of the Syndicate and its minions will be off fighting the rest of us once word gets 'round...and it will rather quickly.

"As for the Master, your guess is as good as mine. Use any magik necessary; should things go awry, the North Wind has offered his lodgings as a hold up. Now remember, we've learned that the Master, oh, how I hate to say that name--NO man is my master--has brought creatures and beasts from plains of existence that do not belong here, nor should they have ever come here, but it is what it is, and we'll deal accordingly.

"We also know that he has unlocked some sort of magik stronger than our own, or this Master has done something to affect our magik and our laws of magik. Some spells aren't working as they should be, as I'm sure you've all noticed. Our biggest hope in winning this war hangs on you, Sadie, the Keeper of the Ataraxia Heart."

Sadie's own heart sank, as did her stomach. How could they expect a girl, a witchling with no powers of her own who didn't even know where to begin looking for said Heart, to save all of humankind's existence as well as that of the magikal realm? She shook her head and her palms began to sweat. Twisting her hair between her fingers, she felt as though her legs were going to give out on her. Swallowing proved difficult with such a dry throat so she tried to lick her lips instead. Her mouth felt as though it were stranded in the desert surrounded by peanut butter cookies.

"Pardon me, Ms. Cabot, I would love to be able to do as you ask, but I know nothing. I don't know where to find this Ataraxia Heart. Perhaps if you were to give me some time to look for it, I could be better equipped to do what you ask of me," said Sadie in a weak voice, trying not to throw up in front of everyone.

"Witchling, we have no time. I believe in you; we all believe in you. Be strong and open to all possibilities. Do what you *feel* inside to be the right thing to do. Stay close to Tara and your mother and my lands, child, *do not* let yourself be caught again. I'm not sure we could save you this time. Now, if there's nothing further, you three must go so we can start this war and, with any luck, finish it for good," Ms. Cabot said with her usual commanding voice.

Sadie knew her last word had much more meaning attached to it than intended.

Before Sadie could protest anymore, Tara, her mother, and eventually she joined hands making the usual W sign over their hearts. Sadie kept her eyes on her mother, hoping for some sort of sign, but Adrienne was lost in concentration. As the spell began to take effect, Sadie looked to the Three and watched them blur and fade from sight. In the midst of the transporting spell, Sadie could still hear the Three speaking to one another.

"Why do I feel as though I sent the lamb to the slaughter?" queried Ms. Cabot.

"Don't worry, Felicity; the girl is stronger than she thinks," said Miss Bruja. "And her heart is pure; I saw it. And I saw something else in it as well." This caused Ms. Cabot, Mrs. Teak, and Grimm to look up from what they were doing.

"She'll figure things out soon enough...I hope."

* * *

No sooner than the room came into focus did Sadie smell the stench of something burning once again. She knew they were back in the place that she least wanted to be, but had to be; and a huge war was about to begin. Tara put her hands over her eyes and then pulled them away a minute later.

"All the rest are outside waiting for our call," she said.

"Good, now, if I remember correctly, this corridor leads to the dungeons. Maybe we can release some of the others to help in the fight, at least, the ones who are still strong enough to fight," said Adrienne.

Sadie just stood there, wondering what she could do, and why she was even there. She still felt she would be of better service if she had been given time to locate the Heart and possibly learn some magik. She squeezed her hand over the smooth object in her pocket.

At least I still have my talisman, though a lot of good that'll do if I don't know how to use it.

Her thoughts were interrupted by a loud wail.

"Just as I thought, this way girls," said Adrienne.

The threesome crept silently towards the dungeons, alert and almost wobbly with the enormous weight of what lay upon them. They rounded a bend and the stench became thicker, stronger, causing Tara to cough a little. Adrienne stopped and looked back at her with admonition.

"Sorry, it's just that the stench is becoming worse. It's hanging in the air like liverwurst that's been sitting in the sun," said Tara. "Speaking of the smell of liverwurst, I hope Alroy is one of the ranks outside. Oh, how he loves a good battle, and I'd hate for him to miss this one."

At the end of the shorter corridor they had entered, there was a faint light they cautiously walked towards. Reaching the door, the smell was so thick they had to cover their mouths with their hands. A substantial, grey-green smoke floated in a layer a foot thick and hung from the ceiling as if it could drip down on them. Adrienne gasped. Immediately, she grabbed hands with Tara and threw up the W, signaling to Sadie that they needed a shield. Tara grabbed Sadie's hand tightly and pulled her closer. Making the magik for the shield had brought them all together in the doorway, and both Tara and Sadie saw what had caused Adrienne's alarm.

A lone creature stood in front of a large fire pit. It was slick with sweat, black and completely hairless. This creature had no eyes and in its place where the nose should be was a protrusion that looked like someone had stuck a pink, glistening octopus on its face. The wiggly appendages seemed to sniff the air of the cell immediately in front of it, and a beak snapped out of the mass. It clicked and clacked open and shut as the creature opened a cell door. Whatever was inside squealed as the creature grabbed it in its long, bony fingers. Turning to face the fire pit again, they saw that it now held a small gnome over the flames. It licked its lips, and then said a few words too garbled for them to understand. The gnome struggled, but to no avail, the creature had a tight grasp on the little being.

Please release me.

Sadie thought she heard the gnome say though his lips did not move.

It had to be the gnome. The only other voice I've ever heard in my head was Mom's, unless I'm slowly beginning to be able to read minds, too.

The fire within the pit roared and rose up, flames licking the ceiling before dropping again. From out of the fire a large, orange colored profile appeared. It was the color of rotting pumpkins. It was shaped like a pig's head with features to match, but had the eyes of a cat on the prowl. It appeared to be just skeletal, no skin or muscle tissue. Two massive black twisted horns jutted from its skull, dripping with blood and flame, and its spiky sharp teeth extended out in all directions.

This enormous and repulsive head was attached to the body of a serpent with gleaming dead pumpkin orange scales, not dissimilar to steel. It had two muscular arms, short like a tyrannosaurus rex, with skinny little clawed fingers that clicked and gnashed together. Sadie shivered as the little gnome wiggled and squealed relentlessly. She couldn't believe the horror she was witnessing, and she didn't want to think about what was to come next.

The black beast dropped the gnome into the pit, and the pig-serpent creature grabbed it between its mangled teeth. In two quick chomps, it was all over with, and the creature descended once again into the flames. A deep red glow came from the opposite corner of the room no sooner than the gnome was devoured. The horrible stench of burning flesh became unbearable. Sadie knew that being transfixed by the scene she'd just witnessed had kept her from noticing it before, but now that it was glowing, it was all she could look at.

On a pedestal the height of about five foot tall stood a glowing red, semi-translucent, heart-shaped object. Sadie heard Tara gasp. She looked at her mother and recognized sheer terror holding her features frozen.

Please let us go.

Sadie looked around and didn't see anyone or anything the voice could have come from. She realized this voice was in her head, much like her mother's voice had been.

Is this the Ataraxia Heart, the heart they all keep talking about?

"The Core of Corruption," whispered Tara.

Sadie was glad to hear this truth because, in fact, she thought the object might just really be the Ataraxia Heart. And she in no way wanted to go near it.

"That's right, how quick you recognize pure evil when you see it, when you yourselves are such self righteous beings. I don't mind saying that I'm a little surprised, I thought you...people knew more. You're right to show such fear in its presence, for it can destroy you before you even know what's happened. All it takes is one word from me."

The threesome quickly peeled their eyes from the glowing orb and found they were looking at a tall man in a black silken suit. A man that Sadie and her mother recognized to be the Master. Sadie gasped as Tara and her mother moved to put themselves between her and him. With the protective shield broken, it was all they could do. The Master laughed. Though his eyes appeared to be red-rimmed and he kept sniffling, he still looked as menacing as ever.

"Don't think you can protect her. If I had wanted her dead, she would be already. As you can see, as you have seen, I can do many, many things since I've released the Soul Seether and gained use of the Core. All I have to do is feed him some of those stinking pure souls, easy to find believe it or not, and I have all the power and magik I need right at my fingertips."

(He snapped his fingers and a wood nymph appeared in his hand.)

"I will soon be Master over all dominions, both here and in any realm I so choose; I just have to keep my pet happy."

He tossed the wood nymph into the pit of fire. Tara closed her eyes and bowed her head as if in prayer.

"You have no idea what you've done. You have no idea just how utterly devastating the Core of Corruption is, or its keeper, the Soul Seether. When the Three banished it, it was put under many spells to seal both up for all eternity. How were you able to release it from the Seether's chest? How did you even find it? What kind of deal did you make with the Soul Seether? You really have no idea just what you've done? And who are you? Where do you come from? I've never seen nor heard of..." Adrienne asked.

"Shut up! I have no patience for your rambling questions. Now I know where your annoying little offspring gets it. You babble and babble, just like your girl-child, and I do not owe you any answers. You will soon either be dead, a snack for the Soul Seether, or you'll worship at my feet."

He inhaled from the purple flowers in his lapel, speaking more softly afterwards.

"And as I just told you, all I have to do is give the Soul Seether what it wants, pure souls, and I get the use of the Core of Corruption for all time. You see, the Three forgot one thing: The Soul Seether can't resist pure souls. It would rather have them than its own heart. We always want what we can't get.

"I tempted it with one, a very pure one. I think you might know whom I'm talking about. I think he was called Whistle. The Soul Seether and its Core were all mine soon after, just as you will be, just as every realm and creature and being will be as soon as I dispose of these pious and bothersome idiots who call themselves the Guild."

He snapped his fingers again and Gok appeared, stroking his sash of scalps as usual.

"Tell me, Gok, how goes the battle raging between us and them?"

The imp wiped a bit of drool from his greasy mouth and hocked up a large grey chuck of semi-solid phlegm. He spit it into the air and caught it again, chewed it up, and then swallowed.

"It seems that we're pretty much tied, Master, pretty much tied. We need to release the Soul Seether to get this thing over with. Can I release it? Can I Master, please, please?" the imp begged without pride.

"In time. First, let our kind have some more fun, killing and destroying those good seekers and doers. I want you to take the one called Tara, you remember her, your friend you were stuck in the bubble with. I want you to bring her to me so I can demonstrate just what I can do."

Sadie felt a strong rush of an emotion she couldn't quite pinpoint course through her body. She also heard *the voice* again, but she couldn't dwell on that. She needed to do something to stall whatever the Master was going to do with Tara. Without thinking she shouted out.

"I have the Ataraxia Heart, and I'll give it to you if you let Tara and my mother go," she said, regretting the words as soon as they left her lips.

What have I gotten myself into this time?

"I was going to use Tara as bait to lure out the Soul Seether in all its evil glory. I was going to torture her in such wonderful and new ways, the likes of which you and your mother have never seen. I was going to do that to coax you into handing over the Heart. Why does my fun always get waylaid? It seems I'll just have to torture her for fun now because you see; you'll give me the Heart regardless. Now that I know it's on you, there's no reason to resist me. I'll take it even if I have to cut you to little bits to find it. Which might just prove profitable if your connection with it is as the Seether's is with its Core."

"First, can I ask why you need the Ataraxia Heart if you already have the Core of Corruption, the Soul Seether, some other creepy pets, these creatures and beasts from other realms and so many of our own kind on your side? What could you possibly need the Heart for? I see no harm in knowing if you're going to kill us anyway," said Sadie.

The Master thought for a moment before inhaling from his lapel once more. Sadie wondered just what it was doing for him. She assumed it must have some magikal power, perhaps it was his talisman. Then he took out a small vial from his inside jacket pocket. It was clear, and Sadie could see purple smoke swirling inside. Her stomach turned when she realized what it was.

He's an addict.

"Well, I don't mind filling you in. Especially as it seems your very own mother enjoys leaving you in the dark."

He flicked his wrist and delivered an invisible slap to Adrienne's face. Adrienne's head jerked to the side, taking the blow, as she looked down apologetically at Sadie.

"Have a seat and I'll tell you a story," the Master said.

He raised his hands, snapped his fingers and Sadie, her mother, and Tara were bound to chairs. Their shield disintegrated.

"Now, where shall I begin?" said the Master.

A Very

Special Pet

Bound tightly to the cold surface of the stone chairs the Master had magikally produced to hold them captive, Sadie's mind raced at all the possible ways to stall whatever was to come. She only hoped he really would give her information on the Ataraxia Heart, as he had said. At least then, she might have a chance at figuring out exactly where it was and what she could do with it. After much silence, save for the roaring hellfire of the Soul Seether's pit, Sadie spoke again in an attempt to buy time.

"Are you going to tell me what you said you would, or do I have to just get rid of the Heart before you can use it against us as well?"

Why do I keep saying these crazy things, these obvious lies?

The Master snapped his fingers and three small fairies appeared in his hand. He held them high over the pit of fire, shaking them like a dog owner does with treats. He was tempting the Soul Seether out for its prize. As it slithered and hissed and rose up from within the fire, the Master laughed hideously. He took another sniff of the flowers in his lapel and another deep breath in from the vial.

The Master then slapped the handful of fairies against the stone wall, knocking them out, and then tossed them to the monster in the pit. The Seether caught them mid air and swallowed them whole. The large, black beast that had previously held the position of feeding the Seether shook, laughing with pleasure at the act, as the Master wiped his hands on his pants.

"Some fairies are drenched in such purity; I do hate the feel of goodness on my hands. The only pleasure I get out of touching them is slapping them against something really hard to knock them out. It keeps them from flying away before I give them up to the Soul Seether. Now, where were we?" he said as he approached his literally captive audience.

"Ah, yes, I was about to explain the magik and mystery of the Ataraxia Heart. Hmmmm," he said as he licked his fingers and smoothed into place his already slicked back, perfect hair. "Where to begin, where to begin? Hmmmmm...as you must know, there is a balance to life, love-hate, up-down and good-bad. It simply must be in order for this world, for any world, to function properly.

"If I gain possession of the Ataraxia Heart, while also in possession of the Core of Corruption, I can disrupt that precious balance in life. You see, the Core and the Heart are actually one, split in two. Evil holds the good and good holds the bad. Does this make any sense to you?

"It's really black and white if you think about it. I can choose to make one more prominent than the other, and I'm sure you know which one I choose. I can do this by controlling how many souls and what kind it gets. By doing so, dark can prevail over light for as long as I so choose. And I will tell you, witches, it will be for all eternity."

"That's not true, since the balance will be disturbed, more or less broken, things will begin to go awry which explains why all of our magik isn't working correctly; it's already started, you idiot. You're upsetting nature's natural balance. Nothing will be as it was. You know that; there will be mass chaos," Tara interrupted.

The Master laughed a full-throated, loud, hearty chuckle and wiped the corners of his eyes as if he'd been brought to tears by her words. He kept laughing as he walked towards the fire pit, still snickering, and threw an imp who had wandered into the room into the burning flames.

Sadie was shocked. If he was able to kill one of his own without regard, what else was he capable of? He stood looking down into the fire as the imp let out a pathetic wail.

"Oh, now that's rich. You three are either the stupidest women I've ever encountered, or you really know nothing of pure evil." He spun around to face them again as his voice lowered. "Evil thrives on chaos."

"But you won't be able to control anything; that's what chaos is, no control, not even by the maniac that loosed it," said Adrienne.

"I'll control everything," the Master offered back with malice in his voice. He walked towards the black, hairless creature. The writhing pink tentacles on its face began to twitch as if in anticipation.

"Gok, bring me the latest capture."

He commanded this of the imp while staring at the black beast. Sadie's stomach churned as she noticed that he looked at it in the same fashion newlyweds look at each other.

Gok left, this time walking. He went down the dark corridor adjoining the room opposite the door from where Sadie, her mother, and Tara had entered. Save for the roaring fire of the pit, the room became silent once again. The constant periods of silence were beginning to drive Sadie crazy. The Master stood with his back to them as he stroked the black creature's slick, wet skin, in between sniffs from his lapel. Sadie looked at her mother, and Adrienne mouthed the words *we'll get out of here* to her, but Sadie didn't have much faith.

Tara turned her head away from the pit and the Master, to face Sadie and mouth, *yes, we will.*

There was a commotion in the passageway as Gok and the victim drew closer. Gok appeared, dragging a rough burlap sack over his shoulder. It was the length of a human and who or whatever was inside kicked furiously. He dropped the sack at the feet of the Master and kicked it once, hard, while drool escaped from his mouth and oozed through the material of the bag. He untied the end and two legs appeared. The black beast's octopus mouth began to snap its beak and its tentacles wriggled furiously. The Master pacified it by stroking its bald head.

"You see, Ladies," he said, grabbing the end of the sack opposite the feet, "I feed the Seether to keep the Core happy. The Seether is the Keeper of the Core. I've learned how to separate the Seether from the Core and in doing so, he belongs to me now.

"He does my bidding so long as I constantly provide him with fresh, pure souls to feed his insatiable appetite. He needs me to feed him, as I need him for destruction, for evil, and for my work here. Evil likes to spread out.

"What? You want to see him complete and whole? Your weak sensibilities would probably balk at him intact with the Core, and it would have devastating effects for you. It would behoove you not to ask to see his one true form."

He dumped the contents of the sack onto the floor. Sadie gasped.

"I see you know this pathetic excuse for a man," said the Master.

"That's David's father," Sadie half mumbled.

"He is a weak, pathetic human who worked for the Guild. He tried to burn down our offices here in Cranberry Grove and for that, he will pay," the Master replied.

Grabbing the man by his bound arms, the Master yanked him to his feet with the same amount of ease with which he dumped him out of the sack. He took off his blindfold and removed his gag. David's father gulped a huge breath while his eyes adjusted to the light of the killing room. He spotted Sadie and began to speak, his voice scratchy and rough.

"Sadie, I tried to watch out for you; I tried to keep you safe like Ms. Cabot asked of me. That was me back in the bookstore--the man who knocked all those books over, the man hidden beneath the black wool coat and hat.

"As of late, the Syndicate has been able to spot witchlings before they turn. The Guild had me keep an eye on you so that they couldn't get to you beforehand. I have no idea how the Syndicate knew of my involvement. Please," he pleaded, turning to the Master, "I have a son and a daughter that need me. They're innocent; they're human and do not belong in this war. They need me as a father; they have no mother. Please spare me."

He turned back to Sadie.

"I'm afraid I've failed you; I've failed the human race, my children, Ms. Cabot, and the Guild. I'm sorry," he choked out as he dropped to his knees.

"Maybe I should have taken the magik they offered me. But I was afraid...I'm sorry...you see, Sadie, I'm your Uncle Marcus."

Adrienne MacDougall let out a gasp.

"I REMEMBER YOU NOW! I knew you looked familiar. I saw a picture once when Dominic and I were married. I tried to find you when he died, but you'd disappeared."

"I know and I'm sorry for that, too. When the Syndicate killed him, I renounced my magik. I was tired of all the evil it could do. I guess, in my grief, I forgot all the good it could also do. I wanted nothing further than to live in ignorant bliss in the human world. And I did...for a while.

"You died in a car crash, well, supposedly died, and Sadie was all alone and coming on the change. I went to Ms. Cabot and told her my tale. I told her all my fears and worries, and she let me help how she saw fit." Marcus began sobbing again. "I am so sorry, Adrienne...I am so very sorry, Sadie...."

"Not half as sorry as you'll be in a moment," laughed the Master. "Oh, and your son and daughter, David and Hannah, such easy, stupid children to manipulate. I recruited them as soon as I saw you in the bookstore."

David's father looked crushed, defeated, and tears began to fall down his face.

"I knew that, no, I could *feel* that you were up to something of a goodly nature, goodness does have such a stench. Bits and pieces was all it took to convince those two rotten children of yours to work for me--bits of magik and pieces of lies, and they turned you in quicker than an imp on a rotting rat's corpse."

The black creature came forward and took the man by the shoulders. David's father, Sadie's long lost Uncle Marcus, seemed immediately transfixed by the creature and swayed in its arms as if in a trance. It was like watching some macabre death dance between creature and man.

"Now, you'll get to see the Core in action," said the Master softly.

The tentacles on the creature grew a little and spread themselves across the face of Marcus. Each one seemed to be a mouth on its own. The beak came snapping out and grabbed his face, covering his mouth and nose. Blood began to trickle down his chin and neck, and the little mouths on the tentacles lapped it up while others held him in place suctioning tight.

David's father's body began to tremble and shake. A white light began to flow from him to the beast and then over to the Core; it was a snakelike coil that worked its way between the three. The air felt heavy, oppressive, and made Sadie, Tara and Adrienne feel very uncomfortable, like they were in the presence of pure evil. And in reality, they were. There was a smell of burnt flesh wafting around the room. The tentacles then released the man's face, and the beak, smeared with blood, slowly receded as well.

As this happened, the Core began to glow more so than when the gnome and fairies were fed to the beast in the fire pit. Its brilliance was almost blinding, and the feeling of dread weighed heavily on the three women. Tara inhaled sharply as if her breath had been taken away.

The black creature released the man from its grip, and he fell to the floor with a thud. Horrified, the three women held their breath as his body began to twist and contort violently. It began to change, to transform; when the spasms and seizures were over, he lay, back to them, in a still heap.

Moments later, Marcus stood up, awkwardly, as if a newborn taking its first weak, unsure steps. Turning their faces, the women gasped in horror at this new version of Sadie's Uncle Marcus, as he slowly gazed upon them for the first time. He had clawed hands and leathery, rough-looking skin. Spiky protrusions tore through his clothes and ran the length of each arm. Veins were apparent just beneath his skin and two small horns were beginning to rip through the flesh of his forehead. His eyes, void of any emotion and a milky white, turned to meet the Master's. It opened its mouth, blood and tissue falling to the floor, and spoke.

"I'm in your service; give me my orders, Master."

"Go and fight with the others to destroy the Guild. Kill any humans that get in your way; they're meaningless, worthless. Bring back any magikal creatures that seem too noble or any humans that seem too good. You'll be able to smell the purity in them. Do your best to serve me, and I'll not destroy you," said the Master.

The new creature that used to be a simple man, David's and Hannah's father, Sadie's long lost Uncle Marcus, left the dungeon to join the ranks of other evil creatures and act out his orders.

I had an uncle....

Turning once again to face Sadie, the Master wiped his hands through his hair and then took a long, deep inhalation from the purple flowers on his lapel. Walking towards Sadie, he began to smile his wicked grin.

"You really don't know anything do you? The Core sucked his pure soul right out of him. It's locked away within its infinite walls. Look at you, surprised, a bit shocked maybe, all three of you are. I guess I underestimated your goody-two-shoes powers. Well, let me ask you something, Sadie. Do you really want to be the keeper of all that evil?"

Sadie's eyebrows furrowed and the corners of her mouth turned down.

What is he talking about?

She looked at her mother who silently and slowly shook her head as she bowed it, chin meeting chest. Sadie turned to Tara who tried to put on a brave face.

"Sadie, whatever he says will be a trick. Do not listen to him. He'll twist the truth to meet his needs, lie to you, tell you anything to try and bring you over to his side. He needs the Ataraxia Heart and he...."

"Shut up, you worthless and wretched witch. Now, Sadie, answer my question," said the Master.

"I don't know what you're talking about," she replied.

And she honestly didn't.

The Master's laughing was getting quite annoying to Sadie. Her bindings were beginning to burn her wrists and her head hurt. The burnt flesh smell was nauseating, and she wished they weren't in this situation. She was angry that she had an uncle whom she could have lived with instead of all those foster homes. She was angry they were all in the position they were in. And she was really aggravated that she still knew nothing about this object everyone said she had. She wished with every ounce of her being she knew more about the Heart.

"The Ataraxia Heart holds within it all the evil that it has destroyed, just as the Core holds all the good souls. The Core is the Heart of the Seether. The Seether just does its bidding. As you will do the bidding of the Heart.

"You see--balance. I'm sure it's quite full, since it's been in circulation a millennium now. Do you really want that responsibility? It's quite a big one for such a young girl, one who's not even capable of wielding all her powers yet. Oh, that's right, you don't even *have* all of them yet," the Master chuckled.

"How do you know about the Heart's workings? How do you know what it does? Leave my daughter alone or I'll...."

"You'll what? Die like the rest of those that oppose me? I have no use for you or your pretty friend here. But, Sadie, now we could rule this new world, all the new worlds I'm making and in great style. You know what they say? 'Keep your friends close, but your enemies closer,'" the Master said menacingly.

Sadie's stomach churned at the thought of doing anything with this man. He was evil to the core, which made his appearance even more repulsive to her even though he was a handsome man. She studied his face for a moment, searching for anything she could possibly use.

She was angry that her mother, Tara, the Three, none of them told her anything about the Heart, yet the Master gave her information about it freely. She wanted to know how it was that the Master knew and could tell her things about it. She also wanted to know why this Heart that thrives on evil would be placed in the possession of such a young and inexperienced girl.

Do I really want that responsibility?

"Sadie, think about it. I'll take the Heart from you and lock it away so that you will never have to worry about it again. You'll never have to worry about being tempted by the evil it carries inside. I'll help you to...."

"No, Sadie, he'll use the Heart to unleash all its evil souls it's holding within. He'll destroy you, not help you. Don't listen to him!" shouted Adrienne, sounding desperate.

Sadie was beginning to see a way out. If she willingly did what the Master asked, she'd be free of the responsibility of the Heart. If she had known it was full of so much evil, she would have insisted her mother take it back immediately. She'd never wanted the task of keeping it anyway.

Please help us.

There was that voice again.

Ignore the voice; focus Sadie.

If she did what the Master asked, maybe he'd let them go. They could find another way to fight him, to fight the Syndicate.

Yes, he'll let us go if I just give him what he wants, Sadie thought as she looked into his eyes.

"No, Sadie, he won't; please just follow what you truly feel," begged Tara.

Sadie looked at her mother again. She loved her so much and didn't want to lose her again. Though she was angry her mother hadn't told her anything about this burden she was in possession of, wherever it was, she didn't want anything between them. She just wanted, no, she *needed*, her help and guidance.

"Mom, please, tell me what to do," Sadie pleaded.

"Ladybug, you know in the deepest regions of your soul what is right and what is wrong. Trust in yourself; I cannot reveal a thing to you about the Heart by decree of the Heart's powers. Remember, you must discover it by yourself.

"If I do tell you, I will surely pay the ultimate price of forfeiting my life for the sake of information, and I think I may be needed here more than in the afterlife. Plus, we've only just found each other again. I need to be with you, Sadie. Believe in yourself and the power of good. The Heart will not forsake you. I can't say anymore," Adrienne answered.

The Master grinned, his smile spreading wide. "I will let you, your mother and Tara go if you just give me the Heart. I give you my word," he said.

Sadie was torn between two worlds. She thought it noble and good to give up one thing for the lives of others she loved. He might even fix Uncle Marcus. But she also had doubts as to whether she could trust his word. On the one hand, she felt like she had nothing to lose by entering the agreement with him, not that she knew where the Heart was to give it to him, but she figured if he knew what he did about it, he could probably figure out where it was.

On the other hand, deep in her soul, she felt it would be wrong to agree to anything with this evil man, though she didn't know why she felt this way. At the same time, she just might be going crazy since she was hearing voices again. She thought about that and realized she could feel the voices more than anything, and they were making her feel other things.

She felt it would be far nobler to die with the conviction of following the path of good and righteousness than to agree to anything with the Master. She studied his face, in the hopes of finding some sort of compassion or humanity, but deep down knew he was void of both. She watched him, stalling; as he took another sniff off his lapel flowers, something sparked inside her. She looked at his eyes, and then she looked at the flowers once again.

Suddenly, recognition and remembrance overtook Sadie as she stared intensely at the cluster of purple flowers in The Master's lapel.

"Catnip!" she exclaimed.

The Master lifted the flowers to his nose and inhaled deeply.

"I don't see how my choice of lapel flower has to do with anything right now, witchling," he said almost in a growl. He seemed angry that Sadie was more interested in his catnip than in his plan to dominate every plain of existence or even the question he had proposed to her. It was as if she were taking away his moment of glory, and now he seemed to be on the verge of madness. Or maybe it was all the drugs....

Sadie's chest began to feel weird, like it was swelling, and her head and stomach had that familiar feeling like when she KNEW her mother was still alive or how she *knew* something was going to happen.

Feel us, Sadie!

Her vision went white with a blinding light, and her entire body filled with a warmth and love she didn't know possible. As her head rolled back, too heavy to hold up on its own anymore, perfect knowledge filled her entire being.

"YOU'RE GRIMM!" she shouted before going limp.

Anger flashed across the man's face, severe and resolute, while his body seemed to ripple. Tara and Adrienne stared in disbelief, then looked to Sadie's limp body and then turned their attentions back to the Master.

"That explains how you knew so much, you were supposedly cat-napping on Arthur when I went to explain all that had happened, to show I wasn't dead and bring everyone back to the North Wind's abode. You're a sick and revolting traitor. Why? Why are you doing this? Is Mrs. Felis in on this, as well? Wait 'til the Three hear about this," said Adrienne.

"They won't hear about any of it," Grimm, formerly known as the Master, said with force.

"And to think, the humans that originated and built the Syndicate for the sole purpose of destroying all witches and magikal beings are actually being led by one." Tara laughed a spiteful cackle and continued. "I'm assuming that's why you took the form of a man. Unless, of course, you really want to be a human...in that case, I recommend counseling and some...."

But her words were cut short by the Master. "ENOUGH!" he shouted and looked as though he would burst from anger.

The doors to the corridor slammed shut and bolted themselves by an unseen force. The hairless black beast dove into the fire pit in a flash of light and sparks. The Core of Corruption stone began to glow a bright red and was now vibrating on its pedestal. The Master walked towards the pit and knelt at its edge. His long thin fingers ran across the rim of the cavity and his head cocked sideways. Looking back over his shoulder, he grinned maliciously at his three captives. Sadie had begun to regain consciousness and saw him through blurry-eyed vision.

"Now, you're going to meet my very special pet," said The Master.

A Good Old

Heart to Heart

Hearing those words coming from the traitor Grimm made Sadie sit up straight in her cold, stone, straightjacket chair. She knew she had to listen to what he was saying, that it was life and death, but she was experiencing something she had never felt before. Her body tingled from head to toe; she felt more alive than she ever had. Something was happening inside her.

Is this what it feels like to know your magik? Because I'm feeling much stronger for some reason.

She shivered, not from fear, but because of the newfound energy coursing through her essence. She knew, without fully hearing what he was saying, that Grimm was about to do something drastic. She also knew she had the power now to try and stop him and, at the same time, the power to rule all the worlds with him.

The voice in her head that was only moments ago so clear was now the chatter and mumble of a thousand voices all at once. There were too many to single out just one, and she didn't need to be distracted by them now. She needed to stall Grimm once more so she could come fully back to her senses and make a clear-headed decision.

This power does feel good. And think of all the getting even I could do with all those nasty kids at school. I could make everyone pay for how mean they were to me. I would never again have to sit alone at lunchtime if I chose to go back. Oh, things would be so different at school...I could zap anyone who picked on me--ever or even in the future. Wait, is this the evil talking? The evil that the Heart holds? I don't care; it feels good.

"Grimm...I've decided to join you. These witches have done nothing for me but put me in the midst of a great war--one that I didn't want to fight.

But now…now that I've seen your power…I want power, too. I won't be stupid like Uncle Marcus.

"I want to get even with all those kids at school who were so mean to me. I want to do…things. You've explained more to me about the Ataraxia Heart in the short time I've been down here than they have in days. My own mother didn't even tell me she gave it to me. Heck, she didn't even tell me I was a witch. "Release me from these bindings and together we'll destroy the Guild. What's that saying I've heard…oh yeah, 'better to rule in Hell than serve in Heaven.' Please…I want to help you release all those dark souls from the Heart. Now that I've been…confined…I can only imagine how they feel," said Sadie. Her face was twisted with anger, and she turned left and right, glaring at her mother and Tara. Grimm studied her features, grinning, and stood up from the pit to face her full on.

"Do you really think I'd fall for that? You'll have to do better than that, Sadie," he said.

"Release me, and I'll prove it to you. Give me a captor to feed to the Soul Seether. Let me torture someone. Let me show you," replied Sadie.

She was, for the first time in her life, steady and sure in her speech.

Grimm appeared to think for a moment. He rubbed his chin while sniffing his lapel. He then pulled that little vial out once more and inhaled deeply. His eyes glassed over, and a smile began to form on his face.

"Sadie, NO! I love you; you know I couldn't tell you anything. Please, don't do this," begged Adrienne.

"Don't bother, sister witch. She's already gone over to the dark side. We're fighting this battle without her now; we must fight her as well as him," Tara said.

Sadie smiled a wicked grin. She stared straight ahead at Grimm, willing him to believe in her with every fiber of her being. Grimm rose and walked slowly, deliberately, to stand in front of Sadie. He knelt down until he was about eye level in front of her. He placed both hands on either side of her cheeks and stared into her eyes for what seemed like an eternity.

"I will loose you from your bindings, but remember: I'm the Master. I can kill you instantly, if not by myself then with the help of the Seether. Don't try anything; you will regret it," he said.

"I am here to serve you," replied a very somber Sadie.

Grimm loosed her bindings by hand and then snapped away the stone chair, out of the dungeon, out of existence. Legs stiff from sitting on the cold stone surface, Sadie stood slowly and a bit unsteadily. She flexed her muscles, which now seemed stronger somehow, and extended her fingers as energy and power poured through her every molecule.

"Now you'll show me your loyalty," said Grimm.

Grimm snapped his fingers, and Zeno appeared. He was bound on all four feet and his hands were tied tightly to his chest. His mouth was gagged, and he had wounds all over his body. As he lay on the floor of the dungeon, looking up at Sadie, his tail swished in aggravated twitches.

"When they caught your Uncle Marcus, they also brought back our favorite old cart horse Zeno."

Turning to face Sadie, Grimm continued.

"Did he tell you he used to be one of our best slaves, hauling precious stones from the mountain trolls' mine? He was really obedient until he escaped. To this day, I don't know how he did it. But no matter now, he's back. And apparently he's losing his touch; he was doing very badly in a fight with one of our creatures from the fifteenth plain. Sadie, I want you to kill him for me."

Sadie walked to kneel in front of Zeno. She had no emotion on her face, save for a blank look in her eyes. Her hand drifted to the ring he had given her as a birthday present, and then she quickly took it off. She wound his long mane through the ring and tied it onto his hair tightly.

"I have no use for this…horse…or the gift he gave me," she said with steely determination. Standing once again, she turned to face Grimm, the Master, and her new master. "The only thing is I don't have all of my powers yet. You'll have to do it or help me do it."

Grimm smiled the most wicked of evil grins and came to stand by Sadie. Zeno shut his eyes, as if accepting his fate, and made no more movement or sound. Grimm took Sadie's hand and raised it with his own. In one swift flick of his wrists, Zeno became ensconced in flames and then began to fade from sight. In a matter of seconds, it was all over with. Adrienne cried aloud while Tara hung her head low.

"Well, that didn't work quite as I had planned, but he's gone nonetheless. I'm gonna have to set up some new magik laws once all is said and done. You can help me with that, Sadie. I don't like my magik not producing the exact result I require. Although, the fire was a nice bonus," said Grimm.

"Let's get on with the program," said Sadie, void of any emotion.

He walked to the pit, motioning for Sadie to follow. Obeying, she did and came to stand right beside him.

"Let's get out my best pet to play for a while, so you can continue to prove your loyalty," he said to her.

"Gladly, I'd like to see what it can do," she said.

"Sadie, please, rethink this. You're good; I know you are. You didn't mean to do that to Zeno; I know you didn't. Please, Sadie, Ladybug, I need you; we all need you," begged Adrienne.

"We don't need her; we can fight without her. She doesn't even have full witch power or know where the Heart is. She's just..." Tara didn't get to finish.

"But that's where you're wrong. You saw what I did to that cart horse, granted with a little help from Grimm. But I am feeling stronger by the minute since destroying him. Watch this," said Sadie.

She pointed at a sconce on the wall with her right hand and reaching into her pocket with her left, gripped her raven skull. Focusing on all the newfound energy within her, sparks of light began to pop and crackle above her head. Immediately a bolt of bright white light, just like lightning, surged forth from her finger and blew the sconce into a thousand pieces. Grimm smiled. Adrienne looked surprised. Tara hung her head once again. Sadie grinned wickedly before facing Grimm.

"Now, show me this pet of yours," she said.

Grimm knelt at the fire pit, bowed his head, and whispered a few words. The flames began to rise, this time a tinted a blue-black color. A low, deep growl was heard from the depths, and Sadie knelt beside Grimm. Her heart pounded faster, harder, as she could now feel the evil that lay within the very walls of the dungeon. There was a gurgling and the flames all but disappeared. Both Sadie and the Master stood up, in unison, and faced the hole in the dungeon floor.

"Step back, you'll not want to be close for what happens next," said Grimm, taking her hand and pulling her away. "I've learned some new magik. It was a gift from the Seether. I've made it possible for the Seether to be functional without its heart--the Core, at my command, of course. All of its energy held together makes for a very powerful entity and ally indeed. And...it's all under my control," he said, smiling viciously.

Standing back against the wall, Sadie planted her feet firmly for what was to happen next. The energy inside her seemed to expand until she thought she would burst. Her heart felt the size of her entire body; in her mind she began to see images of death and destruction.

Release my cohorts, she heard a disembodied voice say, and she knew it was directed at her.

She also knew this voice was different from the previous voices she had begun to hear.

Maybe I really am going mad now.

She looked around to see if anyone else had heard this voice, but all eyes were transfixed on the pit, even Grimm's. Sadie's body began to quiver and shake.

I want my children, the voice said again.

Sadie felt it this time, in both her heart and mind. Grimm held Sadie flush to the wall with one arm as he snapped his fingers on the other hand.

"Get ready; this is going to be phenomenal," he said, almost giggling.

A blast equivalent to a volcanic burst shot forth from the pit. The heat alone made Sadie feel her hair and eyebrows to make sure they were still there. Then a roar that shook the stones of the dungeon and made small bits of dust and debris fall from the walls and ceiling bellowed from within the intense fire.

Sadie was not afraid, for once, and she found this to be empowering. A large, black, clawed hand slowly emerged from the flames. It held the side of the pit, unsteady, feeling around as another appeared. Slowly, a figure began to rise up within the flames, pulled by the hands on the rim. The shape was enormous, with two immense wings, and the black outline of it belied nothing of what they were about to see. Sadie inhaled, and this time didn't choke on the burnt flesh smell that hung thick in the air.

Grimm stepped forward to face the shadowy figure still hidden, engulfed in the inferno. He knelt on one knee, raised both hands skyward and began to speak.

"I have given you the power to live and breathe without the Core beating inside of you. For the first time ever, you can walk the earth and other realms in your one true form. You can exist without the burden of the Core. I am your Master; your creator of new and this is your birth. I command you to do my bidding," he said to the fiery figure.

A low, slow rumble shook the floor. The walls began to drop bits of stone and the Core fell from its pedestal. It rolled precariously towards the edge of the cavity, which now resembled a crater more than fire pit. One of the clawed hands reached out and grabbed the Core quite delicately for such grotesque and mutilated hands. The shape in the fire began to come closer to the forefront until it began to slowly emerge from the flames. Sadie's eyes opened wide, watching its every move.

I want my kindred spirits, she heard the disembodied voice say.

But this time she knew it was the creature in the flames. And it was only speaking to her. It wanted the evil souls contained in the Ataraxia Heart, and it knew she had it.

If only I knew where it was, she thought. *Oh, what I could do.*

With the Core in one hand and the other pulling itself from the pit of fire, the creature emerged to show itself wholly. It was colossal, rippling with muscle and authority. Sadie wondered if it would burst the ceiling of the dungeon they all occupied and crush them all.

It looked almost human, save for the two spiraling, twisting horns protruding from its head and the large black leathery wings with matching black skin. It took a step with its cloven hoof out of the pit and came into full view. Impressive, intimidating with its size and appearance, Sadie still was not afraid.   She looked at her mother and Tara, whose eyes were stricken with fear. She looked at Grimm, who was grinning wickedly with pride at what he had accomplished.

Give me what's mine, she heard in her head.

Watching intensely, the beast surveyed those in the room. Its hooves clopping and echoing on the stone floor, it turned to survey its surroundings and stopped to face Grimm.

"Bow before me, Seether; I am your maker," Grimm said with authority. "And you can stop worrying about the Core; you don't need it to exist anymore. I told you, I'll be its keeper from now on."

The beast hesitated and then looked to the ceiling and let loose a loud bawl. It shook its head and sparks flew from its horns. It spread its wings, sending a gush of heated air across the room. Lowering its gaze, it looked directly at Sadie for several moments before turning to face Grimm.

"Fool, infidel, and weak little imposter. I answer to no one. You are but a cat, a kitten, fraudulently hiding in a man's form. I banish you to your true form without return to this guise for all eternity," the creature said.

Grimm began to contort and writhe in pain. He grabbed his head, then his chest, and fell to his knees. Dropping down on all fours he began to shrink and was lost in his clothing. A cat's tail snaked forth from a leg of the trousers, twitching with aggravation. Roiling with pain and anguish, he had turned from man to the cat they all knew.

When the transformation was complete, Grimm the cat disappeared into the shadows at the far reaches of the room. The denunciation of Grimm had also broken his spells, and Tara and Adrienne were released from their bindings. They held each other as they cowered in fear, along with Grimm, against a far wall. The beast seemed satisfied and not bothered by them, and turned his attentions to Sadie.

"I haven't walked this Earth for thousands of years. It feels strange, but satisfying," he said, flexing his wings and stretching his back. Grabbing hold of the Core, he raised it to look at it more closely. "Now, I can be whole again," he said moving the Core to directly in front of his chest.

Taking one of his long, sharp claws he sliced open his chest to reveal an empty dark cavity behind his ribs. He inserted the Core, which began to pulse like the beat of a heart. His chest sealed itself, and the Core could be seen under his dark, black leathery flesh, pulsing and throbbing.

"Just as you are whole, so am I. No one can really live without their Heart. Yes, you did see me rise up out of the pit without it, but what you saw was the shell of me, a zombie if you will, under that imposter's command. Now, I'm whole once again. Had it not been for my desire to be free from my prison, I would have never have bargained with such an infidel.

"But I knew he'd slip up soon enough, and I could be wholly free once again. Imagine for a moment, girl, what we could accomplish should we take each other's burdens, each others cross in life to bear. Are you not the least bit curious?"

Sadie felt a wave of discovery ripple through her body and once again, she *knew*. The Ataraxia Heart was within her; it was her Heart. The implications of this finding were immense and brought her to her knees as the newest surge of energy and knowing raged inside her. For the first time in her life, Sadie believed in herself. For the first time in her life, Sadie was confident and sure. For the first time in her life, she felt strong. The beast smiled down on her.

"It is good to see such devotion," he growled, "but this act of false commitment stops here. You may have fooled the imprudent and grasping cat, but not me. I know within you lies my failure, my fallen comrades. You hold my brethren inside that Heart of yours.

"I cannot kill you, for it will send them to the unknown forever, and I wish them to stand side by side with me as I take back the night and bring darkness to the world once again. Light has ruled for too long. Now, it's my turn. I've been locked away for too long. You have contained in you some of the most powerful, dark demons and forces that have ever come into existence.

"I need you to release them willingly. I command you to do so or be imprisoned in my flames without end--or at least until I find a way to let them loose from your Heart myself. I'm asking for your Heart, Sadie, but what I really want is your soul."

Sadie kept her eyes to the floor. She could feel the many evil, corrupt souls pounding on the walls of her Heart, imploring release. Simultaneously, she heard the pure, wholesome souls that were trapped within the Core, begging her for her help. It just didn't seem fair.

Her body rippled with energy coursing through every vein, and she felt power to her center. She felt her talisman vibrating inside her pocket. She could feel the fear in her mother, in Tara, and in Grimm. She could feel the power emanating from the Seether. In her mind's eye she saw the battle raging outside between the Guild and the Syndicate; she saw the battles all over the world between the two. And the death and destruction it was causing. Humans, magikal being and creatures, both good and evil, and nature, were being destroyed in huge quantities and on enormous levels.

She bristled with knowledge, and right then, right there she knew what had to be done. Rising slowly, she lifted her head and stared into the eyes of the beast. Turning to face her mother and Tara, her mother imploring her with her tears and Tara looking down at the floor in what some may have thought to be a nod. Grimm cowered at their legs. Turning back to face the beast, she was resolute in her conviction.

Raising her hand to her chest, the beast nodded satisfaction. She began her task and then she hesitated, realizing she didn't have the sharp, steely claws of the beast or a knife to do the job. She spied a long, deadly spear attached to the wall and removed it forcefully with magik, drawing it to her. Grasping the spear tightly she walked towards the Seether to complete her task. Reaching him, standing directly in front of him, she began to speak.

"I am yours to command, and I freely give you my Heart," she said.

The beast grinned maliciously, shutting his eyes tightly, and raising his head to howl his contentment. Within a flash and seeing her opening, Sadie rammed the spear into his chest and hugged him tightly, Heart to Heart.

A massive explosion accompanied by blinding white light filled the dungeon room. Tara and Adrienne were knocked unconscious as they were slammed against the crumbling stones and fell to the floor. Grimm curled up tightly in a ball and was flung up against the wall as well, knocking him out in the process.

Sadie felt the souls of a million beings, both good and evil, flood through her body, touching her very existence. Simultaneously, she felt love and hate, sorrow and joy; she wanted to laugh and cry; when she could take no more when she truly felt as though she would explode, she and the beast were separated by a force more powerful than any the Earth had ever seen before. Everything went black for Sadie as the dungeon, the town of Cranberry Grove and the land for several miles around lay in ruins.

* * *

Blinking her eyes, Sadie saw the blue sky above her. Sprinklings of clouds drifted lazily across the heavens and the air felt warm and inviting. A twinge of pain made her put her hand to her temples; and as she did, she remembered. Her stomach lurched, and she knew she had to find her mother and Tara. She tried to move and found her legs pinned under stone debris. Sitting up slowly, she wiggled out from under the rubble and began to look around.

"MOM!" she called, but got no answer.

She got up, feeling slightly wobbly, and started to search through the debris. Stepping over what remained of iron dungeon bars, she spotted her mother and Tara, holding each other and laying in a heap against some wreckage. She ran to them, nervous at what she might find.

"MOM, please, wake up, it's over. Please, oh, please, don't be dead. Not now, not after everything, I can't lose you again," she said through blinding tears.

Hugging her mother tightly, Sadie cried into her dust-laden hair. She felt an arm on her shoulder and opened her tear-filled eyes to see Tara trying to regain full consciousness.

"Oh, Tara, I think Mom's dead; she won't wake up," cried Sadie.

"Adrienne, open your eyes. It's over, Sadie has saved us all," Tara said in a raspy voice.

Slowly, Adrienne stirred. She blinked her eyes and tried to focus on what was in front of her. Sadie cried harder with happiness and hugged her mother tightly.

"I thought I'd lost you again," she sobbed.

Adrienne hugged Sadie as she also choked back sobs.

"I thought I'd lost you. You were so convincing back there. If Tara had not read your mind and then told me what was going on when the beast was beckoning you, I would have sworn you'd crossed over to the dark side. And your powers, the Heart must have given them to you full force, without the three years transformation. You're such a powerful little witch, and the first of your kind.   "Imagine, my daughter, the only thirteen-year-old witch to ever exist. I'm so proud of you, Sadie. You've saved us all from the Seether and from evil. You've discovered the Heart and used it for its true purpose to destroy evil. But, how did you live and the Seether didn't? Or is he...."

"The Seether is still alive somewhere. I can feel him. But don't worry, we need that balance, remember? And all the souls the Heart held and the Core held, they've all been released and moved on. I can feel it. I *know*. I don't know where they went, but they're gone now. The Seether is still there; we need the balance.

"Though, from what I feel, it'll be a while before he can do any real damage," said Sadie. "Plus, I don't know if you're gonna be mad at this or not, but the Ataraxia Heart and the Core were destroyed when I did what I did."

"Oh, Ladybug, how could I be mad? You saved us; you saved everything from imminent destruction. I never thought it was right for so many good souls to be contained instead of moving on. The bad souls--yes, but not the good ones. I'm sure they're all where they need to be now," replied Sadie's mother with happiness in her eyes.

"Speaking of destruction, we've got to get out of here and find the Three so we can make this right. If you haven't noticed, Cranberry Grove doesn't look so good. Who knows how far this damage reaches. The Three have to put things back the way they were or humans will begin their witch hunts again, blaming us for all of this," said Tara.

Standing up and helping her mother as well, Sadie gave Tara a hug once she was on her feet. The three stood, surveying the damage and shaking off the dust. Sadie spotted something amidst the rabble.

"Look, over there; it's Grimm. Do you think he's dead?"

The three walked to where the body of Grimm lay, sprawled out like a cat that had been hit by a car on the side of the road. Sadie knelt beside him and stroked his fur. Even though he was found to be the leader of the Syndicate, had released the Seether, and was basically rotten to the core, something about seeing him lying there made Sadie want to pet him. It was as if she felt sorry for him.

Grimm opened his eyes and jumped to his feet, alarmed. He staggered a bit, trying to regain his composure. He looked up at Tara and Adrienne and then came to look at Sadie.

"Sadie, thank the gods you were able to stop him. I had no idea the power I unleashed when I made him whole. It was the catnip; it was the human energy, my addiction became out of control. I need help. I was wrong; you can't control such immense evil. I was wrong to try. I'm sorry," he said.

"I understand--to a certain extent. But why did you do it, Grimm? That's what I don't understand." Sadie asked.

"You mean besides not being in my right mind from all the catnip and stolen human energy? Well, I've always wanted to be human--for as long as I can remember. Humans can do so much more than a cat can. Humans have free will and minds; cats have an owner. That's how it started at least, and then things got out of control the more I...imbibed."

"Oh, Grimm, I used to be the same way, minus the addictions, that is. I always wanted to be someone I wasn't. To have things I didn't have. I was never happy with myself or my life. But the one thing I've learned from all of this is that you need to accept and love yourself for who you are. Everything else will follow if you do that."

"I think you're right, Sadie. I'm really sorry. I guess I need help."

Sadie wanted to believe him, yet something didn't quite feel right inside her. She looked up to her mother and Tara for an answer.

"What should we do?" she asked.

"Let's take this traitor to the Three so they can decide what to do with him. It's not up to us. He must be locked away," said Tara.

"No, Sadie, don't let them take me. The Three will put me in the box and that will surely kill me. Please, Sadie. I didn't kill you when I could have; I simply switched the teas that night back there in the bookstore. Please, Sadie, let me go so I can...change...on my own terms."

"No, he has to pay the consequences for what he's done," replied Adrienne.

"You think?" It was all Grimm said, or rather asked, as he immediately vanished.

"He must have been buying some time to get his strength back so he could vanish. I thought something didn't quite *feel* right," Sadie sighed.

"Forget about him. I think he's learned his lesson. I think he's learned he will never dominate anyone or anything ever again. Plus, remember, the Seether banished him from glamouring himself as a man, so he can't lead the Syndicate anymore. That organization is going to be in chaos for a long time, battling amongst themselves for the role of master if they even continue on.

"And I'm sure they'll be plenty mad that they were duped by a cat--a magikal cat, at that. The very thing they stand to fight was in their midst and leading them. They'll be out to get him in numbers. We'll not have to worry about them or Grimm for some time...or the Seether, thanks to my all-powerful daughter," Adrienne said. "The Seether is probably licking his wounds as we speak and terribly mad he no longer has the Core. Without it, he'll have to come up with another way to steal innocent souls."

Adrienne MacDougall took her daughter by the shoulders and looked her in the eyes. She cleared her throat before speaking and got down on one knee.

"Sadie, I have to know, why did you do what you did to Zeno?"

Sadie smiled. When she did, Adrienne looked horrified. Tara, as usual, looked down at the ground.

"MOM! No! I would never have...I'm smiling 'cause Zeno is alive! That ring he gave me had special powers attached to it. When I finally felt the Heart inside me, it told me things, gave me knowledge.

"That ring was magikked by the Source itself. It had the power to grant a second chance at life. I knew if my plan were to work, I had to make it look like I were willing to kill Zeno. That's why he simply disappeared in the flames. It wasn't because Grimm's magik wasn't working right; it was because it worked like the magik of a Phoenix.

"Zeno has risen from the flames, like a Phoenix. Oh, he's alive and well, somewhere. That's the only part I don't know, where he is."

Adrienne squeezed her daughter tightly. Tara smoothed the back of Sadie's head.

"Oh, Sadie, I was a little worried. You can be so...convincing in your actions. I was afraid you sacrificed him to save us or that you, well, I don't know. I'm just glad things worked out the way they did, or I don't know what kind of trouble we'd all be in right now," said Adrienne.

A noise came from the rubble that caused the three to turn towards it with trepidation.

Great, all we need....

Broken bricks and bits of wood tumbled to the ground as a very dusty, very disheveled Crazy Mary moved towards them from the pile of debris.

"Better hurry, better make haste. My crazy sister Ms. Cabot is waiting for you three so she can make things right," said Crazy Mary.

"Um, Cra...um, Mary, I've never really had the opportunity to introduce myself. I'm Sadie, Sadie MacDougall, and I'd like to...."

"I know who you are girl. I've been watching you for ages. Making sure you're safe. We'll speak again when the time is right. Right now, I've got to find my sister's cat; she's hungry, I know it. I wish she would look for her own darn cat; I'm about sick of this. Can't have a life of my own! Now go on, my wacky sister, who's not right in the head, I tell ya, needs to see you all," she responded by cutting Sadie off.

Adrienne took Sadie by the shoulders as Crazy Mary wandered off amongst the mess, obviously looking for something. "Sadie, she'll be alright. And she and her sister have a millennia long argument over who's the crazy one; you'll hear that story one day," said Adrienne.

"But shouldn't we at least help her look for Ms. Cabot's cat?"

"Sadie, Ms. Cabot doesn't have a cat," said Adrienne.

Sadie was confused once again, but she accepted it and realized this would probably happen lots until she got a better understanding of the new world she was a part of.

I guess I'll learn more about this story in time.

Sadie turned and hugged her mother. "Mom, I don't think we should call her Crazy Mary anymore--names like that hurt people's feelings. And who's to say who really is crazy?"

"Yes, Sadie, I agree with you completely."

"C'mon, me lassies, let's go find the Three so they can clean up this mess and make Cranberry Grove whole again," said Tara as she snapped her fingers and transported them from the mess.

A Chance

to Be Normal

As Sadie sat on the carved, dark wood steamer trunk in the corner of the vast hall, she couldn't help but think about how lucky she truly was. Seeing everyone at the celebration party made her so happy. Realizing what a lucky girl she was--even more so. Everyone she cared about had somehow, miraculously, survived the final battle of the long time war with the Syndicate. Well, all of them except Whistle. Sadie's brow furrowed at the thought of her friend.

Cranberry Grove had been fully restored to its former small-town self along with all its human inhabitants. It was likewise for every city and town around the world where the battles had raged. What was also amazing (and good for their sanity as well) was that the Three made sure no human had any recollection of any battle, magik, or "strange events" ever taking place.

Of course, with destruction of this scale, the Three had to call in Mother Nature to help with the restorations. She was more than glad to help since so much of nature had been destroyed, and she always did like a tidy house. When all was said and done, everything looked as if nothing had ever transpired. The Three, Mother Nature, and any others who helped set things right slept for a solid week.

The most important, wonderful, and miraculous thing to Sadie though, in spite of all of these things, was that she now actually had not only her mother back, but also the people who genuinely cared about her. She felt like she fit in and belonged somewhere for the first time in her life.

Her eyes glazed over as she watched her mother laughing with several others. Some mountain dwarves were telling all who would listen how they won the battle against the Syndicate's forces in Colorado with their sheer strength and unequal brute force.

Do all gnomes and dwarves have height issues? What did Miss Bruja call it, Little Man Syndrome?

Sadie felt like crying, and for the second time in her life (the first being when she found her mother alive), she wanted to cry from happiness.

"Don't tell me you're still an unhappy child? I mean, this entire party is for you," said Mrs. Felis as she handed Sadie a package. Saying she handed it to Sadie was somewhat incorrect. She more pushed it with her nose as she was in her true and most comfortable form--a cat.

"No--no, I'm just thinking about how lucky I am, that's all. And I'm glad you weren't involved with all the treachery Grimm created. Well, I just KNEW you weren't. What's this?" Sadie asked taking the brown paper-wrapped article from the floor.

"Just something I thought you needed long ago and think you may need even more today," replied Mrs. Felis, licking her paws.

Sadie carefully untied the string and began to unwrap the parcel. Inside was the familiar green leather embossed book that Mrs. Felis had given her on her thirteenth birthday back in the bookstore. Sadie sighed; it all seemed like a lifetime ago. She stared at the beauty of the book and ran her hand across the cover. As she did, sparkles of light trickled down from about five inches above her fingers. She looked at Mrs. Felis wide-eyed.

"Don't look so startled; you are a witch now. It's not often that one becomes a full witch without the usual three years of transformation from witchling. I'm guessing it all had to do with the Ataraxia Heart and all its glory and magnificence," said Mrs. Felis with a wink.

"But I didn't do any magik just now," said Sadie.

"The Book *knows* you, dear," Mrs. Felis replied, magikking a very old fashioned ink pen out of thin air. "Now, finish what you and your book started."

Sadie opened the book. Inside, where it used to be blank, were titles to spells intricately scribed in beautiful cursive. Sadie was a bit stunned and looked at Mrs. Felis before looking down again at the pages. She turned them carefully, stopping on one with the title *How to Produce a Protective Shield.*

Without even thinking, Sadie began to fill the page with what she knew to be the correct spell. The pen in her hand flew over the paper, writing down exactly what should be written. Mrs. Felis sat in front of her, proud and admiring, like a grandmother would be.

"Having the girl do school work at her own party? Not very celebratory," said a voice off to the side.

Sadie recognized the voice, but knew it couldn't be. She shivered and continued writing in her book.

I must still be stinging from all that's happened, either that or, because of all that's happened; I'm finally losing my mind when I just found myself.

"What? No, hello, how do you do? You were just thinking about me were you not?" asked the voice.

She slowly raised her head and looked over her left shoulder. Floating in the air, a bit above her head was a grey, cloudy figure. It hovered and floated and wore a huge smile on its face.

"WHISTLE!" Sadie shouted as she jumped up from her seat. She set down her book and fountain pen in front of Mrs. Felis before throwing open her arms to hug her long-lost dead friend. Her arms wrapped themselves back around her own body as she swiped thin air.

"Whoa, now, girl, don't be stirring up me molecules just 'cause you be gettin' emotional," said the apparition of Whistle.

"I thought I'd never see you again. Are you a ghost now?"

"Well, aren't we the ever smart child? I suppose next you're going to tell me I died a horrific death or that Elgarbam is a pain in the rump. You always were one to point out the obvious," said Whistle tauntingly, but as much himself as he used to be--although he now looked a bit younger and much sprier.

"I'm so glad you're...okay," said Sadie, unsure.

"It's not bad, not bad at all. It's not better or worse than being alive, just different. And that's all I can tell you. Some things must remain a mystery. Now, where's that incorrigible little wretch Elgarbam? I'd like to play some tricks on him before he knows I'm back," said Whistle as he floated away over the tops of the heads of all the party goers.

Sadie watched him go, and she felt better about his death. Even though he wasn't solid or alive anymore, he was still around. She picked up her book and pen again, looking at the fat grey cat wearing glasses, and smiled at her from the bottom of her heart.

A loud shrieking giggle caught her attention, and she looked up in time to see Miss Bruja being chased around the room teasingly by Sven the Strong, the Viking Warrior from Valhalla. The Lorelei sat on a tufted footstool with several men at her ankles, completely enthralled and obviously smitten.

Elgarbam was swatting an invisible "fly" that was apparently tweaking his ears and knocking off his little red cap. Sadie laughed knowingly. Tara was busy reprimanding several birds that had returned to take up residence twittering around her head. Apparently they had eaten several butterflies that also lived in her aura. All seemed right in the world.

"Well, I'll leave you to it. I've got some work to do for The Guild. The Three are still a little mad that I didn't catch Grimm's deception so they've piled on more missions for me in some of the other realms. Then I can return and take my rightful place as both you and your mother's cat. In the meantime, I've got packing to do and some stocking up on supplies. I'll see you again soon, most definitely before I leave," said Mrs. Felis as she arched her back and stretched. Smiling at Sadie, the cat turned and disappeared into the crowd.

"Sadie!" shouted her mother. "Come join us. We're going to play a game of Who's That Witch?"

"In a minute, Mom, I want to put this book in my room," said Sadie.

"Well, just snap it there," replied her mother.

"I want to do some other things first. I'll be right back," said Sadie. She didn't want to tell her mother she just wanted to be alone for a minute. Though she had come to terms with, accepted, and actually liked her magik and her new life, she was a bit overwhelmed. Now, she was even a bit of a celebrity if only in the magikal realm. And never, ever, being able to be a 'normal' teenager, well, what was normal anyway?

And like Tara always says, Sadie thought, *normal is just a setting on the washing machine if you use one of those blasted human contraptions anyway. Magik is so much more...normal.*

Walking down the sconce-lit corridor to her room at the Guild, Sadie felt a tightening in her chest.

Uh-oh, I know that feeling, she thought.

But she dismissed it as quickly as it came, for there was no reason to fear the Syndicate, the Seether, or anything really at this moment in time and especially not at her party.

It must be all those Forgur cookies I ate.

With the way they made the troll burp, it was no wonder they were having an effect on her as well.

I wonder where that troll is anyway, I should probably check on him.

Earlier in the evening, Sadie had shared a plate of the troll's favorite cookies with him since he didn't want to leave his post. He took his job as security of the Guild offices very seriously.

She felt bad when she saw him staring in one of the windows and joined him outside. If it weren't for Tara arriving and bringing Alroy with her, she felt surely the troll would have had a miserable evening. She didn't want that as she still felt badly for tricking him when she wore the invisibility earrings.

Plopping down on her bed, Sadie closed her eyes and continued relishing all her new friends and family, and her new powers, and full witch status. Though she knew she should probably get back to the party, her party, she just wanted some peace and quiet. Her life had been one problem after another since Halloween and her thirteenth birthday. She had not a moment's time to really rest.

Drifting off to sleep had not been in her plans, but when Sadie opened her eyes, she realized she must have been out for several hours because she was so stiff. The room was dark, and she felt so groggy. Sitting up, she stretched and then made her way back to the party hall.

As she walked back down the corridor, everything was eerily silent. It was dark, as well. Reaching the great hall, Sadie took a deep breath. It was even darker and more silent than her room or the hallway. Squinting to get a better look, she noticed that all the guests were motionless, as if held in suspended animation. Her stomach dropped.

Sadie's heart began to beat faster. She walked over to the closest figure, a satyr still holding his flute to his mouth. She walked around him. He looked like a statue. Sadie began to get that tight, strange feeling in her chest. She saw Tara, in the midst of dancing, the birds and butterflies eerily hanging in mid air above her head like a disoriented tiara.

Her mother was caught mid-laugh and frozen like a three-dimensional photograph. As she walked through the room, her stomach began to tighten and her mouth became dry. There was no sign of any movement or breathing.

"Is this the work of the Seether? Have you healed and come for me already?" She shouted into the echoing hall.

"Not the Seether, Sadie, that thing will be on the mend for some time yet. By the time it's ready to fight you, you'll be long gone. I'm here to take revenge on you for ruining my plans," said Grimm as he slowly walked from the shadows.

"What have you done to them? I demand you fix them immediately, or I'll make you pay--again," said Sadie, her anger building.

"If you do anything to me, they will stay in this state for all time. Plus, you've forgotten your talisman. I know it's back in your room. I don't care if you're a full witch now either. You're still new enough at it that you most likely will need your talisman for quite some time. I know many things, remember? Now, what I want is this..." Grimm began, but stopped to lick a still wounded paw.

Sadie's heart reeled, and she tried to contain herself. Another thing she learned through all of this was not to act rashly as she used to do.

Grimm began again.

"I want you to watch as I destroy the things you value most, like you did to me. I'm going to take from you what you wanted most, a family and people who cared about you, just as you took my power and my being human: what I wanted. Hmmmmm, where to start? Oh, puuurrrrrrfect," he hissed, "I'll begin with that annoying nature-lover Tara and end with your precious mother."

"But I didn't banish you from being human. The Seether did."

"I blame you; he wouldn't have done it if it weren't for you."

"Grimm, are you still doing catnip and taking that energy? I think your judgment is a bit clouded."

"I know exactly what I'm doing. It has nothing to do with my extracurricular activities!" Grimm shouted as he took a bit of catnip out of a pouch he had around his neck.

Grimm walked towards Tara stealthily. Sadie was frozen, not like the rest, but because she knew there was nothing she could do. He had her. If she destroyed him, they would all be lost. If she tried to freeze him as well, there was no one to help her break this spell of his. She was stuck, caught in a catch twenty-two. Exhaling exuberantly, she felt defeated, and after all she had come through to end like this was pathetic.

Grimm jumped and grabbed one of the birds from Tara's aura. He ate it slowly, bits of feathers sticking to his mouth, and the crunching of little bones was grating on Sadie's last nerve.

"Must you drag this out? Must I watch? Can't you just be done with me, leave them alone, and move on to do what you intend? I'll not just sit here and watch this latest horror show of yours," said Sadie.

"I'll do this as I please, not as you wish. But I must say, you've given me a better idea," said Grimm.

Looking directly at Sadie, he whispered unintelligible words and in a flash of dark magik, bound her head to foot. She couldn't move a muscle, though inside her, her heart beat furiously.

Saying more garbled incantations, the crowd of party goers began to come back to themselves, slowly and a bit confused. Sadie felt a bit of remorse at having destroyed the Ataraxia Heart; she could have used its powers now. That's for sure. Grimm sat in front of Sadie and cleared his throat loudly before speaking.

"If any of you tries anything, Sadie dies a most horrible death," he spoke to them all.

The crowd stayed hushed after a slight rumble, and Adrienne stepped forward.

"Please, take me instead of my daughter. I'm the one who really wanted to thwart your efforts, not her," she begged.

Grimm laughed. Sadie felt as though her heart would burst out of her chest. She couldn't move no matter how hard she tried.

What kind of magik does he have?

Grimm walked around Sadie once before returning to sit in front of her. He licked his paw as the anxious crowd nervously held back their magik. Small bits of it crackled and popped above their heads. Adrienne implored him once more.

"Please, Grimm. I am her mother and cannot let you harm her," she said.

"I really don't see what you can possibly do without causing her death to come quicker and your own to come inevitably slower and more painful. I will have my revenge. There's nothing you can do," he replied.

"No, but there's something I can do," cried Mrs. Felis as she leapt from one of the plant stands.

She hit Grimm with monster force, and they began a catfight the likes of which had never been seen. Adrienne ran to Sadie as the cats rolled on the floor, tufts of hair flying and hisses and screams echoing in the party hall. Mother and daughter watched helplessly as the two felines raged in battle. The crowd parted to let the fight move around the room. There was no stopping them.

Sadie's heart began to pulse furiously, making her entire body tremble. Slowly, as Grimm was putting all he had into the tussle with Mrs. Felis, his magik over Sadie began to wane. In her mind, with the power of all the magik she had inside of her, Sadie began to formulate the correct spell to break his hold on her. She wasn't quite sure how, or why, but the words came to her as if they had always been there with her. She burst free from the paralysis in time to see the two cats hit a wall and then come rolling, fighting towards her.

"Mom, what do I do? If I try to stop him, Mrs. Felis will die, also," she asked Adrienne.

"Sadie, you must destroy him. Sometimes the good of the many outweighs the good of the one," replied Adrienne. "This is your battle, and one only you can fight."

Sadie's heart broke. How could she let Mrs. Felis die after all she had done for her, after all she had been to her? When she had no one back in the human world, when she was all alone, Mrs. Felis had been her friend.

She watched as Grimm sliced a huge rip in the old cat's side. Wincing, Sadie reluctantly raised her hand.

How can I do this to her? She's always been so good to me. And she's our cat; I should be protecting her.

Grimm took another slice out of Mrs. Felis, and her friend screeched in agony. Speaking in a tongue she barely understood, Sadie pointed her right finger at the cats while her left went into the sign of W over her chest. Grimm bit off a part of Mrs. Felis's ear, and Sadie heard her cry in pain.

With every ounce of her magik, Sadie called for complete and total force. A bolt of light shot from her finger and hit the cats full on. There was an explosion, some settling of smoke and sparks, and then total silence. When the smoke cleared, there was nothing left of either cat.

Sadie cried and went into her mother's arms. Adrienne tried to console her. Tara also went to wrap her arms around them both. All of the creatures and people in the room murmured consolations to them and each other, as the party was no longer. It had taken on the somber tone of a wake.

"She was a good cat, a good soldier of the Guild," said Ms. Cabot.

"She'll be missed, that's for sure. She taught me many things," said a young cat that belonged to another witch.

Sniffling and wiping away tears, Sadie spoke. "I feel so horrible; I didn't want her to die."

"You're forgetting I've got nine lives," spoke Mrs. Felis as she stretched in her best Halloween cat arch. She leapt down from a ledge high on the wall.

"Grimm was on his ninth; me, I've only used six. Sadie, don't you think you should keep better track of your talisman?"

Mrs. Felis strutted over to Sadie who picked her up immediately.

The crowd roared with happiness and music began to play. Satyrs played flutes while nymphs strummed harps. All in attendance began to dance and sing, and the party became a party once more. Sadie set Mrs. Felis down while Tara and Adrienne hugged her once more.

"Please, I can't breathe," choked Sadie.

"Sorry, Ladybug, I just can't believe what a strong, brave, and smart young woman, sorry, young witch, you've become. Have I told you how proud I am of you?"

"The lass has definitely got strong character," said Tara, beaming. "I'm proud to call her my friend."

"I'm just an average girl with not-so-average friends whom I love very much," said Sadie. "I may not be unremarkable anymore, and I'll

NEVER be normal now, but I'm still just...me. All of you make me who I am."

*   *   *

Sitting on the foot of her bed, Adrienne watched as her daughter put her book and her talisman into her trunk. Sadie whispered a few words and the leather crate magikked shut, locked up tightly. She then turned and ran and jumped into bed, like she used to do when she was much younger and thought monsters lived under there.

For some reason, even though the party had gone on until the sun began to rise, Sadie felt giddy and wide awake. She felt as though she were right where she was supposed to be and that all was right in her world. As she got under the covers and pulled them up to her chin, she spoke her thoughts aloud.

"I don't feel so...awkward anymore. Why is that? Does magik make your problems go away?"

Adrienne smiled at her daughter. Standing up and then moving to sit next to her on the bed, she stroked her hair.

"No, *you* make your problems go away. I think you've finally become comfortable in your own skin; that's all. You've come into your own, Ladybug. But remember, you've still got much to learn. Life is about learning the whole way through, not just what you learn in school or what you learn when you are young. You learn and grow and change the entire time you're alive. I'm still learning. I've learned much from you," Adrienne said. "Hopefully, you'll learn many things from me. We've got each other again, and we'll go through life together, learning, laughing, making mistakes and changing along the way; it'll all be worthwhile 'cause in the end, you, me, all of us, will have lived a full, open life with, the Gods be willing, much happiness."

"But what about the Seether? He's gonna come back," said Sadie.

"Yes, and you'll battle him again, I'm sure. You two share two parts of one heart remember? Even though the Ataraxia Heart and the Core are no more, you two will always be connected because of what happened.

"But also remember, he'll always be there for good reason. Without bad, how would we know good? Without love, how would we know hate? There's always gonna be bad and evil in the world, just like there will always be good to fight it and overcome it. All you have to do is follow your heart. Don't you worry about that now, Sadie. When the time comes, you'll be able to do what you have to do," said Adrienne.

Sadie smiled, beginning to feel sleepy. Adrienne tucked the covers in around her daughter and kissed her on the forehead.

"I'm so glad to have you back, Mom. Even when everyone was telling me I was crazy and picking on me and teasing me, telling me you were dead and I was nuts for thinking otherwise, I *knew* you were still alive somewhere, somehow," Sadie murmured, getting sleepier.

"But you stayed strong--strong enough to keep on going even when you were at your saddest. Strong enough to handle learning you were a witch and strong enough to save me and the whole world, not to mention all the other worlds," replied Adrienne.

"When can I see these other worlds?" asked Sadie.

"Soon, very soon, but for now, get some sleep, little witch. Tomorrow you've got some much-needed training, and I want you to clean your room, and then we've got some sea nymphs to visit this weekend along with the mountain trolls.

"We've got your cousins Hannah's and David's trial to attend. Your Uncle Marcus wants to visit you, to get to know you now that he's been restored to his former self. Though he's chosen to still live without his powers in the human world, he's family. Some family we want, like him; some we don't and just have to accept, like David and Hannah.

"Oh, and I told the North Wind you'd come by to visit; he's so lonely you know. And I want you to help Tara with the herb garden, and I'm sure you'll have much homework, and…."

"Geez, some things never change," Sadie mumbled as she drifted off to sleep.

www.ingramcontent.com/pod-product-compliance
Lightning Source LLC
Chambersburg PA
CBHW050940120626
46552CB00001B/296